The Last King of Lydia

TIM LEACH is a graduate of the MA writing course at Warwick University, where he has also taught creative writing on the undergraduate programme. This is his first novel.

The Last King of Lydia

Tim Leach

ATLANTIC BOOKS
London

First published in hardback and trade paperback in Great Britain
in 2013 by Atlantic Books, an imprint of Atlantic Books Ltd.

Copyright © Tim Leach, 2013

The moral right of Tim Leach to be identified as the author
of this work has been asserted by him in accordance with the

Hardback ISBN: 978 0 85789 917 0
Trade paperback ISBN: 978 0 85789 918 7
EBook ISBN: 978 0 85789 920 0

Printed in Great Britain by the MPG Printgroup, UK

Atlantic Books
An imprint of Atlantic Books Ltd
Ormond House
26–27 Boswell Street
London WC1N 3JZ

www.atlantic-books.co.uk

For Gill and Michael

Contents

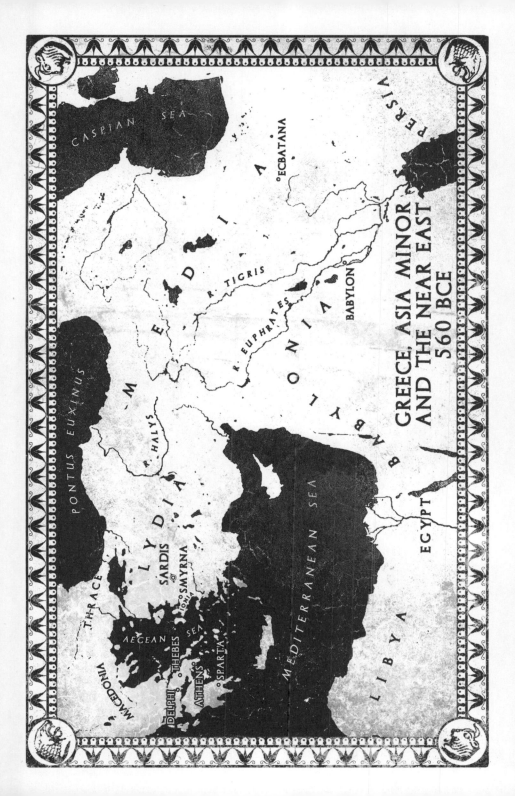

GREECE, ASIA MINOR
AND THE NEAR EAST
560 BCE

PERSIA

CASPIAN SEA

°ECBATANA

M E D I A

R. TIGRIS

BABYLONIA

R. EUPHRATES

BABYLON °

PONTUS EUXINUS

R. HALYS

LYDIA

THRACE

SARDIS
° SMYRNA
IONIA

MACEDONIA

AECEAN SEA

DELPHI ° THEBES
° ATHENS
° SPARTA

MEDITERRANEAN SEA

EGYPT

LIBYA

The Pyre
547 BC

The preparations for the execution began many hours before dawn.

In the heart of the royal palace, servants had uprooted and removed trees and rare plants from a courtyard, and raised a high wooden pyre in their place. In the darkness of the winter morning, they untied sacks of dry timber and stacked it neatly around the pyre. They brought out a finely carved table from one of the royal dining rooms and placed it on a balcony that overlooked the courtyard. On the table they laid bowls of dates and olives, flasks of wine and silver bowls of water, and they placed a pair of braziers nearby, ready to warm the cold air when the time came.

On the far side of the palace, in a cellar that had once held grain and which now served as a dungeon, a door was unlocked. Insistent hands shook the prisoner awake and led him from his cell through the dark corridors of the palace. The guards who escorted him could see well at night and saw no reason to light torches to guide the way, and so the prisoner moved slowly. He was a man who had never had to move in darkness.

His guides did not beat or otherwise punish him for his hesitation. They led him around corners and up stairs with soft taps to his shoulders and chest, as an experienced rider can direct a horse with gentle pressure from his knees. They did not bind his wrists with iron, gave him water when he requested it, and before they had gone far they led him to a chamber pot behind a screen and gave him privacy. There, too, the guards handed him the simple white robe in which he was to die, and let him change into it without being watched. They went further and further into the palace, until they were almost at the courtyard, and not once did a man so much as raise his voice to the prisoner. The guards had long since learned the way to make a royal prisoner docile. So long as you allowed a king the illusion of servility he would go with you calmly, even as you led him to his death.

The barber who was assigned to the prisoner did not observe this principle. He had never seen a king die, and as he cropped the prisoner's hair and trimmed his thick, black beard, he placed little nicks in his scalp and chin, apologizing for his clumsiness each time, even as he keenly watched the royal blood flow. The guards did not share the barber's curiosity. They were veterans of many wars of conquest, and they knew that a king bled and died like any other man.

After the barber had finished his work, the captain of the guard observed the blood that had stained the prisoner's robe. He barked a curse, and gestured to his men to hand him another robe. They always carried a second in case a prisoner were to soil himself on the way to his execution, for it was an impious thing for a man to be put to death in stained clothing. The captain took the clean robe and handed it to the prisoner, gesturing for him to put it on.

The prisoner spoke out in protest, and although they did not speak the same language, the captain understood him well enough. He looked for some means by which to screen the prisoner's nakedness, but there was nothing in that room to serve that purpose. He glanced out of a window and saw that morning light was rapidly spreading across the sky. They had no time to waste.

The captain gave an order to his men and, as one, they turned on their heels to face the wall. After a moment, the prisoner pulled the dirty robe over his head and put on the clean one, hunched over in an attempt to conceal his nakedness. The barber glanced swiftly over his shoulder at the naked king, but the captain cuffed him sharply and told him to keep his eyes down.

Wearing the new robe, the prisoner straightened and turned towards the guards. He did not speak. The guards would wait until he said that he was ready. For a single moment, he retained the right to command with which he had been born. For the last time, he was free. He stood silent for as long as he could, before clearing his throat to signal that he was ready.

The captain pushed open the doors to the courtyard. The space opened up around them, vast and threatening after the narrow corridors. The prisoner looked up and shuddered as he saw the pyre loom before and above him like a beckoning finger. At the very top, where the fire would be hottest, there was a simple wooden throne for him to sit and die in.

They led him up the steps, the wood creaking beneath their feet. The prisoner's place was far above the ground, so high that he was level with the upper balcony. The man who was to watch the prisoner die was not one to stoop or peer down on a spectacle. He too was a king, and would offer the other this last act of respect: to be high above the slaves and soldiers as he died, to stand equal with the king who would take his place on the throne of Sardis.

They shackled the prisoner to the chair at the top of the pyre. One of the guards held a bucket in his hand, and after they had secured the prisoner he turned to his captain in enquiry. The captain nodded, and the guard began to daub the prisoner's robe with oil so that it would burn faster. After this was done, the captain inspected the bindings one last time, and reassured himself that everything was as it should be. He nodded to the prisoner, as if in thanks, and then he and his men descended the steps to wait.

The preparations had been completed ahead of time. The servants lit the braziers on the upper balcony, and the guards lounged at the base of the pyre, rolling dice for coins and favours, trading memories of women they had bedded and battles they had fought. The prisoner on the pyre stared ahead without expression, watching as the day began to dawn, and the dew rose from the wood like smoke.

At the very moment that the sun broke over the horizon, Cyrus, king of Persia, emerged from the doors of the palace. He sat in the cushioned chair, his long fingers toying with the dates in the bowl that lay in front of him as his taster sampled the food and the drink on the table. This servant turned to him and nodded, and Cyrus ate lightly, as was his custom, paying no attention to the condemned man. He raised a cup of wine and took one sip, then put it down. At last, he looked at the man on the pyre. They had gone to war to destroy each other, had traded countless messages, threats, and ultimatums through heralds and emissaries, but it was the first time that the two kings had met face to face. Cyrus stared at his prisoner with an idle curiosity; the condemned man blankly returned his gaze. The Persian king raised an eyebrow and inclined his head slightly, to indicate that the prisoner might speak if he wished, but the other man said nothing. Cyrus leaned back in his chair, then made a slight gesture to the men who waited below.

Four dark-skinned slaves lowered their torches to the pyre at the same instant, holding the flames to the dry wood until the fire had caught and there was no danger that a gust of wind would extinguish it. That might be taken as an omen, and this was not a time for omens. A servant on the balcony lit a bowl of strong incense and placed it on Cyrus's table. It would not do to expose the king of Persia to the smell of burning flesh.

The prisoner stared down and watched as the fire spread languidly from one pile of wood to another. He looked up again towards Cyrus, but the Persian king no longer watched him. Sheets of parchment had been unrolled in front of him, and the king was lost in the matters of state. Just once, he leaned forward to observe the fire and see how far it had progressed, like a man who has come early to a race and wishes to see if the entertainment is likely to begin soon. Apparently satisfied that there was still plenty of time, he went back to looking over his papers.

The prisoner first felt the heat against the soles of his bare feet. There was only a slight increase in temperature, but it was filled with the promise of pain to come. He tilted his head back until it rested against the wooden stake behind him, and looked up at the sky. He had heard that in some nations it was taken as a sign from the Gods if it rained hard enough to extinguish an executioner's pyre, sparing the condemned man. He didn't know if the Persians believed that. It did not matter. The sky was clear.

The first curls of smoke began to reach him, and he sucked at them greedily. It would be better if he were to fall unconscious before the fire touched him, but there was no hope of that – the dry wood burned cleanly and gave off little smoke, and he could hear the fire advance. It would reach him soon, kill him slowly.

He closed his eyes, his lips moving in prayers to the Gods in whom he might no longer believe. His face remained calm and unmoved, even as the flames rose higher and nearer. Then he flinched, as a memory struck him. A low groan escaped his lips.

Cyrus heard this cry and looked up. He saw the prisoner shuddering again, like a soldier run through with a spear, his head hanging low and his eyes open. For the first time that day, the blank mask that he had worn crumbled.

'Solon,' he said, as a coil of thick smoke ran up his body and wound round his neck like a noose.

'Solon.'

The Philosopher
558 BC

I

'All hail Croesus, king of Lydia, son of Alyattes of the Mermnadae!
Wise Leader, mighty Warrior loving Father and benevolent Ruler!
Know this, humble Lydians, know that you stand in the presence of
the greatest king that these lands have ever known. Under his great
leadership, we Lydians have truly become the most blessed nation
on the earth. For who can match our nation in wealth? Our wondrous
city for splendour? Our women for beauty? Our warriors for skill
and valour? Even the Gods themselves might be humbled by our
king's treasuries, and his wealth is matched only by his kindness to
his people, his nobility of spirit, his ruthlessness to his enemies,
his . . .'

Croesus sniffed, and yawned.

The king of Lydia was suffering from a slight cold, and would
have preferred it if the herald could have been more concise. He was
sweating under his heavy purple robes, for the room was thick with
heat – a necessary ostentation to show that the king lived untroubled
by the winter cold. He drummed his bejewelled fingers impatiently on
the arm of his throne, producing a priceless clatter of gold against
gold. He knew the entire speech by heart now, and had to stop himself
from mouthing the words. He sometimes joked to his more favoured
courtiers that he was tempted to try and conquer yet another nation,

lose a city or two, marry another woman, just so the herald would have something new to say.

It was the first day of the new month, a day when any freeborn man or woman could attend and petition for his favour. Long before dawn, they would queue to cast etched stone tablets into golden urns, and a certain number would be drawn by lot to receive his royal favour.

Some invented elaborate stories to win a moment with their king. These impostors tended to be identified before they reached the court, but occasionally a particularly skilled liar would slip through. In front of the king, their stories invariably unravelled, and they would be thrown out as timewasters and fabulists. Most of those attending were genuine supplicants, many of them having travelled for days or weeks to have their plea heard. Some were tradesmen who sought relief from their creditors, others young men caught up in blood feuds. Some were widows looking for help raising their children, others criminals begging for clemency and absolution. Together they became an endless stream of troubled humanity, each hoping for the word of the king or the handful of coins that could transform their lives.

Croesus was usually no friend to the poor, for the fortunes of wealthy men always rely on the poverty of the many. Yet, when confronted with a supplicant face to face, he was invariably moved to pity, and would pronounce the most generous judgement that he could.

He listened attentively to the first visitors, but grew drowsy and distracted as the day drew on. The business of politics was mainly conducted after dark, at the dinner tables and in the private rooms of the nobles, and he had to be well rested to keep his wits about him at these late-night encounters. His illness fatigued him, and the heat from the braziers and the weight of his ceremonial robes proved too much. He was fast asleep for the last set of supplicants.

Yet judgement continued without interruption. As Croesus drifted off, a courtier stepped forward beside him. This courtier listened to the particulars of each plea, leaned down and pretended to listen to the king, and then gave the royal verdict. In mimicking his lord, he always erred on the side of generosity and clemency. The guards moved closer to the crowd and kept a watchful eye for any who might be tempted to point and laugh and spoil the illusion, but few ever did. They needed to believe in the benevolence of the king more than anyone.

The noise of the departing crowd woke Croesus. He had fallen asleep leaning on his left arm, and as he sat up he began to massage it back to life. Seeing that the hall was empty of outsiders, he took off the heavy ornamental crown and rolled his head back and forth to relieve the cramp in his neck. Beneath this gold headpiece, a narrow silver band remained in place tight against his scalp so that his royal status was not compromised. This hidden crown never left his head, even when he slept, bathed, or lay with a woman.

Croesus beckoned his personal slave forward, a short, powerfully built man with a shaven head.

'I fell asleep again, Isocrates.'

'Yes, master.'

'Were there any problems?'

'No, master.'

'I wish I could stay awake, but . . .' He shrugged.

'The demands of state. It is understandable, master. But the system works – the people get their judgements either way.'

'I've heard that in some of the kingdoms to the east, the king is considered a god that mere mortals are not permitted to see.'

'The idea appeals to you, master?'

'On days like this it does. I could build a wall of black obsidian with a terrifying face of gold – the face of a god king. I would hold these sessions as usual. Someone else could pass judgement and speak

13

through the mask on my behalf, and I could sleep comfortably on a couch somewhere. What do you think?'

'With respect, master, I doubt if it would go well for you.'

'Oh? Why not? Speak freely.'

'They don't come this far just for your blessing. They come to see you.'

'How touching.'

'Besides, they are mostly farmers, wise to a showman's tricks. They accept that you might doze off, but I would be careful of taking it any further.'

Croesus gave the slave an amused glance. 'You make it sound as though it is the people who choose to keep me on the throne.'

Isocrates gave a low bow. 'My mistake, master.'

'That's quite all right. But I suspect you may be correct, as usual. It is one of your most irritating habits. Try to be wrong more often.'

A smile twitched across the slave's lips. 'I will do my best, master.'

'Well,' Croesus continued, 'if I do build my golden face, I promise that you shall speak for me. You've a much more kingly voice than I do. Deep, resonant, powerful,' Croesus said, and ticked off each of these qualities on a finger as he spoke. 'Your mouth was born to command, Isocrates, even if the rest of you is destined to serve.' Isocrates politely bowed his head in acknowledgement of his master's wit. 'Now, why don't you go see what that messenger wants?' The king gestured towards the entrance of the throne room. 'He has been hovering around for some time now, but hasn't had the nerve to come forward and speak to me.'

'I expect he is too intimidated to interrupt you, master.'

'You'd better relieve him of his burden.'

The messenger delivered his message to the slave, shot a single brief glance at the king, then hurried from the chamber.

'What was our nervous friend's message?'

'Solon of Athens has arrived at the court, master, and requests an audience with the king of Lydia.'

'Does he now!' Croesus picked at his lips with his thumb. 'I didn't think the old man would ever respond to my invitation.'

'In which room should we receive him?'

'For an Athenian? The Marble Room, of course.'

'Might it be better to show him something he has never seen before? Perhaps the Emerald Room?'

'Oh, no. They are a proud people, the Athenians. They don't think much of us. If we show him the Emerald Room, he'll think it gaudy. Barbarous excess. Marble is the only beauty these people respect.'

'I bow before your wisdom, master,' said Isocrates.

He turned to the court, clapped his hands together, and as one the courtiers and slaves stopped what they were doing and prepared to move.

Many travellers came to Croesus's court, and all testified to its grandeur, yet each returned to tell a different story. Some said the throne room was a splendid chamber where every surface seemed to be etched with gold, others that it was filled with crystal lamps and lined with polished stone so that the air seemed to catch fire with reflected light. When two such travellers met in a distant land, a fierce argument would inevitably break out, each insisting that he had seen the true throne room of Sardis and decrying the other as a liar.

In truth, the palace at Sardis held many throne rooms, and every few months, one would be stripped and redecorated. It was an endless, opulent carousel that each visitor saw but once. The stories spread, echoed and contradicted one another, and some visitors even described throne rooms that had never existed. They told of impossible architecture, doors that opened through magic or automation, thrones that hovered in mid air, the humblest courtier dripping in gold like a king. When these stories made their way back to Croesus, he was well pleased. He desired a place in myth, not in history.

Within a matter of minutes, the entire court had relocated to a starkly beautiful marble hall, the perfect white stone shipped all the way from Attica at colossal expense. Ministers sat at their desks hard at work, courtiers stood in groups and laughed and gossiped, sculptors and architects debated aesthetics, and slaves moved amongst them all, dispensing food and wine, listening closely for a chance item of gossip that might win favour with their masters. No one would have suspected, on entering this throne room, that they had all been there only for moments rather than for hours. The courtiers were accustomed to such changes. On busy days with many visitors, they would all move from room to room half a dozen times before the day's work was done.

Croesus went into an antechamber to prepare himself. He changed into a robe the colour of bone, and his attendants pulled the emerald and sapphire rings from his fingers and replaced them with finely patterned silver bands. He waited patiently as one of his slave women powdered and repainted his face. Once he had inspected himself in a polished stone and found the reflection to his liking, he entered the new throne room. He took his place on the marble throne and made a small gesture to the slave at the door.

'Solon of Athens! Philosopher, statesman, and poet!'

The doors opened, and Croesus observed a small, shrunken old man make his way carefully into the throne room. The king noted the way his visitor walked tenderly on his gout-ridden feet, took in the simple robes that he wore, the absence of gold at his wrists and neck. A man with no fortune, or one who had purposefully taken on the appearance of the sage, the beggar, Solon could indeed have been mistaken for a vagabond, except that his eyes were sharp and alive with thought, and he politely greeted the members of the court with a politician's easy grace.

Croesus descended the steps of the throne with his arms outspread. 'Such a distinguished visitor honours my humble court, Solon.' He embraced the Athenian and kissed him. 'You must be weary from your travels—'

16

'Yes.'

Croesus blinked in surprise, but continued '—so rest with me at this table and take—'

'Do you mind if I relieve myself first?' Solon said.

Croesus stared. 'What?'

The old man smiled. 'My insides aren't as spacious as they used to be, I'm afraid. They have shrunk, like the rest of me. As they command, so I must obey.' He gave a little shrug. 'Nature.'

A titter passed through the room. 'Of course,' Croesus said. 'My apologies.'

'My thanks, good king, my most humble thanks.'

Isocrates led the Athenian to a doorway at the far end of the throne room. Solon opened the door and put his head inside without entering. He shuffled back to the table and resumed his seat opposite Croesus.

Croesus frowned. 'Is something wrong?' the king asked.

'Forgive my little deception.' He smiled. 'I have heard such stories of your wealth. I wanted to see if even your chamber pot was made of gold.'

Laughter again, and it showed no sign of abating. Croesus chose to smile magnanimously.

'A good trick. Very fine. Will you sit and take some wine?'

'I will. My thanks.'

Solon sat and drank, propping his tender feet on a stool, and Croesus waited for him to speak. To observe the splendour of the court, to enquire about the king's family, or any of the other customary greetings. Solon said nothing.

Eventually, Croesus broke the silence. 'I am honoured to have you visit my court. Truly honoured. They say you are the wisest man in the world.'

'Do they?' Solon said absently. 'You see, I have always been puzzled by these people, "they". They seem to hold all kinds of strange opinions, everyone claims to be speaking on their behalf, yet when you want to talk to them,' he leaned forward, gesturing theatrically around the throne room, 'they are never to be found.' Croesus laughed politely. Solon continued, '"They" say you are the richest man in the world.'

'If they say that, you can trust their opinion. They do not lie in my case, and so I assume they are truthful in yours . . .'

Solon shrugged. 'A flawed assumption. But a comforting one.'

Croesus cleared his throat. 'You have had a long journey?'

'Long and unpleasant. I'm really much too old for this sort of thing.'

'Well, we shall try and keep you entertained.'

'Oh, I am sure you will try.' This provoked another little laugh, quickly stifled, from somewhere in the crowd.

Croesus said nothing in response. He leaned forward and looked closely at his guest, his eyes narrowed.

Solon bowed his head. 'Perhaps there is a place where we could speak privately?'

'There is a balcony with a fine view that I was planning to show you, after a tour of the treasuries. The tour is customary, but perhaps you would rather—'

'No, no. My feet ache, but I would like to see your treasures. Please, do show me. I came here for two things – to see the famous riches of Lydia, and to meet the man who possesses that wealth. Would you indulge an old man?'

'Very well.' Croesus rose abruptly and walked towards the stairwell. He stopped, looked over his shoulder, and said, as though in a challenge, 'You will not forget what you are about to see.'

They ascended the stairs to the upper levels of the palace, and passed through a set of silver doors, then a set of gold doors. Finally, they reached the maze of the treasuries.

The first room was given over to the treasures of lands conquered by Croesus – enormous gold bowls etched with the histories of nations, the crude crowns of barbarians and the intricate sceptres of richer peoples, all now overthrown and subject to Lydia. The second room was dedicated to the artefacts of Lydia itself – marble sculptures of gods and goddesses, carved ivories and intricate golden jewellery. At the centre stood a statue of a horseman with a scarlet breastplate and black braided hair, a member of the invincible cavalry that had won Croesus his empire.

The next chamber contained arms and armour from the heroic past. There were jewelled swords from ancient times that were reputed to have killed gods and monsters, but were now so fragile that a single tap of a fingernail would be enough to destroy them; shields that had turned aside thunderbolts and the spears of giants, and gold-edged breastplates that had been worn by heroes in a hundred battles, each bearing a single ragged tear for the wound that had finally brought the hero down.

In the following room, a forest of rare fabrics hung from the ceiling in thick drapes, so that, moving through the room, one was caressed from all sides by priceless silken fingers. They hung so thickly that Solon, wandering absently, found himself out of sight of both Croesus and the walls of the room, and had to call to the king to find his way out.

The next room seemed to be filled only with knee-deep sand. Many, on seeing this, wondered at first if it were home to ancient treasures that had long since faded into dust. But the sand had a peculiar hardness underfoot, and when the curious sifted the sand through their fingers, they realized that it was pure gold dust, enough to buy the city of Athens twice over.

Yet another room was devoted to priceless paper, its bookshelves packed with scrolls and rare parchments. Each roll of paper (so Croesus said) contained the answer to some historical mystery – the secret thoughts of a general before a famous battle, the lost writings

19

of ancient thinkers, the solutions and proofs to mathematical problems long thought impossible. Yet all these secrets would remain for ever unread, for if any of the ancient papers were unrolled they would crumble instantly into dust.

The treasuries stretched on through the entire upper floor of the palace, a labyrinth of riches. Croesus paid little attention to the ancient relics he had seen a hundred times before. Instead he watched Solon. The Athenian's face was unreadable, and he said little as he walked. Occasionally he would ask one of the slaves to tell him the history of a particular item, or he would stretch a hand towards a treasure and give Croesus an enquiring glance to see whether he was permitted to touch. For the most part he was silent, and, finally, Croesus was moved to ask him what he thought.

'Hmm?' Solon looked up and smiled politely. 'Oh. Yes, they are remarkable. Quite remarkable.'

'Perhaps they are not as impressive as you expected? There are many chambers left to see. Something in them might—'

'No,' said Solon abruptly. Croesus was no longer offended by these interruptions. The habit of an old man with little time left to him, and none to waste. Solon continued: 'No I don't think so. You came closest with this library of yours.' He gestured at the bookshelves and the crumbling parchments that filled the room. 'This knowledge appeals to me more than the swords of heroes. Yet these works have no value if they cannot be read.'

'If everyone could read them, then they would cease to be valuable. My interest in them would come to an end. There is no pleasing you, is there, Solon?'

'Perhaps not.' Solon gave the room of treasures one last, wistful glance. A thought seemed to strike him. 'Where are the coins, by the way?' he said.

'What?'

'The famous coins of Lydia. They are minted here in Sardis, are they not? And yet they are nowhere to be found in your treasuries?'

'That is so,' Croesus said shortly. 'Shall we go? I'm sure you are ready to sit down.'

Solon looked at the king, his politician's mind sensing weakness. Then a weary expression passed over his face. 'I am tired,' he said.

Croesus led him out from the treasuries and, after several turns up a tight and narrow staircase, they emerged onto a balcony at the highest point of the palace. The king gestured outwards, his palm down and fingers spread, as if hoping to hold the city that he ruled in a single hand.

Solon looked down on Sardis. From this position, one seemed to look on some strange twin city. The closest buildings appeared to be two or three times the size of those just a little further away, as if Sardis were a city where giants lived alongside ordinary men, or where men lived beside dwarfs.

It was merely a trick of perspective. Half of Sardis, including the palace, was built imposingly on a steep-sided hill, a set of high walls contouring and elaborating on its natural defences. Here, the wealthiest citizens of Sardis lived, packed tight in tiny homes, sacrificing space and comfort for the prestige of living near to the king. The rest of the city, an uneven mass of mud-brick and reed houses, sprawled over the plains below. From here the common people, rich in space and poor in everything else, looked upon the dense peak of wealth that allowed no place for them.

Solon's eyes turned towards the sound of running water, found the Pactolus river. All knew the story of this river, of how Midas had washed away his curse in its waters, how it ran with gold that any shepherd could pan from its waters. Sardis – the impregnable city, built alongside a source of inexhaustible riches.

'My greatest treasure,' said Croesus. 'A king could not wish for a better place to call his home.'

They sat and took food and wine, and then Croesus dismissed both his slaves and his guards.

For the first time that day, the two men were alone together, and free to speak their minds.

2

They sat in silence for a time. Both men, practised politicians, trying to remember what it was to speak openly in private to a man you did not know. They looked out across the city, not at each other. Solon sat with his fingers interlaced, thumbs tapping against each other in an irregular rhythm. Croesus repeatedly took a date from a bowl, lifted it a few inches, then dropped it back on the pile again.

Finally, the older man broke the silence. 'So. What do you want to ask me, Croesus?'

Croesus turned to look at him. 'What makes you think I want to ask you anything?'

'Everyone wants to ask me something.'

'Perhaps I do. Perhaps I haven't yet decided if you are worth asking anything of.'

Solon laughed. 'I am a disappointment to you?'

'So far, yes, though you may yet redeem yourself.' Croesus shrugged. 'I sense I disappoint you as well.'

'Not at all.'

'My palace means nothing to you. Nor do my treasures. You seem to have a rather dim view of me as well. I am not a fool, you know. I don't care to be mocked in my own throne room.'

'My apologies. I am not a very good guest. I am an old man, and

23

I really have no patience for the theatre of throne rooms. But you are a new king, and depend on such theatrics. Perhaps you even enjoy them. I once did.'

'And the treasuries? I have never seen a man so indifferent, confronted with so much of the wealth of the world.'

Solon thought for a moment. 'I am glad to have seen them,' he said. 'But they do not move me. I was curious to see if I could be impressed by such riches. But I find that I cannot. I must seem ungrateful.' He clapped his hands together, leaned forward. 'Come, let me be of some use to you. What is it you wish to know?'

'Let me turn your question back to you, first. Do you want to ask me anything?'

Solon smiled apologetically. 'Not particularly.'

'Why did you travel here, if it was not to speak to me?'

'I have been travelling since I retired from politics. This was simply another place I had yet to visit. The final city on my travels, you understand – I will return to Athens now. Perhaps you will forgive my lack of courtesy, given how long I have been away from home. Twenty years is a long time.'

'Do you love your home?'

'Athens? Oh, yes. More than anything, though my countrymen can be foolish. They once gave me command of an army because of a poem I had written about wise leadership. An army for a poem! They will not believe *that* a century from now.' He shook his head. 'A foolish people, but I have hopes for them yet. It will be a great city one day. I only wish that I had been born a little later, so that I would live to see it.'

'Are you enjoying your retirement?'

'Not at all. It is a wretched business, being at the end of one's life. Travel makes it worse. Wonders are wasted on a homesick man.'

'Why did you leave Athens in the first place, if you loved it so much?'

24

'It was a way to trick the Archons. You see, I was able to pass a number of reforms in spite of their objections.'

'Reforms?'

'Yes. In Athens, the wealthy rule in their own interest while the rest suffer in silence. It is the same everywhere, of course, but I wanted to change my own home for the better. Everyone does, I suppose. I spent my life flattering and bullying a group of stubborn old men, so as to enable the passage of a few simple laws.'

'And what was this trick of yours?'

'A quirk of Athenian law. One of the only laws that I didn't try to reform, in case I ever had to make use of it. If the person who passes a law is not in the city, the Archons cannot repeal that law for ten years. It is supposed to discourage political assassination. So they were kind enough to let me pass my laws, thinking that they could overturn them in a year or two. But I announced my retirement and left the city, and they were stuck with my reforms for a decade.'

'Very clever. I applaud you.'

'I'm not proud of it. It is a foolish law, and it was low of me to take advantage of it. But I hoped some good might come of it.'

'Did it?'

'No.' Solon said. 'It is as I thought it would be. They endured my laws for a decade and then they repealed them . . . Now I hear that a tyrant has come to power. Psistratus.'

'You know the man?'

'Oh yes. I loved him once. Now I must go back to fight him, in whatever way that I can. It will do no good. He will ignore me and humiliate me, and I will die of old age long before he falls from power. So you see, my life has been an empty gesture.' He was silent for a moment. 'Perhaps I should have stuck to poetry. I was never much of a poet, but it certainly made me happier than politics.'

'Your politics does sound like a tedious business. A lifetime of work for a few petty changes. I think I prefer my system. A single man commands and is obeyed. Or do you believe a tyranny like mine puts unworthy people in power? A lottery of birth, some call it. Were your politicians the finest men in Athens, the most fit to rule?'

'No. Quite the opposite, if anything.'

'Oh?'

'Yes. It seems to me that, almost always, only the evil and the insane crave the power to rule.'

Amused, Croesus said: 'Do you count me as such a man?'

'No, because you were born to power. You never had to seek it.'

Croesus raised an eyebrow. 'In that case, are *you* evil? A madman? You, after all, rose to supreme power in Athens.'

'No.' Solon shook his head. 'I flatter myself enough to believe I belong to another class of men who try to rule.'

'Who are?'

'Men who are outraged that the worst of men are those who rise to the top.' He finished his cup of wine and placed it down carefully. 'Of course, I became a politician like any other, relying on bribery and trickery to get my way. I realized too late that there are few truly evil men in power. They are mostly weak, ambitious men who fool themselves that they are doing the right thing. That is why I retired. And now I am at the end of a wasted life.' He leaned back and looked out across the city. 'Why so many questions, Croesus?' he said. 'I cannot believe you are so interested in the life of an old statesman like myself.'

Croesus shrugged, taking up a handful of grapes and chewing on them thoughtfully. 'I am trying to discover why you are such a miserable man, given the fame that you have earned for your wisdom.'

'Wisdom doesn't guarantee happiness. Neither does fame, for that matter.'

'You should try wealth. It works for me.'

'Ah. Now I sense we are coming to something important. Perhaps it is my unhappiness that disappoints you, more than anything else.'

'Yes, you are right.' Croesus paused. 'I do have a question for you.'

'Ask, Croesus.'

'Who is the happiest person that you have ever met?'

Solon thought for a long time.

'Tellus,' he said at last, tearing off a piece of bread and dipping it into olive oil.

'Tellus,' Croesus said carefully, sounding out the name.

'Yes.'

Croesus looked at Solon, but the Athenian did not elaborate. 'I haven't heard of him,' Croesus said shortly. 'Who was he?'

'Tellus? He was an Athenian.'

'A wealthy man?'

'Oh no, but he was wealthy enough to keep himself and his family.' Solon cleared his throat then spoke again. 'There are many reasons to call him happy. He had many children, and he lived long enough to see his children's children grow. He was fortunate enough to live in a time when Athens was prosperous and justly governed. He fought in battle against the city of Eleusis, and it was by his efforts that the enemy was routed. He was wounded, and died a few hours later, but he died knowing that he had saved the city he loved. The people of Athens gave him a great funeral at the place where he fell. He was the happiest person that I have known.'

'Well then, who is the second happiest person you have known?'

'May I name two men jointly in answer to that?'

'Certainly.'

'Then I would name a pair of Argive brothers, Cleobis and Biton.'

'Go on,' said the king.

'They were two farmers who had more than enough to live on, and they were considered the strongest men in their village. They honoured the Gods. During the festival of Hera, their oxen were late returning from the fields, and their mother was too ill to walk into town by herself. So these two men yoked themselves to a cart and pulled her six *stades* to the temple. They were the toast of the festival, the entire village praising their filial love and their strength, and their mother prayed to Hera that her sons be granted the ultimate blessing. And they were. The two men went to sleep that night and never woke again.'

'You call this happiness?'

'They were happy when they died, were they not? What more can we hope for? Besides, their names will not be forgotten. The townspeople made statues in their honour and sent them to Delphi. You can still see them there, if you ever visit the temple.'

'In all this talk of happy men,' Croesus said, speaking slowly, 'there is one name that you have, perhaps, forgotten to mention.'

'Whose name is that?'

'Mine.'

Solon looked at Croesus. Then he laughed.

'Come, you toy with me,' Croesus said. 'You promised that you were done with mockery.'

'I don't mean to mock you.'

'Do you hold my happiness in such contempt that you would place me behind these farmers?' Croesus asked. 'Look around you. My empire is the greatest in the world. No one has ever possessed such wealth as I do. I have a noble son to carry on my name. My people love me. I am happy. What do I lack that would put me above these men?'

'Death, Croesus. Perhaps if you were to die at this moment, I might be able to grant you the title that you seek.'

'Explain yourself.'

'Croesus, I don't judge anyone happy until they are dead, and I know how they met their end. That is the moment to judge someone's happiness; the moment when his entire life is behind him. You are prosperous now, but the Gods have a habit of making life difficult for such people; they do not like to see us mortals become too powerful. Or too happy, for that matter.' Solon paused. 'How old are you, Croesus?

'I have lived for thirty-six years.'

'So you are only halfway through your life. Do you know for how many days you will live?

Croesus snorted. 'What man knows that? Only the Gods know that.'

'Well, in the absence of their authority, let us fall back on probability, and calculation. You may live to seventy. In those seventy years, by our calendar, you will have seen twenty-six thousand, two hundred and fifty days.'

Croesus raised an eyebrow. 'Quite impressive.'

Solon waved the praise away. 'I have done this calculation before. Now, half of your days are gone, and they have been happy ones. You are in an enviable position. But what of the thirteen thousand days that remain? How many of them will be happy? Until you die, you can't be called happy. Just lucky.'

'You speak of happiness as though you were a merchant tallying taxes and profits. Or a farmer, weighing up happy and unhappy days like ripe and rotten apples from a year's harvest.'

'Do you study mathematics?'

'I'm afraid the subject does not interest me.'

'Oh, it should. On my travels I have had many conversations with a rather brilliant young Ionian. Just a boy, but something of a prodigy. He believes that all things can be expressed through numbers. If so, surely there must be an equation for happiness. If you want to know what happiness is, then set your mathematicians to it. You have the wealth to hire the best in the world, and they'll figure it out for you soon enough.'

Croesus paused. He half opened his mouth to speak several times, but each time he thought better of it, clearly searching for the perfect retort.

Solon leaned forward and spoke again. 'You sought words of wisdom from the famous Solon? Here they are. Look to the end, no matter what you are considering. Often enough the Gods give a man a glimpse of happiness, and then utterly ruin him.'

Finally, Croesus spoke, calmly and without anger. 'A wise man should judge wisdom, and a happy man judge happiness,' he said. 'What does a miserable old man like you know of happiness?'

'I have offended you.'

'No,' Croesus said. 'I am irritated, and a little bored, but not offended.'

'I shall leave tomorrow.'

'No. Stay for a few days. Relax and enjoy yourself. We shall not speak again, but try to enjoy your stay in my city. You seem to struggle with pleasure, yet I hope you find some of it here.' Croesus clapped his hands, and Isocrates came forward onto the balcony. 'Isocrates is my personal slave. A Hellene, so you should have plenty to talk about together. He will see to your needs this evening.' The king stood up, walked forward, and leaned on the balcony with his back to his guest, in a gesture of dismissal.

Solon stood and bowed. 'I thank you, Croesus.' He paused. 'I wish you all the happiness in the world. That is, after all, what you seem to seek.'

After Solon had left to go to the guest quarters, Croesus looked at Isocrates. 'Something else?'

'A Phrygian nobleman called Adrastus begs an audience with you.'

'Do I know him?'

'You know his family.'

'Very well. Send him to me.' Isocrates bowed and left.

The king of Lydia turned back and looked out over Sardis, out over the pale buildings, over the thousands of his people who busied themselves with their lives and knew nothing of the thoughts of their king. He looked down at the rings on his fingers, then back to the couch on which the old philosopher had sat a few moments before.

He shook his head. And laughed.

3

'So. How was the famous Solon?'

Croesus leaned back and sighed. 'Disappointing.'

At this, his wife laughed.

They sat, together with their eldest son, in a walled garden court-yard – a private refuge in a palace where all eyes watched their ruler, looking for his blessing, or waiting for his mistakes. A rare space for the king to be in, for a few rare moments on the uncommon days when he could spare them, could be a man with his family.

'Disappointing?' his wife said. 'How so?'

'Just an old man, like any other. A wretched old man, worn out by the world. Oh, he is clever, no doubt about that. But he reeks of disappointment. May the Gods preserve me from such an ending.'

'What did you expect from him, Father?' said his son, Atys.

'Something better. Something more. I don't know.'

'Did you ask him anything?'

Croesus scratched his beard and turned his head. 'Yes.'

'And what was it?' his wife said.

'I asked him who was the happiest man he'd ever met.'

'And he didn't say you?'

'No.'

'Oh, Croesus. I know you too well. Must you be the happiest

man in the world, as well as the richest?'

'I thought they were the same thing.' The three of them laughed together. Croesus leaned forward, and gave his wife a chaste kiss on the cheek.

Theirs had been a dynastic marriage, but they had been fortunate enough to grow fond of one another. Croesus remembered seeing Danae for the first time, knowing that they would be married within a month; he had been grateful, at least, that the woman his father had chosen for him was a tall, copper-skinned beauty. Over time, he came to value her thoughts much more than any other quality, for he could bring her any uncommonly tangled problem of the court and she would find a way to unravel it. He had never come to love Danae, but he trusted her.

He looked across at his son. Here, he thought, is one that I do love. Everything about the boy radiated potential. His clearly defined features, already the face of a man at fourteen, had a rare beauty that drew people to him, like iron to a lodestone. He spoke well, learned quickly, and above all he enjoyed playing the roles that were appropriate to him. He loved being the magnanimous prince, just as he would one day enjoy acting as the benevolent king.

Croesus clapped the boy on the shoulder. 'What do you think, Atys? Is your father the happiest man in the world?'

Atys thought for a moment, for it was his habit to consider all questions seriously, even those asked in jest. 'I think I am surely happier than you,' he said, 'since I have such a great man as my father.'

'Listen to the little flatterer!' Danae said. 'He has got the tongue of a courtier, not a king.'

'No,' Croesus said, 'no, he is very clever. He has claimed the prize for himself, yet forced me to feel gratitude in conceding it to him. He is a king. A trickster, but still a king, quick in pursuit of all the honour and prizes on which he can lay his hands. As he should be.'

'And what of me?' Danae asked, a playful smile dancing on her lips. 'With such a husband and such a son, surely my happiness out-strips both of yours?'

Croesus threw up his hands in mock defeat. 'Must everyone deny me this? My wife, my son, Solon the Athenian . . . I suspect conspir-acy. But I shall be the greatest king the world has ever known, and is not the king the man that all others aspire to be? Is not the happiest king the happiest man? Dispute the logic of that, if you will.'

'Did you ask him who was the unhappiest man he had ever met?' asked Atys.

'No. But I think I may have met him today myself.' Croesus shook his head. 'Poor Adrastus.'

'Adrastus?'

'A young man who came to throw himself on my mercy. He is from the east, a Phrygian. He killed his brother by accident, and was hounded from his city as a fratricide. Cursed by the Gods, they said.'

'Will you take him in?'

'Of course. It was an accident. He shall be one of your compan-ions, Atys.'

Atys opened his mouth to reply, but fell silent at a familiar sound. A scraping walk, bare feet dragging over the stones. The family fell quiet and still. They looked to the entrance to the garden, and waited for Croesus's second son to come into view.

Gyges felt his way along the walls like a blind man. His wide eyes appeared to take up most of his head, which was, as always, covered in long, thick hair. He could only rarely be bathed, depending on his unpredictable whims, and so his appearance was that of a wild man, or a prophet. But prophets spoke, and wild men howled. This son could do neither.

When he looked into the boy's eyes, Croesus was always grateful for his silence. They seemed to stare through walls, through people, as though they saw through to another place entirely. A terrible place, judging by the fixed expression of horror on the boy's face.

The king would have preferred to have Gyges kept in some comfortable set of rooms, but his son would not stand to be confined. He would not shout, scream, or make any noise louder than a whistling gasp, but he would pull at his hair, pound on the walls, tear out his fingernails in his attempts to prise open doors and windows if they were barred against him. He was surprisingly strong, and had, on occasion, knocked down a guard or servant who had tried to restrain him. So now they let him go free in the palace, with only one slave, named Maia, tasked to follow him. It was her company alone that he would accept.

Gyges shuffled forward to the edge of the garden. He did not like to walk on anything but stone, and so stopped just before his feet touched earth, as spirits are said to be halted by the shallowest trickle of running water. He stared at his family without apparent recognition. Then he reached out and pointed to Atys, let his hand fall, then raised it again and pointed at Danae. The finger fell once more, and then seemed about to rise a second time. Gyges hesitated, and then instead raised his hand to his chest, the palm facing Croesus, the knuckles against his heart. He turned and walked away, feet dragging against the stones until he was out of sight, Maia following silently in his wake.

None of them spoke for a time. Danae picked at the gold leaf on her necklace. 'A blessing or a curse, do you think?' she said at last.

'Neither,' said Croesus. 'He's no prophet. He sees some other world. He should have been born in that world, not this one.'

Danae did not argue with this. Looking at Gyges, she saw something – a creature worthy of pity, an accident of flesh, a warning from the Gods. But she did not see a son.

In a private chamber in another part of the palace Solon sat and massaged his aching feet. Isocrates stood in the corner of the room, waiting for the Athenian to ask for wine, music, or simply to be left alone. But the guest made no requests, nor did he ask for his solitude. He was, perhaps, waiting to see when the slave would finally speak.

'Gout?' Isocrates said, after a time.

'Yes.'

'It is bad?'

'Yes, I'm afraid so.'

'You have tried remedies?'

'Yes, many. None that worked.'

'That's because you haven't tried my cure. Wait here.'

'You don't have to—' But Isocrates had gone. Solon shifted on his chair, clenching folds of his robe in his fist and releasing them, in a distracted, rhythmic motion. It was not long before the slave returned with a silver bowl in his hand, containing a dark red liquid. 'Drink this,' he said.

Solon took a sip, and winced at the bitter taste. 'What is it?'

'Crocus root in wine.'

'It tastes foul,' he said as he drank it down. 'But I am used to bitter medicine.'

'Within a week or so, you will feel much better. I will give you some to take with you, and instruct your servants in how to find and prepare it.'

'Oh, that won't be necessary. Just give me a year's supply – I am sure your master can afford to spare it. I don't suppose I shall last much longer than that.'

Isocrates shrugged. 'As you will. Though I imagine that the Gods will play a joke on you, and let you live longer; punishment for the arrogance of presuming to know when you will die.'

'Ah. But then I shall have tricked them into giving me a few more years of life, even if I must be uncomfortable . . .' Solon paused, looking on the slave, and saw his arms were strong and his stance confident – almost too much so, for a man in his position. He had the

36

physical presence of a labourer or a wrestler, not a subtle man of the court. 'You don't speak like most slaves I have met,' he said.

'Is that a complaint?'

'It is an observation.'

'I think you prefer honesty. I can flatter well enough, if it is necessary.'

'So you are whatever others want you to be?'

'Something like that.'

'And do you spy on your guests for your king, after you have put them at their ease?'

'Sometimes. Not this time. He doesn't have much interest in you.' Isocrates allowed himself a small smile. 'Then again, I would say that, wouldn't I?'

Solon waved a hand. 'It doesn't matter. There's nothing that I would say to you that I would not say to him.'

'What can I do for you? Would you like a massage? Shall I find someone to play music for you? We have a lyre player whose musicianship is quite exquisite.'

'I have always found the Lydian lyre a little shrill for my tastes.'

'Would you like a woman? Or a young man, if you prefer?'

'I am almost eighty. A dried-up old man. I have very little to offer a woman these days. Or a man, for that matter. I think you mock me.'

'Not at all. There is no predicting the appetites of an old man – they can be the most voracious of all. I once had to bring in half a dozen women in succession before a seventy-year-old Thracian could be satisfied.' Isocrates laughed at the memory 'He was an old goat.'

'Well, I am not he,' Solon said. 'But I will accept a massage. This old body aches.'

'Very well. That is a service I can perform myself.'

Solon undressed and lay on a stone bench at one side of the

37

chamber. As he began to massage the old man, Isocrates found him almost insubstantial, the slack flesh moving aside at the slightest touch, presenting bone.

Solon felt the hesitance of the hands working across his shoulders. 'I suppose I feel like death, don't I?'

'Like a plucked chicken with not enough meat on it.'

Solon laughed. 'You are a good soul, Isocrates. I like you. Do you enjoy working for your master? Is he good to you? If not, perhaps I can buy you for myself.'

'He is good to me, and to my wife.'

'You have a wife?'

'Yes. We met in this household.'

'Unusual for a slave. Or is the custom different in Lydia?'

'No. It is forbidden. But Croesus permitted it, as a reward for my services.'

'And children? Have you been grateful enough to provide your master with more property?'

'No.'

The tone of his response was cold and final, and Solon chose not to press him further. 'So, how did you come to rise to such a prominent position?' he said instead. 'Were you a high-ranking man before you became a slave? Forgive me for saying so, but you do not look like one.'

'No. I was a baker, when I was first taken as a slave. So was my wife. We met in the kitchens here.'

'Ah. That makes sense. Your massage does have something of the kneading board about it. I feel like a particularly damp piece of dough beneath your fingers. How does a baker get from the kitchens to the throne room?'

Isocrates finished on Solon's shoulders, and began to work his way down the Athenian's back. 'Perhaps you have heard about what happened at the succession of my king?'

'I heard something. There was a half-brother causing trouble, as I recall.'

'That's right. Pantaleon. Croesus was his father's choice as heir, but when the king died, Pantaleon tried to usurp the throne. His step-mother and other conspirators came to me, gave me poison, and instructed me to kill the king.'

'I had heard there was a baker involved in this story. That was you?'

'Yes.'

'You used it to poison them instead, did you not?'

'Yes. They were staying in the palace at the time, and it was simple enough for me to serve them with their own poison.'

'Remind me not to make an enemy of you,' Solon said. 'They would have made you a rich man. Perhaps even a free man. Instead you became a murderer. Why do it?'

Isocrates hesitated, his hands pausing for a moment on the old man's back. 'I don't know.'

'I think you do.'

'Croesus is an innocent,' Isocrates said, after a moment. 'And they were such schemers. It didn't seem right, to murder an innocent man to put people like them into power. And those who use poison surely deserve to die by it. Is that a proverb?'

'It should be. So, you are a baker, a poisoner, now the personal slave of the king. You have many talents, it seems.'

'I like to think so.'

'I am not sure he is worthy of you. I cannot tell you the number of courts that I have visited where the slaves had more wit than their masters. I have begun to think that perhaps our cities would be much improved if the masters and the slaves were to change places overnight.'

'You do my master wrong.'

'He asked me the most foolish question today. Sitting there with a look in his eyes like a shy boy in front of a beautiful girl. I thought he had some profound dilemma to present to me. A good philosophical puzzle, perhaps. Instead he asked me to name the happiest person I had ever met.'

'And you didn't say him?'

'No. I told him it was Tellus. That vexed him.'

'And who is Tellus?'

'An Athenian, like any other.' Solon smiled. 'Your Croesus, he is a decent man, and not a bad king by all accounts. But he's a fool.'

'He's no fool.'

'Then what is he?'

Isocrates shrugged. 'Inexperienced.'

'Ah. There you have it. He hasn't seen much of the world, has he? An innocent man. That's why he thinks he's happy.' Solon paused, turning the thought over. 'Thank you, Isocrates. You have given me the answer I was looking for.'

'How do you mean?'

'There was something in his character that I couldn't quite understand. I am thinking of writing something, you know, on the characters of kings and of their closest slaves. The chapter on Croesus would have been incomplete without that little observation of yours.'

Isocrates finished his massage at the base of the other man's back, stepped backwards, and bowed. Solon sat upright, stretched and muttered appreciatively.

'My thanks to you,' Solon said. 'In return, I shall give you something.'

'My duty is my reward.'

'I doubt that's true. I have no coin to give you, but perhaps you will accept a secret.' And before the slave could respond, Solon leaned forward and spoke a few words in his ear.

Isocrates stepped back and looked at the other man warily. Solon smiled. 'I know slaves have little use for other men's secrets,' he said.

'My apologies.' The old man yawned.

'You are tired,' the slave said. 'I will leave you.'

'Yes, I am tired. Sleep comes easily when you are as old as I am. Practice for what lies ahead.' Solon rubbed at his face. 'Thank you for your company, Isocrates. I don't suppose I shall see you again. I doubt that your master will spare you during the rest of my stay here.'

'You are right. Good luck with your writing.'

'Oh, that.' Solon waved a hand dismissively. 'I will never finish it. I'll die long before it is done, and if it is not finished by me it will have to be burned. There is nothing more dangerous than leaving a half-finished work behind when you die. Some fool will come along and finish it for you, and your legacy is tainted.' He paused. 'A shame, though. You would have warranted a most interesting chapter to yourself. Instead, you will be forgotten by history.'

'The only slaves that are remembered are those who were foolish or treacherous, or died badly. To be forgotten is not so bad.'

Isocrates went to leave, but stopped at the doorway. Solon looked up at him. 'Something else?'

The slave turned back. 'I am curious. Why start your work, if you know you will never finish it?'

Solon paused. 'I remember, a few years ago, at one court or another, listening to a boy recite a poem. It was quite beautiful. After he had finished, I asked him to teach it to me. Another man in the room looked at my grey hair – what is left of it – and asked me why I was bothering to learn the poem, old man that I was. I told him, "So that I may learn it and then die."' He shrugged. 'What else is there to do?'

Isocrates kept his head low and his pace steady after he left the guest chamber. He looked at no one as he walked through the narrow corridors of the palace, and paused only to flatten himself against the wall when someone approached.

As he walked, he felt eyes pass over him briefly, then slip away just as quickly. He wondered whether any of those men and women, if asked about it an hour later, would say that they they had seen him at all. He doubted it. They would not be lying. They had simply trained themselves not to see him or any other slave, any more than one would notice a door or a well that one used every day. If any of them had noticed him, they would have assumed that he was running an errand for his king. None would have suspected that he might be running an errand for himself.

It took him some time to find whom he was looking for. There was no predicting what her movements would be, where she would be found or even if she could be found at all. Many times, he had squandered what free time he had travelling from one room in the palace to another, chasing phantoms through the corridors of Sardis. This time, he was fortunate. After only a short search, in a small courtyard at the gate of palace, he found Maia, the slave who watched the king's second son.

As always, she was with her charge. He watched as the boy slowly paced around the dusty courtyard. The guards who stood near by were careful to stay away from him. Any other mute they would have laughed at and toyed with, and so, unable to mock a royal prince and not knowing what else to do with him, they tried to ignore him. They watched Maia instead.

She was not one of the beautiful slaves. Plain-faced and heavy-set, Maia had little to draw the wandering eye to her. When, on occasion, Isocrates was asked by another slave why he had chosen her as his wife, he would say, and only half in jest, 'Because she's patient.'

It was a quality that well suited her to her task as the boy's guardian. For the most part, she left Gyges alone, staying just out of arm's reach. Occasionally, judging his mood, she would move quickly to pick up something for him to play with. A loose reed, a cracked piece of pottery, a rag of cloth, whatever came to hand. He was known to reject any toys that were given to him, accepting only these improvised, adapted objects which he used for games that no one else could understand.

Isocrates watched them together, his wife and the boy, as they moved around the courtyard in a strange, broken dance, sometimes drawing close, but never touching. For a moment, he allowed himself to imagine that it was his son at play there, not the king's.

Maia looked up for a moment from her charge, and saw her husband standing in the doorway. He smiled, opened his mouth to call to her, but her eyes warned against it. She made a slight gesture with her hand. He looked up, and saw, from a balcony, the king of Lydia looking down on the courtyard.

Croesus was watching Maia playing patiently with his son. Sometimes, a hint of a smile worked its way on his face, when Gyges acted like any other child, absorbed in his own secret games and invented world. Then the boy would turn away and hiss or moan, make the alien sounds that no other child made, and the king's half-smile would twist in on itself – whether from pain or disgust, Isocrates could not tell. For the most part, the king's face was unreadable. Perhaps he was trying to pretend to himself that he too was watching another man's son.

A sound from the courtyard made Isocrates look back to Maia and Gyges. He saw her crouch down by one of the piles of rubbish that were scattered on the ground. It was not until she started moving backwards, still crouched, that he saw she had found a stray dog hiding there. She coaxed it out with patient words and gestures, and it came forward warily, blinking at the sun.

It was an ugly thing, its coat uneven with mange, its left ear little more than a ribbon of scarflesh from one fight too many. Maia led it past Gyges. The boy ignored it at first, but when it drew close, he reached down and ran a shuddering hand through its coat, gentle and forceful in turn. At his touch, the dog turned back and licked at his hand, a brief moment of affection, before it wandered away, sniffing at another pile of rubbish for some stray bone or hunk of rotten meat to chew on.

Gyges smiled, a brief, brilliant smile, and gave a gasping noise that might have been his version of a laugh. With a motion as natural as it was unexpected, he reached out and took Maia's hand. She was too surprised to react or pull away, and Gyges passed a finger over her palm, once, before he started back, turned away, and wandered to the other side of the courtyard as though nothing had happened. Isocrates looked up to the balcony, and saw that the king had averted his eyes from this sight.

Taking his opportunity, Isocrates walked across the courtyard. Maia turned away from him as he approached, and curled one hand behind her back. Without slowing as he walked past, he reached out to her and, for an instant, let his fingers pass over hers. A passing touch and he was gone, walking between the guards and through the doorway to another quarter of the palace. He wondered how many days it would be before he could steal another touch from her.

Before he went back into the palace and back to his duties, he risked a glance over his shoulder, to see if Croesus had seen him. But the king had gone.

4

That night, Croesus dreamed with the clarity of a prophecy.

He dreamed that he was born deep under the earth. He passed centuries in the still dark, feeling the slow expansion and contraction of the ground beneath him, listening to the discordant sounds that echoed down from the surface as cities rose and fell, seas were born and died. He rested, and was at peace within the earth.

But then light and air broke into his home. Bronze picks cut him away, loaded him onto carts, and took him from the place of his birth. He was a piece of iron, removed from his mountain tomb to become a slave to men. He travelled for many days over mountains and hills, through small towns and villages where blacksmiths and tradesmen tried to buy him. His owners would not sell; he was of a noble lineage, too good to be beaten into a horseshoe or part of a plough. Soon, the convoy crested a hill that was familiar to him from his waking life, and looked down on the city of Sardis.

In the armourer's forge, he sweltered in the fire. He turned red, then white with the heat, but he felt no pain, even as the hammer fell on him and pounded him flat. He felt his form become sharper and sleeker. He was changing into something deadly, something beautiful.

He had to await his destiny, hanging in an armoury deep within the palace. Somehow, the wait in the armoury, though it spanned only a few years, was far more painful than the centuries he had slept in the earth. Could there be a worse fate than to be moulded into something remarkable, only to waste away the years unused, to rust and break and be discarded? Occasionally his metallic pulse would quicken as human hands took hold of him, but it was only to be cleaned and sharpened or paraded in ceremony. At night, when men slept but forged iron could talk freely, he and his companions in the armoury spoke of the duels they would fight, the great battles that they would win, if only they were given the opportunity.

He witnessed the coronation of his waking self as king of Lydia. Borne by a soldier on the walls of Sardis he watched the parade go past, watched as the new king waved to the cheering crowds and smiled at the chanting of his name. As a man, that day had meant everything to him. As a weapon he felt only the hope that he might finally go to war. A new king always went to war.

The wars came, but he remained in his armoury, growing older and weaker. As the years passed, some of his fellows descended into a senile madness, boasting of wars they had never fought, claiming to have been the personal weapons of renowned warriors who had died centuries before. Some rusted, were taken away, and never returned. Croesus wondered if he would prefer that fate, to be cast out to rust and dissolve back into the earth, rather than this eternity of waiting. But that was not his destiny.

He was taken from the armoury, bundled with half a dozen of his fellows, covered with hide and strapped to the side of a pack animal. For days he jolted along the road, listening to the excited chatter of his companions, roused from their stupor and going at last to war. He lived in darkness, shielded from the elements, waiting. He was reminded of his first days beneath the earth, and he prayed that the journey would not end, that he would remain for ever in this same exquisite state of anticipation.

But the battle came at last, the air alive with the screams of fearful men, the animal cries of the enemy, the sound of iron against iron, iron through skin, iron into bone. He circled the edges of the conflict, waiting patiently. He felt the practised hand that gripped him with a dry palm, waiting to make a throw that would count.

The entire world stood still. His master let him fly, and he felt the air roar, sensed a single figure growing large and filling his world.

He struck deep, tasted blood. Buried in flesh and bone, he could feel the dying heart beat through him, and knew that the wound was mortal. His master's hand gripped him once more, and with a single motion he was pulled loose and hung suspended above the body of his enemy. He saw the face of the man he had killed.

It was his son, Atys.

Croesus woke. He sat alone, his wife far away in her own private quarters, and shook silently in his bedclothes until he found the strength to move. He went to a basin of water and washed his face, swallowed a goblet of wine. He could still feel his son's blood on his face, still taste it on his lips.

He cried out for his guards. They entered the room in a moment, checking the corners, prodding the curtains with the tips of their spears, their hands running over Croesus to search for a hidden wound. He waved them away. 'Listen to me.' He voice trailed off, and his eyes flickered across the bodies of his guards. He saw the iron daggers and iron short swords strapped to their waists, the iron-headed spears they clutched in their hands. He thought of the thousands of iron weapons in Sardis, of a death waiting in every part of the palace.

'Leave all your weapons here,' he said. 'Then go to my son and guard him with your lives.'

They exchanged uncertain looks. 'Guard your son without our weapons?' one of them asked.

'Yes,' Croesus said, 'exactly that. Go, now.'

It was not for them to question the king further, and so they placed their weapons before him and left to obey their orders. Croesus sat on the stone floor and ran his hands over the blades, trying to feel for anything that felt familiar. He held each one up in turn to his ear, as though hoping that it might whisper its name to him. In his dream, each of the weapons had spoken with a different voice, and the individual patterns of the iron had been as diverse and familiar to him as the faces of his own family. Now they all looked the same, had no voice of iron to mark them apart. He spent the rest of the night crouched there, cradling the blades in his arms, trying to discover if one of them might be the weapon that would kill his son.

In the morning, a new decree was announced in the city. Croesus commanded that all iron weapons outside of the armouries were to be taken from the men's quarters and hung up in the women's quarters. All the armouries were to have their guard doubled, and no weapons were to leave them without his permission. Soon after, the palace guards were rearmed with bronze weapons. The guards complained to their captains when the soldiers of the city jeered at their inferior, effeminate weaponry, but the edict stood.

The fear was choking at first. For weeks afterwards, he would spend much of his free time in one armoury or another, touching each spear and sword and arrowhead in turn, trying to locate his dream self, his iron double. But, gradually and inevitably, the fear receded. He had been granted a vision, and surely no vision would come without the ability to change that future. The Gods would not be that cruel.

The absence of iron weapons soon became nothing more than another strange custom of the Lydian court. Rumour spread in the neighbouring countries that it was an aesthetic choice, that Croesus, in his vanity and his love of glittering wealth, found bronze more pleasing to his eyes than iron. The king enjoyed this rumour, and began to spread it himself.

In time, he almost came to believe it.

5

The priest brought two sets of hands together, pronounced the old words, and they were married. The watching crowd cried out, and Croesus tried to give his voice to the celebration. But no words came, only air – a soft sigh of relief.

Five years had passed, five years in which Lydia had grown stronger. Tribe and city, island and township – all people west of the Halys river soon came under the power of Croesus. Some fought or endured siege for a time, others surrendered as soon as the flag of bull and lion was seen on the horizon. After the wars, the eastern tribes brought Croesus offerings of honey, necklaces of gold beads, patterned silver bracelets. The Ionians gave him red wine in black and brown amphorae, the black the colour of Nubian skin, the brown the colour of wet earth, the deep red wine like blood and water.

Five years of conquest and prosperity, and only now had his son chosen to take a wife.

He had made countless introductions to the daughters of the Lydian nobility, but his son, smiling shyly, had rejected each one. Croesus could have forced his son to respect his wishes, but found he did not have the heart for it. He wanted more than anything for his son to be married, but, it seemed, was powerless to bring it to pass.

49

The king waited, and each day he woke and prayed for his son to fall in love.

He looked around the temple, at his family. Atys sat drinking wine with the other young men as they pledged countless toasts to the health of the new couple. Occasionally one of them would lean in close to Atys to whisper something in his ear. Obscene suggestions, judging by the way Atys blushed and shook his head. Amongst them, drinking quietly, was Adrastus, the man who had thrown himself on Croesus's mercy five years before. Croesus remembered how the priests had poured pigs' blood over Adrastus's hands, reading the spooling gore as it ran down to the floor and pronouncing the omens to be good, the blood guilt cleansed. The priests had received a gold statue four cubits high from Croesus in return. Good omens did not go unrewarded, and Adrastus had been taken into the royal household without complaint.

He looked at the women. Danae moved through the crowd, mollifying disappointed fathers, entertaining visiting ambassadors and diplomats. He looked at Iva, the woman his son had chosen at last to be his wife. She had a delicate beauty, and it was not difficult to see why Atys had been drawn to her, though she was thinner than Croesus would have liked, and shy too. She was the daughter of a minor nobleman, and it was a match that gave no political advantage, but to the king that no longer mattered. He saw Maia sitting with the new bride, talking quietly. He supposed she was telling Iva of what would happen in the night ahead, telling her not to be afraid. Beside them both, Gyges sat with a bewildered expression on his face, looking in on a strange ritual from this other world. He had, at least, understood enough to remain quiet during the ceremony. The king wanted no ill omens on this day of all days.

Croesus turned away from the wedding crowd, and found Isocrates at his side, waiting silently for orders.

'Isocrates.'

'Master.'

'Everything is well with our guests? No trouble from the Ionians?'

'They seem to be behaving themselves. Do not worry, all is as it should be. It is a fine wedding.'

'Yes. I suppose it is.' Croesus smiled.

'You are happy, master?'

'Relieved. It's a difficult thing, having one's happiness depend on those one cannot control. Don't you think?'

'I wouldn't know, master.'

'I suppose you wouldn't.' Croesus turned away, but did not dismiss his slave. 'I'd like you to do some investigating for me.' He gestured to the milling crowd. 'Talk to the Athenians. They have a small delegation here. Afterwards, send our messengers and emissaries to the city.'

'Yes, master. And what am I to enquire about? The state of the Athenian army perhaps? Or their relations with Sparta, with Delphi?'

'No, no. Nothing like that. I want you to find out about Tellus.'

'Tellus?'

'Yes.' Croesus looked closely at his slave. Few would have noticed a change in the man, for he had given no obvious outward sign. The slightest tensing of the slave's body, a particular flatness to the eyes – it took a man as familiar with him as Croesus to notice this response. 'You have heard of him?' the king said.

'I do not think so,' Isocrates replied. 'Whom do you mean?'

'A man of some fame. Dead now, or so I have heard. Killed in battle against Eleusis. Solon spoke of him. It shouldn't be hard to learn more of him. Not for a man of your talents.'

Isocrates bowed low to hide his eyes. 'As you wish.' He turned to walk away.

'Isocrates?'

He looked back at his king. 'Yes?'

'You are sure you have not heard of Tellus?'

'No, master,' Isocrates said.

It was the first lie he had ever told his king.

6

Far north of Sardis, the woods of Mysia sprawled across land that lay beneath high mountains. They were dense, broken only by the path of the great Macestus river, and the occasional natural clearing where the trees would not grow. It was in one of these rare clearings, at the same moment that Atys's marriage was taking place in the great city to the south, that a hunter lay on a bloodied patch of earth. He lay, quiet and still, and waited to die.

It was a monster, larger than any boar he had ever seen or heard of before. They had heard the rumours, he and his friends, and had gone out into the woods to hunt it. To protect their lands. In pursuit of glory. They were all experienced hunters, careful and skilled. It hadn't mattered. The boar had killed them all.

He had set the spear perfectly as the boar charged at him. Again and again, he re-created the moment in his mind, trying to think what he could have done differently, but there was nothing. The spear had been positioned without error, but as soon as the point touched flesh, the shaft had shivered and snapped as though the beast's hide were made from stone. It had carried on its charge at full force, and for an instant, when it was only a few spans away from him, he had seen himself reflected in the boar's eyes. He had seen his death there. Then the sharp pain as the tusk entered his stomach, the taste of wet dirt in his mouth as he rolled against the ground again and again until he came to rest against a tree.

Then, he lay still and listened to his friends as they died.

He was alone now. Distant but growing closer, he could hear the thud of the boar's hooves against the grass, the angry snorts that escaped its nostrils. He had pulled himself upright, his back against the tree. His skin was cold, cold enough to make him shiver in the heat of the midday sun, but he could feel a thick warmth seeping down into his groin and to the top of his thighs. Hesitant, he reached down to touch his wound. His fingers brushed against a hot wet coil. A piece of himself exposed to the air, and he pulled his hand back as though it had been burned, and turned his head away. He didn't want to look at his wound.

His eyes fell on the high mountain that loomed in the distance. He wondered if that was where the boar had come from. He had heard it said that gods lived there.

As he lay dying, he hoped that the boar was a god. It would be a good thing, he thought, as the padding and snorting of the boar grew louder behind him, to have been killed by a god.

Again, he smelled the stench of the boar. He felt its hot breath against his neck.

Rumour travels faster than horses. By the time a delegation from Mysia had arrived in Sardis to plead for help, the city was already alive with stories of the boar.

It had killed a dozen men already, it was said, and every village and town for a hundred *stades* around lived in fear of it. Crops remained unplanted, and animals wandered wild in the fields whilst their keepers remained barricaded indoors. It was like a monster out of the old myths, and the people of Sardis argued endlessly as to whether it was merely an overgrown monstrosity or the child of a god. Auguries were taken by priests throughout the city to try and provide some answer to the mystery, but their results were inconclusive and contradictory, and each night the air in the city was alive with the scent of burning fat from a dozen different temples. The stray monster of a distant land had come to obsess the Lydian people. Perhaps, invincible as their empire was, they wanted an enemy to be afraid of, a threat against which to unite. If so, they found it in the beast haunting the woods in the north.

After the Mysians arrived at court, Croesus let them make their plea in front of a public crowd. After they had finished speaking, he threw up a hand to quiet the room.

'My honourable subjects,' he said. 'I grieve for the sons that you have lost, and am dismayed that your people have been reduced to fear and terror. No doubt the Gods have seen our prosperity, the great wealth and strength of our kingdom, and have chosen to test us.

'You all remember the story of Heracles, do you not? He fought against the Erymanthian boar. Perhaps this boar we hunt is a descendent of that monster. Heracles captured the boar, but we live in harsher times, and we will not be so merciful. This monster's head will hang from the gate of the palace, and his pierced hide will become one of my greatest trophies.

'I will dispatch my own hunters to kill the beast. Any man of Lydia may join them, as servant or huntsman. The man who strikes the killing blow will be awarded ten talents of gold, with another talent for each man who proves himself valiant. We will end this terror, and our country will be at peace once again.'

Croesus paused for a moment, looking out over the crowd to judge the impact of his speech. He could feel, in the air, the particular silence that the actor and the politician both crave. Whatever happened next, whether the boar were taken or not, his part in the drama would not be faulted.

'Who will go with them?' he said.

A voice, familiar and strong, came from the crowd. Croesus recognised its sound and tone, but his mind refused to believe it at first. Then a man pushed to the front and advanced beyond the others to stand alone, and the king could deny the truth no longer. It was Atys.

His son had grown into a striking man, skilled with horse and spear, and yet Croesus could not help but see a child standing there. And he fancied that in his son's eyes he could still see a child's desire, the desire to win his father's pride.

Croesus said nothing for a time, his face impassive. Several times he parted his lips to speak, but each time he swallowed his words. 'No,' he said at last. 'You shall not go.'

'Why not?'

'It would not be fair to our people, to risk their future in this way.'

'I will be protected by the very finest, travelling through the lands of our allies. There will be no danger.'

The king shook his head. In the past, whatever challenge confronted him, the words had always come without effort, entire speeches conjured from nothing. Now, no matter how eloquently he tried to shape his thoughts, they distilled themselves down to a single word.

'No,' he said again, not much above a whisper.

'Why,' said Atys, 'then I shall sneak from the palace at night to join the hunters.'

'My son—'

Atys turned to the people who packed the hall. 'What do you say, people of Lydia. I will be guided by your will. Shall I go with them?' A roar broke out from the crowd, loud enough to fill the throne room, and Atys turned to his father, triumphant. The crowd roared again, surging forwards past the guards towards the prince. They brushed the backs of their hands against his hair, placed their fingertips to his forehead and the nape of his neck. A few were bold enough to clasp his hand, all hoping for a touch of their champion.

Feeling the hunger of the crowd, knowing that now, truly, it could not be undone, Croesus descended the steps of his throne and advanced into the mob. The people parted before him, and he embraced his son tightly.

'Atys, my brave son, let me congratulate you.' His voice dropped. 'But in private.'

'Father—'

'What were you thinking?'

'My father—'

'No, don't tell me. I know it all already.' Croesus paused to breathe, his face white with anger. 'You think it a sport to humiliate your father.'

'I meant no disrespect.'

'It was very clever. Cornering me like that. Very sharp.' He lifted a finger and held it in front of his son's face. 'But don't ever do it again. Ever.'

Atys bowed his head and said nothing.

'Why do this?' Croesus said, his anger ebbing.

'For glory, father. For the glory of it.'

'Of course. Why else?' Croesus hesitated. 'I am afraid for you, Atys. I am afraid.'

Atys nodded. 'There will be danger. But the prize is worth the risk.'

'You talk like an epic's hero. This isn't you. Talk like my son.' He paused. 'Stay here.'

Atys said nothing for a moment, weighing his answer carefully, the way he had ever since he was a boy. 'Do you remember,' he said, 'when I was young, when we spoke in the garden after you had seen that man from Athens? Solon was his name.'

'Yes. I remember.'

57

'I said I must have been the happiest of us all. Because I had you as a father.'

'Atys—'

'How can I become a king like you when you hide me away in the palace like a woman? When you make me run from the sight of iron because of some dream?'

Croesus did not speak for some time. He had told his son of the dream, soon after iron had been banished from the palace, and as a boy Atys had believed it with the trust of a child for a father who cannot be wrong. Now, as a man, he did not. 'Do not mock my dream,' Croesus said.

'Then think it through. This prophecy is a blessing. I cannot be killed by this boar.' Atys tried a smile. 'He isn't going to come to battle with spear and shield, is he? That's what your dream means, that I cannot be killed by a beast, no matter how terrifying it is. Please, let me go.'

The king leaned in close to his son, and stared at him in silence for a time. 'I hate that you put me through this,' he said. 'I hate you for this.' He turned his back on Atys. 'You may leave.'

'I'm sorry I displease you, Father.' Croesus could hear the pain in his son's voice, but he would not turn around.

'Go then. And send Adrastus to me.'

He waited for a time, his mind empty, and listened to his son leave. Then he heard the sound of another pair of feet against the stone, and the soft noise of Adrastus's robe as he bowed.

'Adrastus,' he said, 'you did not volunteer for the hunt?'

'No. A man with my poor luck has no place on a venture like this. Have I displeased you, my king?'

'No, no.' Croesus voice grew hesitant, absent. 'Have I been kind to you, Adrastus?'

'My lord, you have given me back my life.'

'I see.' Croesus dropped his head and looked at the ground. 'I think

58

you must be the most loyal man I know, since you owe me the most. That makes sense, doesn't it?'

'My lord?'

'Go with the hunters, Adrastus. Protect my son.'

Once again, Adrastus bowed low. 'With my life, my lord.'

7

Late at night on the plains of the north, the hunters gathered around
a fire. They passed around a heavy wineskin, trading stories and crude
jests. They were not too crude – Atys's presence tempered their
language. They sat and talked and looked at the stars for some sign or
omen that might guide them, for there are few who need the luck of
the Gods more than hunters.

After the wineskin had made its way around the circle several
times, one of the men produced a small skin drum and began to beat
a syncopated rhythm. The others, yelping and whooping, staggered
to their feet and began to dance. Atys smiled and waved them off as
they implored him to join them, but insistent hands dragged him up,
and soon he was moved amongst them, his quick feet picking up the
step.

The drum sang faster and faster, and the men danced with it,
all knowing that the first man to stop dancing would be no man at
all. They expected Atys would be the first to cry off, but he was
strong and determined, and kept up with the best of them. They
danced at a furious pace, until finally one man's legs shook and gave
way and he fell to ground. The others collapsed only a moment
later, laughing and howling insults at the man who had fallen first.
The drummer slowed his rhythm, allowing them to recover. Soon,

the beat would bring them all to their feet again.

Out on the edge of the camp, Adrastus sat alone. He watched the dancing, waiting for the noise to die down so that he could return to the fire and sleep in the warmth, for he knew he would not be welcome at the camp until then. He looked out to the east, towards Phrygia. The distant home he would never see again.

He heard a noise behind him and turned, his hand reaching for the spear at his side. Atys threw his hands up in the air in mock surrender, a wineskin slung over his shoulder, his legs still unsteady from his exertions at the fire.

'May I approach and sit, fearsome sentinel?' he said.

'Of course. My apologies.' Adrastus spread his cloak out on the ground, knocking the dust from it with a few strokes of his hand, and Atys sat down beside him.

'You should not talk to me, you know,' Adrastus said. 'None of the others do. They know I am bad luck.'

'If you were bad luck, you wouldn't have found your way to Lydia. You wouldn't have had the fortune to have a man like my father take you in.'

'And I wouldn't have a man like you as my friend.'

'That as well. Come,' Atys said, 'join us by the fire? It makes me sad to see you out here.'

Adrastus smiled. 'No. I wouldn't want to make the others uncomfortable.' He looked over his shoulder. The music had ended, and the men sat watching them. 'You see, they observe us. Don't stay too long, or they will think that I am drawing your good fortune from you, like an evil spirit. But I thank you. You are kind to me.'

'You are a friend to me, Adrastus. When I am king—' He checked himself.

Adrastus laughed. 'Don't stop. There's no harm in it. What prince doesn't dream of being king one day? You would be a poor son indeed if you lacked ambition.'

'No. It's bad luck to speak like that. But there will always be a place for you at my side.'

'Thank you, Atys.'

They sat in silence for a time.

'Did you have a wife, back in your homeland?' Atys said.

'Yes, I did.'

'Do you miss her?'

'A little. We were never in love. Not like you and Iva. But she was kind to me, and fond of me, I think. She wept when I left, and they were tears for me, not for her. You understand what I mean by that?'

'Yes. You should marry again. There are plenty of women who would be honoured to have you for a husband. You are in the king's favour. I could ask—'

'No.' Atys started at the interruption. 'You may not believe that I am cursed,' Adrastus continued slowly. 'But I am glad that I have no children. I did a terrible thing, and that is my punishment. To live alone, and have no children to follow me.'

Looking at him, Atys suddenly felt like a boy again, a boy who knew nothing of grief. Adrastus gave him a companionable touch on the shoulder. 'Good night, Atys. And don't drink too much of that stuff, or you'll feel rotten tomorrow.'

'I'll bear it in mind. Sleep well, Adrastus.'

In a dark, peaceful part of the palace in Sardis, Maia allowed herself the luxury of leaning against a wall to rest her tired legs; she watched Gyges as he knelt on the ground and traced patterns in the dust.

He had been at work for perhaps an hour, tracing a complex sequence of symbols, then standing and scuffing the marks out before kneeling and beginning over again. Once, many years before, Croesus had summoned scholars to examine the marks his son made in dust and sand. He had hoped that they might divine some trace of

62

meaning there; the boy worked with such fixed intensity that it seemed impossible that the symbols he drew could mean nothing. For a time, the king had spoken of how he and his son would soon spend hours side by side, talking silently together in the dust, once his men had solved the riddle of the script.

The scholars studied the boy's work for many months, trying to deduce what Gyges could possibly be drawing. From the images, they tried to extrapolate an alphabet, numbers, some sequence or sign. All had reached the same conclusion. There were no patterns there. They were simply the idle scratchings of an idiot child.

Maia became aware of a presence at one entrance to the room. She did not have to turn towards it to know it was the king. He came more often now, since Atys had left for the north. She sometimes wondered what strange need he satisfied when he came to see his second son; whether, in the lines of Gyges's face, he saw some shadow of his other child.

Most days, he tried to remain unseen, though the king was not as adept at hiding as he thought he was. She always affected not to see him, unless he came forward to speak. She did not know whether Gyges mimicked her pretended ignorance or whether he genuinely did not notice his father, but either way, he never gave any sign that he registered his father's visits.

'Maia.' The king spoke softly, but the sound of his voice, of any voice, was still startling to her.

'Master.' She turned to face the king, and kept her gaze to the floor.

'You may look up. My son, he is well?'

'Yes, he is,' she said. 'He misses his brother.'

'Really.' Croesus gave a pained smile. 'How can you tell?'

'Oh, he has his moods, like any of us. I think I can read them now.' She paused. 'Perhaps that is presumptuous of me. I speak too much, master. Forgive me.'

'No, no.' He shook his head. 'An interesting thought. I should have known you'd be clever, if Isocrates wanted you for a wife. You are a Hellene like him, are you not?'

'Yes. From Phocaea.'

'Do you need anything? Does my son need anything?'

'No, master. We are well taken care of.'

She saw his eyes wander across her face without interest, then stop and fix on her cheek. He clicked his tongue in displeasure. 'Did Gyges do that?'

'Do what?'

He pointed, and she raised her hand, brushing over a small, dark bruise beneath her eye. She shook her head. 'No, master, he would never hurt me. I fell in the courtyard. That is all.'

'Ah. I am glad.' He looked at his silent son. 'It is an onerous enough duty that I have given you without you taking blows for it as well.'

'Oh, not at all. I am happy to take care of him.'

'Why?'

'He makes me feel peaceful.'

The king cocked his head for a moment, as if he expected some trick. Then he smiled. 'I want to reward you. For taking care of my son.'

'I deserve no reward, master.'

'Oh, but you'll have one.' He smiled broadly. 'You can have children. If you want to. No better gift than that, is there?'

She stared at him, her mouth slightly parted.

'I imagine you have refrained out of duty,' he continued. 'Fear, perhaps, of what I might say. There is no need. When I gave permission for you and Isocrates to marry, I meant for you to have that freedom.'

'Thank you, master,' she said slowly. 'But I can't accept.'

'What?'

She paused for a moment then spoke again. 'I am not able to have children, master.'

64

'I see. I am sorry.' He hesitated. 'I must see to my wife. You will tell me if my son needs anything? Anything he wants, it shall be his.'

'Of course.'

'And if you need anything. You must tell me that as well.'

She bowed, and waited until his footsteps had faded away entirely before she straightened again. She turned back to her charge, and, to her surprise, found Gyges watching his father go.

Just for a moment, she thought she saw him smile.

8

On the second day in the Mysian forest, all the signs were that the boar was near.

The birds had ceased to sing, and they saw no mark of any other animal, for man and beast had both fled the creature in the forest. Sometimes close, sometimes distant, they would hear a splintering crash as a bush or tree was uprooted and torn aside; the sound of the alien animal clearing its path through a forest that was not its home. Soon the air was ripe with the tang of boar; some thought they could taste the rusty, faded scent of blood. The dogs howled and whined on their leashes, tormented by a creature they could smell but not see. The men were silent. None of them had spoken since the forest fell quiet.

They moved up to a small clearing. Adrastus went first, peering at the undergrowth. He saw nothing, waved his companions on, and went to step forward himself. Something compelled him to look again. His eyes picked over the trees and thick bushes, and fell on a large shadow in the darkness. It was so still that for a moment he took it for a trick of his eyes, his imagination giving a moment of life to a fallen tree.

The great shadow blinked at him. Two black eyes covered over with brown skin for a fraction of a second, then opened again. The boar stepped forward into the light, six cubits from tail to snout and tall as a man's chest, a monster of muscle and scar. It screamed once, as though issuing a warrior's challenge, and charged.

The first wave of spears flew forward in a moment of lethal motion, most splintering away from thick skin, some biting and sticking and making the boar's skin run black with blood. The dogs followed, tearing and ripping at ankles and flanks, and for a moment, Adrastus thought the boar would surely stumble and fall to the ground under their weight.

But the boar stood firm. It shook the spears from its skin, twisting them loose against trees and hooking them out of its flesh. It turned first on the dogs at its side, crushing them beneath its hooves, spearing them on its tusks, breaking their backs against the trees. It moved slowly at first, then with gathering speed, as if performing some terrible dance repeated over and over at greater pace, each killing blow coming quicker than the last.

Atys watched, without fear, as the boar tore the life from the dogs. He held the spear high, the shaft balanced against his shoulder to conserve his strength, waiting for a break in the pattern, a second of stillness to see his weapon home.

It came at last – a moment's hesitation, as the boar looked up from the dogs and towards the men, as it fixed its tiny black eyes on Adrastus. Atys let his spear fly, saw it split a leg open like a rotten log. The boar dropped to the ground and screamed.

From the other side of the clearing Adrastus marked the point high on the proud chest where a muscle of hate beat strongly, put there by the Gods to test the world of men. He lifted his spear and drew it back, then cast it into the air with a single turn of his body.

It seemed as though the boar watched the spear come, as though it had always been waiting to greet that piece of iron. It twisted aside and dropped its shoulder, one final movement of the dance, and let the weapon pass.

The spear sang through the air, its flight still strong and true, and found a different home in flesh.

They sent a messenger riding ahead with their two best horses to bring the news to Sardis. The hunters followed slowly, weighed with grief and marching in silence. The corpse was wrapped in hides, preserved with what spices they had. At the tail of the defeated party, Adrastus walked alone.

When they reached the sight of home, none of the party raised a cheer or made a sound. They could see the gathering at the gate to the city, the tall bronze spears of the royal guard glittering in the sun, and knew that Croesus was there to meet them.

On the day the messenger had come to him, Croesus did not weep. He had seemed puzzled, his mouth slightly open, like an actor in a play who hears a line that is not his cue, yet is still expected to speak, to respond appropriately to the unknown and unknowable. Waiting, as in a nightmare where death is inevitable yet endlessly deferred. Hoping that the messenger was mistaken, that some other man's son had been taken, not his. Now the hunters returned with a corpse, not a miracle, the end of hope lashed tightly to the back of a horse.

Adrastus came forward when they reached the gates, the hunters parting before him. He took his dagger and cut the body loose, took the stiff, heavy weight in his arms and walked to the gates.

He stood before the king, and waited.

Croesus said nothing. He made a small motion with his hand, and Isocrates and another slave came forward to take the body away. The king looked back at Adrastus, inclined his head questioningly. Adrastus gave the dagger in his hand to Croesus, knelt and offered up his throat. The king's hand gripped the dagger, went white. He placed his left hand on top of the kneeling man's head.

Adrastus waited for the fingers to curl into his hair to hold his head

68

back, for the blade to bite at his throat. He heard the dagger fall to the ground, felt the fingers moving gently over his face. The touch of a father.

'It's not your fault, Adrastus,' he said. 'It is my fault.' He leaned forward and kissed Adrastus on the forehead, as he used to kiss his son. 'You are welcome to stay in the city. I hope you do. But I shan't see you again. You understand that, don't you? I cannot stand to look on you.'

Adrastus watched him go, his eyes empty of hope.

North-west of Sardis, another city rose from the plains. At dawn or dusk, a lost traveller might have mistaken this place for Sardis itself. He would see towering shapes looming ahead of him, a human order imposed on nature's formless aspect. It was only on drawing closer that the traveller would realize that he had been mistaken, that he had arrived instead at a silent city of the dead.

A hundred barrows rose from the ground, each white stone tomb covered with a great mound of clay, as if a god had reached from the sky, lifted earth with the palm of his titanic hand, and scattered it over the barrow to honour the dead. The finest Lydian stonework was to be found buried in these great barrows. In this land, the living passed their lives in crude houses of reed and mud brick, the dead lay in flawless marble. What honour was there in building a great house that would change hands with every generation; that would become the prize of some other man, some other king? It was the last home, the one place that truly belonged to only one man, that was most worthy of a great architect's craft.

One tomb towered above the rest – the tomb of Alyattes, Croesus's father. There were those who came from distant lands to stand in the shadow of this great barrow, to marvel at what men had learned to build. Beside this great tomb, as was the custom, lay the tomb for the next royal burial, in the shadow of Alyattes's, a respectful fraction of the size. Croesus had commissioned it long ago, thinking that it would be his own resting place. He had never thought he would use it to bury his son.

The funeral procession gathered by the barrow, in a semicircle to the west, facing the setting sun. Looking over the mourners, Croesus could see only a sickly reflection of those who had gathered at the wedding a short time before. Every member of the Lydian nobility was there, some in sympathy, others out of duty or ambition. Danae and Iva clung to each other, the mother and the widow both exhausted by their grief, only together finding the strength to stand. His eyes fell last on Gyges, who had followed them all the way from the city. For once, Croesus did not care what impression his troubled son might make in the eyes of others, but the boy remained still and silent throughout the ritual. Croesus wondered if this was his way of showing grief, if here at last was something of their world that Gyges could understand.

The priests came forward and made their sacrifices. They lifted the viscera in their hands, weighing them, smelling them, tasting them, and they declared that the auguries were good. They knelt on the ground, and began to chant. They faced west, waiting for the sun to fall from the sky.

As the sun touched the horizon, the chants grew louder, more forceful. From the base of the barrow, six slaves began to walk up the side of the mound, bearing a casket on their shoulders. They marched towards the mourners, the setting sun at their backs, and laid the casket down. One by one, the nobles came forward to place their gifts in the casket. Last of all, the hunters came forward and laid down their notched and broken weapons.

The sun sank fully below the horizon, and the slaves came forward again, bearing torches in their hands, as if they had caught some last spark from the fading sun. Just as they reached the bier, as they were about to bend down and set their torches to the wood of the casket, a voice rang out, calling for them to halt. The voice of the king.

The priests eyed him with uncertainty as he walked to the casket, fearful that the king might commit some sudden blasphemy. Croesus passed the torchbearers, and knelt. He reached into the pile of hunter's weapons, shuddering as his hand brushed against the casket, and drew out one of the weapons in particular. A spear. He stood and raised the weapon, gripping it tight enough to feel his pulse echo through the wood and return to his hand, like an answering call. Though the tip had been carefully cleaned and polished, he recognized it for what it was.

He placed the spear on the ground, and with one stamp of his foot, like a man who breaks the neck of a sick dog, he broke away the point. Croesus picked up the spearhead and placed it within the folds of his robes, close to his heart. He walked away, and listened to the rush of the flames as the slaves cast their torches down, as the fire took what remained of his son. He did not stay to watch.

The priests made their final prayer, a plea for the Gods to be merciful and accept the prince's soul, and the crowd gave a single, brief cry, like the first gasp of a child. Some remained for a time to watch the flames, others left immediately and followed close behind the king. One by one, the mourners turned and made their way back towards the city.

Up on the hills, a single figure watched the procession depart. Watched, and waited for the night to come.

9

When, later, Iva entered Croesus's private chamber, at first she could not see the king. A few small candles, lit and scattered seemingly at random, gave little light. As her eyes adjusted to the near dark, she found him, seated in shadow, so still that she mistook him for a carved sculpture. He gestured silently for her to sit opposite him.

'You asked for me?' she said.

'Yes, I did. Will you take some wine?'

'I . . . yes.' He poured out a cup, added the smallest trace of water to it, then placed it on the other side of the table. He did not pour any for himself.

'You were very brave at the funeral today,' he said. 'It is not an easy thing to bury a husband.'

'Not an easy thing to bury a son,' she ventured.

'Yes. Well.' He looked down and picked absently at the engraving on the table. 'Did he ever tell you that I dreamed of his death?'

'Yes.'

'I suppose you laughed about it together. Laughed at me. The foolish thoughts of a silly old man.'

'No. Atys would never laugh at you.'

'I'm sure. I pressed him to marry young, you know. But he always refused the women I brought him. Fine ladies. Most of them from better families than yours. But he wanted to wait, to marry for love. He loved you.' He looked up from the table. 'Did you love my son?'

'Yes,' she whispered.

'Are you carrying his child?'

She stared at him and said nothing.

'I see I shall have to repeat myself. Are you carrying his child?'

'No.'

'Are you sure? He did not leave so long ago. Perhaps—'

'No. I am sure. I'm sorry.'

'I see.' He nodded slowly. 'A shame. It would be better if there were a child.' Croesus poured himself a cup of unwatered wine, and drank it down in a single draught. 'What should I do? Leave my empire to my idiot son?'

'I don't know.' She hesitated. 'Perhaps your wife—'

'My wife? No. Her womb is stopped. Since she gave birth to Gyges. He has been a curse in many different ways.'

She said nothing.

'It really would be better if you had a child.'

'I don't understand.'

He hesitated. 'You are very beautiful,' he said.

She looked to the door.

'They won't let you,' he said. 'The guards, I mean. Not without my order.'

'My lord—'

He poured her another cup. 'Come. Drink with me. Don't look so frightened. You misunderstand.'

Her hand shook slightly, but steadied as she took the silver cup and drank deeply.

'Was he kind to you, my son?' the king said.

'Yes.'

'He was shy when he was courting you, was he not?'

She felt the ghost of a smile pass over her face. 'Yes. I could not

73

understand why the king's son seemed so nervous around me. I thought that was just his way with everyone.'

'It was just for you. I hope he was not so shy when he took you as his wife.'

She flinched. 'My lord—'

'Forgive me. I knew him so well when he was a boy. But they grow away from us, our children. There comes a time when we don't know them at all. You must have known him better as a man than I did. I wish I could have known him as you did.' Croesus blinked, and did not understand why he still could not see. It was not until he put a hand to his face that he realized he was weeping.

She looked up at him, and he saw pity in her eyes. He took her hand. He felt her tense, but she did not pull away. He leaned forward, and kissed the top of her head. He felt her relax slightly at the fatherly gesture. Then, with his other hand, he tipped up her chin and kissed her mouth.

She submitted to the kiss, but when he tried to take another, she turned her head away.

'I can't,' she said.

He said nothing.

'Please. Let me go.'

'You owe me a son.'

'Let me go. Please, my lord.' She stood, hesitant, and looked again at the door.

He stood up and seized her arms. She twisted out of his hands and he felt a sudden anger at how easily she escaped him. He seized her again, gripping tighter this time until she cried out in pain. He shook her, once, like a dog shaking a rat, and she turned her face away and closed her eyes.

He put one hand to her robe. He had the idea that he should tear it loose, that this was what he should do next. He tugged hard, but the heavy fabric held firm, and he merely spun her around and pulled her off balance. Then he hit her, an open-handed slap to the face; he regretted it at once. It wasn't necessary.

He put his hands into the folds of her clothes, searching for the place where he could loosen the fabric, his eyes firmly fixed on her body, away from her face. He tugged, frustrated, until at last the stubborn folds began to come away. Inside her robe, he felt his hand touch cold skin.

Now he had to get her to the floor. She stood rigid, unresisting but not acquiescent, and he pressed a hand on her shoulder and a hand on her throat to push her down. She fell awkwardly; the harsh slap of skin against stone echoed through the chamber. She sobbed once, and from the door she heard the creak of leather and metal. One of the guards outside, shifting uneasily from one foot to another. Only a few feet away, unable and unwilling to help her.

Croesus knelt beside her, raised his hands to her again and opened her robe. He went quite still. She opened her eyes and looked at him. He stared at her body, his eyes hidden from her. Hesitant, fearful of what she might provoke, she placed her hands on his shoulders, and pushed them back until she could see his face.

He did not meet her gaze. She felt his hands trembling.

'Croesus?' she said softly.

Slowly, he lay down beside her and bowed his head, his shoulders shaking. She breathed heavily, her arms limp by her side. She pulled her robe to her. Then, slowly, she rolled to her side and embraced him on the ground, holding his head against her stomach.

He wept against her empty body, the tomb of his hopes. The place he wished to bury another son, but could not.

On top of Atys's barrow, two guards sat in the dust and cast dice for pieces of copper beside the embers of the fire. When the sun rose, the priests would come to bury the ashes deep within the barrow. It would be placed in a hidden chamber, away from the centre, in an attempt to mislead the swarms of grave robbers who visited the barrows like jackals in the night, mining for the gifts of the dead. Until the morning came, the guards were to watch over the casket, to ensure that no thief came to take the treasures from it.

Some time after midnight, they heard a sound in the darkness. Someone was walking towards them. They did not get to their feet to issue a challenge. A robber would not be so careless. Before night had fallen, they had seen the figure up on the hills. They knew who was coming, and when Adrastus came into the light of the fire, they did nothing more than nod once at him before returning to their game.

Adrastus stared at the casket. He thought of the moment when the spear had left his hand. He had seen Atys on the far side of the boar even as the shaft slipped through his open palm, and had closed his hand again in an attempt to summon back the death that he had thrown. He had grasped only air. Atys had spat blood and screamed as he died. Adrastus thought of his brother, how his face had turned from laughter to horror when Adrastus had slipped and the sword slid home, all those years before.

Adrastus put his hand to his chest, feeling for the heartbeat to fix its location in his mind, running his fingers over the ribs that were his obstacles. He clasped the sword in his hands, his arms shaking. The guards stopped their game to watch, but made no move to stop him.

Life called out to him, and he wavered for a moment longer. He thought of the things he might do, now that he had no fear of death. Perhaps he would take a wife. Perhaps in love he would find forgiveness.

He leaned forward and thrust the sword into his stomach, wrenched it loose, and fell.

The blood flowed thickly and freely, but not swiftly enough. He cried out with the pain, but death did not come to him.

The two guards watched without expression. After some time, one of them came forward and knelt beside him. He leaned down close and whispered a question in his ear. Adrastus nodded weakly in response. The guard stood up, reversed his spear so that the tip pointed straight down. With a single thrust he ended the life of the man who could kill no one, not even himself, except by chance.

In the palace, in his favourite garden, Croesus sat on a bench with his wife, lit only by the flickering torches. They sat close but did not touch, both of them far beyond tears.

'Do you know,' Croesus said, 'I don't think I would have minded. His death, I mean. If he could have given me a grandson.'

'You don't mean that.'

'Don't tell me what I mean.'

The silence grew between them.

'I remember you asked me once,' he said after a time, 'when I would stop worrying about him?'

She nodded dully 'I remember.'

'I told you that I would stop worrying when I was dead. But I meant I would stop worrying once he had given me an heir. How terrible that is.'

She said nothing, and in the quiet he thought of all the memories he would have to uproot and destroy. Memories of Atys when he was born, tiny and silent, filled only with possibility. As a boy, roaring and charging around the gardens of Sardis, tripping and crying, then standing and running once again. As a man, his character shaping and forming like iron in a mould, becoming something remarkable. Each memory had been a treasure to him, now a splinter in his mind. He would have to forget them all, he thought. There was no other way.

'I'm sorry,' Croesus said eventually.

She looked him in the eyes. 'What do you have to be sorry for?'

'I don't know.' Croesus swallowed deeply, but the tears would not come. 'I was weak,' he said. 'I loved him too much.'

'Croesus . . .'

'I will never love that way again.'

The King
552 BC

I

Even as a child, Croesus had loved to play at being king.

It was a part that he liked to play only when he was alone. Croesus had no shortage of slaves and other children to keep him company, all of them happy to play any game the prince chose. But he would not play at being a king in the company of others; if the game were even referred to, he would blush, then shout and scream until he had driven them all away. It was a secret fantasy that Croesus liked to explore when alone, and, for him, solitude was as much of a luxury as company is to the lonely child.

Whenever he could escape his army of helpers and drive away the children who were assigned to play with him, he would run to some abandoned room in the palace and there hold court. As soon as he was sure he was quite alone, he would construct a throne: an upended wicker basket, a chipped stone step, an old, high chair that he had to clamber on to. He needed nothing more than this. His shyness had made him secretive, and he learned to make do with this single prop which could resume its usual function as soon as he stood away from it and affected to ignore it. Ideally, the room he adopted as his court would also feature an obsidian mirror or a chunk of polished stone, and he would position himself so that from time to time he could glance at his own reflection and judge his performance.

Once seated on his makeshift throne, he had to wait only a few moments before the room filled with movement and noise. Generals and statesmen, slaves and guards; the air took shape to produce them all. The abandoned room became draped in rich silks, the floor tiled with gold, the tables littered with goblets of sweetened grape juice and Egyptian honeyed fruit.

Sometimes he held court as a silent king, barely moving, unspeaking. He would rule through the most minute gestures; a fractional nod of the head would be enough to reprieve a man from execution. A hand, held palm down, cutting briefly through the air to exile a traitor for ever. Two fingers straightened from a closed fist would silence an imaginary courtier as he spoke out of turn.

At other times, he would practise his oratory. He would rise from his throne (or hop down from it, depending on its height), strike a pose, and prepare to speak. He believed that the longer the speech, the greater and more persuasive it would be – the aim was not so much to speak clearly, but to speak continuously for as long as possible. He would deliver, even at a young age, rambling orations, lasting for more than half an hour, an apparently unending stream of words stitched together from speeches of his father's, and from the pronouncements of kings in the stories his mother told him.

Croesus could not remember much more of his childhood than this. In the months that followed the death of his son, he explored the recesses of his mind, searching for an innocent memory to escape into, some moment that could make sense of the world again. He had only the vaguest sense of his early years, and while he could recall the occasional event, moments of particular joy and shame, the actual sensations were lost to him. Recalling the past, it was as if he somehow viewed another man's memories, a man from some alien world that he could not understand. But this game of kings, that he had played ten thousand times in as many different ways, was the one memory he did still retain in all of its detail, and of all the times that he played the game, there was one instance that he remembered most clearly of all.

It was autumn, and he was eight years old. His mother was beginning to show the first signs of the wasting sickness that would end her life a year later. There would be no more innocence for him after that, and no more happiness for his father. Alyattes, but on that autumn day that pain was a long way off. His mother had fainted in court, and in the middle of the ensuing distraction he had managed to steal away for an hour of play.

He was in the middle of a speech, promising a dozen sacks of jewels and a hundred slave women to a wandering hero, when he became aware of an intruder at the doorway behind him. A scrape of leather against stone, the faintest sound of rustling cloth, were enough to let him know that he was being watched. Slowly, afraid of what he would see, he turned to face the doorway.

His father, Alyattes, stood there with a small, ambiguous smile on his face. He was a lean and wiry man, dressed in red robes that hung on him a little loosely. These robes tended to trip him up whenever he forgot himself and hurried somewhere, which was often.

Beneath his father's gaze, the boy hung his head. His father was the only person Croesus could not rage at when he was caught unawares. In front of Alyattes, he felt the heat in his throat and lungs, the pain around the heart of a deep and confused shame. He stood still, awaiting and dreading the mocking remark, the reprimand or, worst, of all, the pretence that his father had observed nothing.

'I am sorry to have interrupted you,' Alyattes said lightly. 'I thought you would want to know that your mother is recovering now.'

'Should I go and see her?' Croesus tried to keep the reluctance from his voice, but he knew it was there. He had no desire to return to the court and comfort his pale-faced mother. He wanted to finish his game.

'In a little while. Can I show you something first? A new invention of mine.'

'Of course,' Croesus said quickly. The shame at being discovered would be with him for weeks, and he was relieved to have any distraction.

'Come here.' Alyattes went to one knee, and Croesus walked over to his father. 'Close your eyes, and open your hands.'

Croesus felt a little object drop into his right hand. Keeping his eyes closed, he rolled it forward on to his fingers. Hard and cool and metallic, he could tell no more than that. He opened his hand, opened his eyes, and looked down at it.

It was an ugly thing. Small, like a shrivelled grape in size and shape, pale yellow in colour. It wasn't even pure gold, he realized, recognizing the shade with an already practised eye, but electrum, an amalgam of gold and silver. An image was stamped on one side, but Croesus could not tell what it was. He asked his father.

'It's a lion.'

'The sign of our household,' Croesus said quickly, just as he would give an answer he knew his tutor would like. Looking again, he thought to himself that the design was like the drawing of a clumsy child.

'Do you know what this thing is?' Alyattes said.

'No, Father.'

'It is a coin. What do you think it is worth?'

'Not very much.' He expected to see anger on his father's face, but Alyattes nodded calmly, as though this were the expected response. 'Is that the wrong thing to say?' Croesus said.

'No, no, quite reasonable.' Alyattes shrugged. 'It's a lump of electrum that any man could sift from the Pactolus. Not pure gold or silver, which is a shame. I should have liked it to be gold. You're right – it should be worth very little.' He leaned forward. 'Can I tell you a secret?'

84

Alyattes pointed at the image of the lion. 'Without that stamp, it is valued at whatever some metal trader tells you it is worth. With that mark, it's worth as much as *I* say it's worth.'

Croesus frowned, and tried to understand. Alyattes continued: 'It's harvest season, now. The farmers are gathering their wheat from the land.' He reached out a finger and tapped the metal disc in Croesus's palm. 'If I say it is so, one of these coins will buy the crop of a poor farmer's field. Forty of them, and you've got the worth of everything that farmer will ever produce. The entire value of a common man's life, and I could put it into a bag that you could wear at your waist and you would barely feel the weight. Men will spend their whole lives chasing after these little pieces of marked metal. They will be willing to kill for them. Think about that.'

'What will you do with it, Father?'

'I will use it to raise an army, and go to war in the East.' Alyattes reached forward and ran his hand through his son's hair. 'I will win you a great empire. Won't you like that?'

Hearing this, Croesus tried to hide his disappointment. His father had gone to war several times already in the boy's short life. Croesus liked to hear stories of the battles, but the wars took his father from him for months, sometimes even years, and they made his mother unhappy.

'Isn't there something else you could do, Father?'

'With these riches, what is there to do but go to war?' Alyattes asked. 'You can barter bread for eggs or a horse for sheep in the marketplace, but with this you can buy a new world. That is what my coins are for.'

Alyattes reached down and took the coin back from his son, and Croesus found his fingers reaching for it even as it was taken from him. His father held the metal oval between finger and thumb. 'Listen to me, and try to understand. I love this,' he said, gesturing to the coin, 'more than I love you. And I love you very much. But this . . .'

85

He shrugged. 'It is a remarkable thing. A remarkable thing that I have made. It will change the world.'

Alyattes stood and turned to leave, and as Croesus watched his father walk away he felt for the very first time the sensation that no child can forget – the sense that one's father or mother is wrong. There was something else to be done with this invention, he was sure of it. It could create something greater than a war.

'Can I keep it?' Croesus said, just as his father was about to leave the room.

Alyattes turned back, and smiled approvingly. He threw the coin to the boy, and Croesus took it from the air with a hasty grasp of his hand.

2

War is an infection that breeds in the minds of kings. Once caught, it may come on slowly or burn hot like a one-day fever. It will not die until it is treated with blood.

For Croesus, the first infection came from the sight of a map.

In the early years of his rule, he had fought several small wars of conquest, the inevitable actions of a powerful king surrounded by weak rulers. A dozen cities fell beneath the banner of bull and lion, but the wars meant nothing to him, and they did not compare with the grand campaigns of his father's life. Occasionally, he would glance without interest at a crude map of his empire, but he never felt any desire for anything more precise. His world was Sardis and his family. What more did he need than that?

Yet, after Atys's death, he asked his cartographers to draw up two maps, accurate in every measure, flawless in detail. For a year, his people rode to every corner of the kingdom, counting the beats of their horses' hooves to measure distance. They waited for clear days and climbed mountains to better view the land, producing sketches from the heights of icy peaks. They corresponded with the mapmakers and librarians of distant cities, waiting months for the arrival of crumbling, faintly inked copies of maps they had thought long lost.

At last, the work was finished. In one of the king's throne rooms

87

they first unrolled a handsome scroll of the Lydian empire, deeply inked with the conquered cities, the dividing rivers, the great Aegean sea that bordered the empire to the west.

Croesus looked at the empire he had inherited. He let his hand brush over the soft skin of the scroll, thinking of the thousands of lives that lay beneath each stroke of his finger, all of them paying their fealty to him. From the sea to the west to the river Halys in the east, all these lands belonged to him. He stared at it until he had the image of his empire firmly fixed in his mind. Then, he asked the cartographers to uncover the other map.

Hesitantly, they unrolled the second scroll. This one showed much more than Lydia. It did not venture across the Aegean to the Hellenic city states, but it stretched far to the east and south. He looked on Egypt, Media, Assyria, the nomad plains of the Massagetae, the great city of Babylon. The cartographers, bound by the king's orders, had not played tricks with the scale as they might otherwise have. There was no hiding the vast expanse of land that lay to the east, the hundreds of thousands of men and women who knew and cared nothing for the king of Lydia.

Croesus noticed that one of the mapmakers was shivering nervously. The king smiled at him. 'Don't fear me. I cannot rule the whole world, can I?' Croesus raised his hand, intending to click his fingers and dismiss the mapmaker and the troubling vision he had summoned. He hesitated, his finger and thumb pressed against each other, but not yet making a sound.

He looked over the map one more time. He began at the far edge of his kingdom, the western city of Phocaea. His eyes roved south to Smyrna, the port where ships from half a hundred nations arrived with jewels, silks and spices. He travelled north, reached the banks of the Hermus river and followed it until he reached Sardis. He paused briefly at his capital, then struck east, heading for the Halys river at the border of his lands.

From there, he imagined his eyes as a marching army. He went beyond the Halys, taking Cappadocia and the great city of Trapezus. He led his conquering gaze south, down the Euphrates to Babylon. He lingered there for a time, imagining what it would be to rule the greatest city in the world, a city unmatched in beauty and spectacle by any other. Then he went east again, pausing at another great river. It was the Tigris, and beyond it lay the land of the Medes.

In his father's time, the Medes and the Lydians had been enemies. After many a bloody and inconclusive war, Croesus's sister had been married to Astyages, king of the Medes, and the two peoples had lived in peace for decades. In his mind, Croesus broke the thirty-year peace in a matter of moments, his eyes passing over the Tigris, into the land of the Medes, and seizing his brother-in-law's kingdom.

But his gaze was still hungry, and continued its march east until finally his eye chanced on the river Medus in the heart of Persia, and came to rest there. For some reason, it seemed like the right place to stop.

Gazing at the maps, he understood why war had so captivated his father. He was grateful for the kingdom of the Medes on his borders, the peace treaty with Astyages that he could never break, for he did not trust this ache that he had, this longing for the East. Without his son, there was such an absence in his life. It would be so easy to fill it with a war.

Croesus tried to leave his thoughts of conquest buried deep in the heavy, yellowed curls of the map. He left the throne room for the one place where he would be able to forget them.

As he descended through the palace, Croesus shed his followers like so many layers of unwanted clothing. First, he disposed of the noblemen who begged favours from him, dispatching them one by one until there were none left to bother him. The band of slaves that trailed after him, half of them in service to him, the other half monitoring his movements on behalf of his nobles, was dismissed with a few brief commands. He kept his guards with him for most of the journey deep into the palace, but dismissed them too before he descended the last stairwell.

Alone, he reached a door in a dark and forgotten corridor of the palace. He took a gold key on a silver chain from within the folds of his clothes. He unlocked the door and went inside.

Croesus was in darkness. By touch and memory he made his way to a table at the end of the room, taking one of dozens of oil-soaked torches that had been left piled there. He felt his way to the far end of the table, his hands fumbling for the flints he knew were there, and he struck sparks until the torch caught.

The room flickered into view. The table and floor were furred with dust, and no slave had cleaned here for years. The floor was covered with many trails of footprints, but they were all exactly the same shape and size. They all belonged to him.

He paced around the abandoned room, filled with broken shards of pottery and crumbling chunks of stone. He reached a rotting wooden chest which, when he was a child, had once served as a throne. He poked at one corner with the toe of his boot, and watched the wood crumble into splinters, accompanied by an eruption of insects and tiny grey spiders.

He drew aside the heavy drape at the far end of the room, felt cool air from the tunnel behind it. He reached up and pulled on a cord hanging by the wall. Deep down below, too distant for him to hear, he knew a small silver bell would be ringing. Now they would know that he was coming.

He held the torch in front of him to light the way, and began to descend. He made his way along the narrow corridor, the ceiling just high enough that he could walk without stooping. It had been made specifically for him.

The passage wound down, until glimmers of light began to appear in the distance. The air grew brighter, then too bright, as though he were heading towards the heart of the sun. The end of the passage opened up into an enormous chamber, and the king entered the lower treasury.

He had begun work on these chambers as soon as his father had died. It had taken years to plan and excavate, and he had kept the digging as close a secret as possible. The slaves who had laboured there had been dispatched to work in the mines at the far corners of his empire immediately after the project had been completed. Croesus sometimes wondered to whom they might have told their secrets in the few short years before rockfalls and rotten lungs had silenced them all, but this did not genuinely concern him. If the bandit kings and petty officials of the outer kingdoms knew of the treasury, he did not fear them, but he wanted none within the palace to know the details of this chamber. The treasuries of the upper floors held hundreds of diverse and priceless artefacts. This lower floor was devoted to a single form of treasure.

Thousands of gold and silver coins were piled high throughout the room, forming towers and buttresses and fortresses. Elsewhere they were piled into hills and mountains of gold and silver. Dozens of burning torches ringed the chamber, the polished stone walls and glittering coins reflecting and amplifying the light until it was intense, near blinding. But it did not trouble the king. Croesus had grown used to staring into the sun of his riches.

His father had long desired gold coins. Alyattes had known that gold and silver both hid within the electrum of the Pactolus river, but his alchemists were never able to discover the technique of separating them. His dream had been to stamp the seal of Lydia on golden coins that would fill the markets of Sardis and the Hellenic cities on the far side of the sea. But he died unsatisfied.

Croesus's metallurgists had finally perfected the art of turning electrum into gold and silver. They had tried every possible combination of heat and pressure that they could imagine, to no effect. One day, in sheer desperation, they added salt to the molten metal, as though it were a gamey meat in need of seasoning, and once the fire was scorching hot, the silver separated to the top, enabling it to be skimmed away like scum from a stew, and the bottom of the crucibles shone with pure gold.

Croesus had kept finding reasons to postpone the day when the coins would enter circulation and replace the electrum coins that had so fascinated his father. Soon, every merchant and tradesmen in Lydia would tally his life in these ovals of gold and silver, each one marked with the lion and bull. But, for now, the coins remained within this sealed chamber. They belonged to him alone.

The room was still, near silent. He could hear the crackling of the torches, the occasional thud as a sack of coins arrived down one of the steep tunnels that led from the mints above ground. Soft beneath these other sounds were the shuffling, hesitant footsteps of the money counters.

They were all blind. These slaves lived within the treasury, in a small antechamber separate from the coins. Food and water reached them through the same shafts where the coins came from above. They would never be permitted to leave. They would grow old and die in a world of gold.

Croesus had no idea what they spoke about to pass the long days, what couplings occurred down here in the darkness, what half-remembered poems were recited, the imaginative journeys that they went on together to escape their closed world, the petty fights and squabbles that broke out over the few luxuries they were allowed. He could only imagine what they did to alleviate the maddening boredom of shifting and polishing and ordering the endless mountains of coins.

When the silver bell rang, they knew to light the torches and be silent, until they could be certain he had gone. Even without sight, they always knew where he was; the king's confident footsteps identified him as one who bore the privilege of vision.

He approached a large, loose pile of gold coins. He thrust his hands into them, gently working his fingers into the heavy metal until his forearms were buried. It felt as though he held his hands in a stream of cold water, and he sensed his burning blood cool.

The small pile of silver near his feet was a healthy slave. In the mound of gold next to it he saw a galleon; the larger mound that towered over it was a fleet. From one corner of the room, where gold and silver mingled freely together like captains and spearmen, he could hear the marching feet of ten thousand soldiers.

On to even larger mounds, and he saw towns, cities, entire races of people locked into the gold and ordered at his command. He saw an empire, stretching across leagues and nations and rivers and seas, all contained within a single, high-chambered room, and perceived by him alone.

He did not yet know what he would do with his wealth. The possibilities were overwhelming, each idea giving way to another as soon as he thought of acting on it. But he knew that, given time, he could find the right use for it. All creation was there, waiting to spring into life. He only had to choose what form it would take, and he could shape a universe with his vision.

My father was right in one thing at least, Croesus thought as he stood amidst all his wealth, new worlds waiting to be born. This is worth more than love.

3

Two years after Atys died, word came that the empire of the Medes had fallen.

The conquest had been sudden, like some disaster of the earth or sea that is precisely managed by the Gods. An exhausted messenger arrived at the court of Sardis to bring word that a Persian army was marching on Ecbatana, the capital of Media. Before Croesus could decide whether to send the man back alone or accompanied by the entire Lydian army, another messenger arrived with the news that the Medes' army had been destroyed and Astyages had been captured. Cyrus of Persia now sat on the throne of the Medes.

Cyrus. The name meant nothing to Croesus, but rumours soon followed the messengers. That he was of a Persian noble family was all that could be said with confidence – all else was the stuff of folk-tales. Some said that Cyrus had been raised by wolves, that he fed only on the flesh of kings and drank only the waters of the river by which he had been born. Others claimed that wild beasts formed the vanguard of his army, while immortal demons served as its elite warriors. Persian sorcerers were said to have destroyed the army of the Medes with lightning from the sky and earthquakes that shook men to death; not a single blow was struck. Croesus soon gave up any attempt to identify the truth behind these wild tales. A new power had risen in the East. The only thing that mattered was how to respond.

At the council of war, they began with numbers. The respective sizes of the Persian and Lydian armies, the cost of mercenaries, the yields of croplands, the wealth of mining regions. Above all, they sought to calculate what Lydia stood to gain and lose. The fate of a dozen nations was reduced to numbers inked on parchment and etched in wax: a balance sheet for a war. It was only after they had finished their calculations that they talked of what should be done.

It was unacceptable, one man said, for the Persians to rule an empire. The Hellenes to the west could be bargained with and understood – they were a civilized people. But there was no negotiating with the Persians. Who knew how they would use their new-found power?

Others of the council were unconvinced by the case for war. Sandanis, the commander of the army, was the leader of this faction. An old man now, with the loose-skinned and weary features of a soldier who had spent a lifetime fighting enemies abroad and politicians at home, he had led the army even in the days of Croesus's father. Repeatedly and forcefully, he argued that Lydia had grown strong through trade and good governance; why risk it all on war with the East? What did events so far away have to do with the Lydian empire?

It was only after the discussion had continued for some time, growing increasingly heated, that the men around the table realized that the king had yet to speak.

One by one, they fell silent and turned to face their ruler. 'Forgive us,' said one of the young noblemen. 'We have spoken at great length, and not waited to hear you, as we should have done.' He coughed apologetically. 'What, may we ask, do you think?'

What did he think? Croesus almost laughed. How could so grave a decision be made on the basis of doubt and suspicion, but nothing more? He could feel the excitement around the table at the thought of war, but he found himself unmoved by it. It mattered little to him who ruled over the lands to the east – Astyages had been his brother king in name only. Given a little more time, another year or so, he believed he would find the right way to use his wealth.

And yet, for all this, when he came to speak, he could not find the words for peace. 'I thank you all for your counsel,' he said. 'What an embarrassment of riches you have given me; enough to put those of my treasuries to shame!' Laughter broke out around the table. 'I have no hunger for war,' Croesus continued, the words coming easily now, 'but will the Persian be satisfied with his new-won kingdom? I think not.' He looked across at Sandanis. 'Do not worry,' Croesus said. 'I will not be rash. We shall consult with the oracles, and with our allies. I have detained you all too long from your own affairs.' He gestured towards the door. 'You may leave.'

The king drummed his fingers on the marble table, smiling and nodding as each of the noblemen departed the council chamber. He sat in silence for a time after they had gone. He turned to Isocrates.

'Your thoughts?' Croesus said.

'Of war with Persia?'

Croesus shook his head, and nodded at the empty chairs. 'Of them.'

Isocrates shrugged. 'Divided. They will follow where you lead.'

'Yes. Or where the Gods lead.'

'That is true, master.'

'We must have a prophecy to guide us. To which of the oracles should we turn? Abae?'

'The prophet at Abae is a stubborn old man, master. He doesn't like foreigners. If you were a Hellene, I might recommend it, but as a Lydian . . .'

'Ah. That is unfortunate. You know much of these matters?'

'I rely on the opinions of men who are wiser than I, master.'

'Well, what do these wiser men have to say of Dodona?'

'I have yet to hear him give a favourable word for war. He lost both his sons in battle many years ago.' Isocrates hesitated for a moment. 'He would give you a prophecy to prevent a war, not to begin one.'

'What about Ammon, in Libya? Astyages always swore by him.'

'I wouldn't trust a Libyan on a matter like this.'

'Prejudice from you, Isocrates?'

'Forgive me, master. But I think prophecy is a matter best left to the Hellenes.'

'Perhaps you are right. Look at what happened to Astyages, after all. I imagine you have objections to Trophonius at Lebadaea as well?'

'Athens has bought him out. He will not give a good word to any other city or nation.'

'Well, it appears our choice is made for us. Delphi it is.'

'The Pythia does give the best prophecies.' He tried to smile. 'I hesitate to say it, to you of all people, master, but you know it will cost you dearly?'

'Do not be concerned with that. What else needs to be done?'

Isocrates thought for a moment. 'We will need to offer a reason,' he said. 'As to why we've favoured Delphi, over the others.'

'Their feelings will be hurt? I wouldn't have thought they would be so sensitive.'

'It doesn't pay to anger a priest. They don't mind if gods ignore them. Just when men do.'

'Very well,' Croesus smiled. 'Make something up, will you?'

'Me, master?'

'Who else? Use your imagination. I'm sure you'll come up with something fitting.'

The story spread quickly.

None could say exactly where it had come from. Some said it had begun at the dining tables of Lydian high society, where a noble close to the heart of the palace had first told the story to impress another man's wife. Others claimed that it was first told in the market squares of the lower city, where the storytellers had gathered to share the rumours of the day. It seemed to appear in many different places at the same moment, as though it were some singular vision that the entire city had dreamed together.

First, the story said, the messengers left the city. None who listened to the tale had mentioned these messengers before, and yet now everyone seemed to remember watching them go, a dozen riders heading from the city half a year earlier, each with two horses, each bearing the mark of a king's messenger. The more men spoke, the more they found themselves agreeing on what these men had looked like, what they had worn, how well they had ridden their mounts.

The messengers left the city together, riding west to Smyrna. There, so the storytellers said, the group divided, one man taking a ship south towards Ammon, the others sailing west to Hellas. These divided again as soon as they touched the shore, scattering across the land, to Abae, Dodona, Lebadaea, and Delphi. They each came to the oracles with gold enough to ask a simple question, but they did not seek the favour of the Gods at once. They waited, counting the days carefully. They waited for the date on which they had all agreed.

A hundred days after their departure, the messengers went in supplication to the prophets and asked the same question of them all. A simple question that did not request that the Gods bless a union, end a feud, save a blighted crop, or otherwise shape the fate of nations. They only desired to know what was it that Croesus, king of Lydia, might be doing at that moment.

On the hundredth day, as this question was being asked in half a dozen different places on the other side of the world, Croesus retired to his chambers, dismissing every courtier and slave who tried to accompany him. Alone, he lit the coals beneath a bronze mixing bowl and poured oil into it. He cracked the shell of a tortoise and cut the meat into pieces. He skinned and gutted a small lamb and, for hours, he mixed the strange, alien stew together. When it was done, he offered the greater portion to the Gods and ate the rest himself.

Each of the oracles responded in their own way. Most spoke in riddles, metaphor and myth. Only one was different, and soon, the words from Delphi, from the Pythia on her sacred tripod, were repeated in every corner of Sardis.

> *I know the number of grains of sand and the measure of the sea,*
> *I understand the mute and hear the speechless.*
> *Into the depth of my senses has come the scent of hard-shelled tortoise*
> *Boiling in bronze with the meat of a lamb,*
> *Laid upon bronze below, covered by bronze above.*

The messengers could not have offered bribes for this information, for they had not known what Croesus would do. Only Croesus and the Gods had known. Croesus, the Gods, and the priestess of Delphi.

4

'Well.' Croesus shook his head. 'I said use your imagination. I never thought you would go that far.'

'Are you displeased, master?' the slave asked.

'Far from it. The story is so absurd that no one would think you had invented it. You are full of surprises. Though you do realize that I will have to retell it a hundred times before the year is out? Your revenge on me, I suppose, for making you think on your feet like that. Someone is sure to ask me to actually butcher a lamb or a turtle one of these days. Do I look like a butcher to you?' He laughed. 'But you have done well. The people now believe in Delphi. We must make sure that the oracle gives them something worth listening to.'

'What do we do now, master?'

'We prepare an offering,' Croesus said, 'that not even a God could refuse.'

Often, in the months that followed, Croesus travelled to the great wooden doors of the furnace room. There, he listened to the sound of the chisels, the roaring, hungry fires, the barked instructions that the metal workers and sculptors gave to the slaves who worked in the room day and night. He listened each day, sometimes for hours, but he did not go inside. He tried to busy himself with other matters. He met with his general, Sandanis, to discuss the preparation of the army. He discussed the changeable attitudes of the nobles with Isocrates. He entertained the rulers of the subdued Ionian nations, gauging the price of their loyalty. Each night, he dreamed of what lay behind the foundry doors.

At last, when the work was only days from completion, he gave in to his desire. He summoned his master craftsman, and asked to be shown the gifts.

Croesus felt the sweat break out across his skin when the doors of the foundry were opened. The air was thick and heavy with heat; the furnaces had been burning for months without being extinguished. The workers wore only loincloths which clung close to their bodies with the sweat, and even the light tunic that Croesus wore felt like an encumbrance in the burning air. The fire gave light to the windowless room, illuminating pools of sharp colour surrounded by shadows; in the low red glow he watched gold and silver bubbling in pools, pouring through gates and into moulds. Everywhere he looked, the king saw his wealth being transformed for the Gods.

'Show me the gifts,' he said.

The master craftsman bowed. He led the king to a far corner, where heavy gold ingots were stacked one on top of the other. Each was a cubit long, half a cubit wide.

'We're up to ninety now,' the craftsman said. 'We're hoping to reach a hundred and twenty by the time we're finished.'

Croesus knelt down and spread his fingers across the ingot on top of the stack. 'How much does each weigh?'

'As much as a small man.' The craftsman grinned, revealing a mouth full of yellowed teeth. 'Or a large woman.'

Croesus nodded, his face impassive. 'What else do you have?'

In another corner, two enormous bowls towered above them, each one fit for a Titan. One was made of gold, the other of a quarter-ton of silver.

'Wine bowls?' Croesus asked, raising an eyebrow.

'The priests like something practical amongst their gifts, or so we've heard,' the master craftsman said. 'Statues and golden ornaments are all very well, but you cannot mix wine in them, can you? Perhaps the Gods like a drink as much as their priests do.'

'I see. You expect them to use these? How much do they hold?'

'Five thousand gallons each. Not the kind of quantity you'll want to mix for your evening meal, but it should serve them well for bigger occasions. Festivals, and the like.'

Croesus nodded again. 'Show me more.'

The king saw elaborate silverware, casks, goblets, jewel-studded brooches, elegant statues in gold and bronze and marble. There was no limit, he thought, to the different forms that his wealth could take. There were infinities of splendour, and he could spend a lifetime discovering them all.

He made his way to the centre of the room. A lion, cast in solid gold, stood proud and defiant, like a ruler surveying his kingdom. The likeness was perfect, as though the Midas of legend had crept into the hills and laid his hands upon a lion mid-roar. In the outlines of its frozen golden mane, its bared teeth and flat nose, Croesus fancied he could see some resemblance to that crude image he had seen long ago, stamped into the electrum of his father's first coin. A faint smile crept to the king's lips.

'Are you pleased, my lord?' the craftsman asked.

'I have never heard of a greater offering,' the king said. 'It is magnificent, and I thank you. But there is one thing I haven't seen. The second statue?'

'Of course, my lord. Just this way.'

Away from the furnaces, almost lost in shadows, was another perfect likeness in gold, this time of a woman. Croesus circled it, counter clockwise then clockwise, studying it from every angle, paying particular attention to the familiar face. He reached forward and traced his hand across the cool golden skin, to see if his hands could find some fault that his eyes could not. He shook his head. 'It is remarkable,' he said. 'Has she seen it?'

'Who, my lord?'

'Maia, of course.' Croesus looked again at the statue. 'You carved her in gold,' he continued, 'but have not shown it to her?'

'No, my lord.' He hesitated. 'We did wonder, my lord, why you asked for a statue of a slave. Perhaps you could enlighten me? It would settle a wager.'

Croesus smiled, but did not look at the craftsman. He stared into the empty golden eyes of the statue. 'She can't have children,' he said.

'My lord?'

'She can't have children. She told me that once. So I thought I would give her immortality in some other way.' Croesus shrugged. 'A whim of your king. Pay it no mind. You have done very well.'

'I'm sure there is plenty more we can do,' the craftsman said. 'What else, my lord? Name anything.'

'No. This is perfect. Wait.' Croesus thought for a moment, then nodded. 'My wife has some very fine necklaces. I shall have them sent down to you immediately. They will be a fine addition to the offering.'

'Your wife? Won't—' the craftsman began to say. He checked himself.

Croesus affected not to hear. 'When will it all be finished?' he asked.

'Three weeks.'

'Very good. We shall dispatch it all in a month.'

'A month, my lord? Why the delay?'

The king's smile broadened. 'It will take another week to bring the animals into the city once your work is finished. A gift of this size requires an appropriate sacrifice to mark its departure, don't you think?'

5

The main square in the lower city was vast, designed for great public occasions. But on this occasion, it was not large enough. The scale of the sacrifice was unprecedented.

Twelve thousand sheep, goats, bulls and pigs, each flanked by the head of a household, filled the square and packed every street that led into it. Even the rooftops were alive with women and children, for everyone in the city had come to bear witness.

Above them all, on the balcony of the palace, Croesus looked down on the streets of the lower city far beneath him. He inhaled the smell of Sardis, listened to the sounds that filtered, faint and distorted, from the streets below him. The air was thick with the earthy stink of the animals, the chatter of the people as they waited for the ritual to begin. There had been many arguments between neighbours as to where they would stand, who would be closest to the central square and claim the greater glory. Some had been settled with fistfights, others with quiet bribes to nearby soldiers or priests. The poorest stood cramped in the side streets and back alleys, the richer shop-keepers on the main thoroughfares, the nobility in the centre square itself. All waited for the king.

Croesus signalled, and the soldier beside him blew a single, long note from the bullhorn that was slung round his neck. The chattering roar of the people ceased. Each of the twelve thousand men gripped the hair of the animal at his side and looked up to the king. They did not wait for him to speak, for he was too distant for them to hear him. They awaited a sign.

Croesus glanced over to the other side of the balcony. The goat, its coat pure white, ruminated calmly next to him. Sensing the king's gaze, it inclined its head to face him. Its black rectangular pupils passed over Croesus with little interest, until it caught sight of a roll of parchment thrust into his belt. It lunged forward, its lips parted and snuffling for the paper, but Croesus pushed its questing nose away, letting his fingers trail down through its coarse wisp of beard. He took a silver cup of water from the edge of the balcony and raised it high in the air as a signal to those who waited below.

In the square and the streets beneath the citadel, each man took a cup of water, lifted it high, and poured it over the head of the beast in front of him. Each animal, feeling the water running over its head, instinctively nodded as if in unwitting agreement, giving its consent for the sacrifice. Croesus lifted his curved knife. Twelve thousand blades shone an answer back to him.

Then the knives fell, digging and cutting and sawing, and waves of blood poured out like an onrushing tide. The air was filled with the screams of the dying animals as they slumped to their knees and the blood boiled up through their mouths. A moment later the sound was drowned out as the people of Sardis roared in celebration.

The king's hands trembled, and a priest stood nearby to second his attempt if he faltered. But he had been well instructed and made no mistake. He reached forward and opened the animal's throat with a single cut.

The goat gave a single barked bleat, of confusion more than pain. It dropped its head and choked, then fell to its knees. It moaned mournfully, shivered and rested its head on its forelegs. It watched its own hot blood spread out around it like a crimson blanket. Its eyes grew dim, and then half closed, a tiny glint of gold visible through the thin slit of the eyelids. It lay still, and waited to die.

Croesus blinked back sudden tears. He put his hands into a basin of water, watched the tendrils of blood eddying into the water like smoke through the air. He shook his head, and smiled uncertainly at his wife. 'Well, it is finished.' She said nothing in response, and Croesus turned to his slaves. 'Prepare this' – he gestured at the carcass – 'for my evening meal. Minus the Gods' share, of course.'

He watched them take the beast away, and felt a kind of weary relief. This sacrifice committed him. The moment for doubt, the moment when he could have changed his mind, was past. The pressure of choice had lifted, and now he had only to follow the course through to the end. He turned to share the thought with his wife. But when he looked back, Danae was gone.

For a single, irrational moment he thought she must have thrown herself from the balcony down into the square below, passing from the world with a single sudden step. Then he saw a long piece of fabric fall back into place over one of the entrances to the balcony, disturbed by her passage. He hurried inside to follow her.

Far below the balcony, the streets of Sardis were wet with blood. The stones of the square were thick with the holy gore, which mixed with the earth and dried in blackish whorls. The priests walked calmly through the crowd, finishing off wounded animals where an inexperienced hand had botched the job.

The rooftop onlookers came forward, daubing their foreheads with the blood that ran on the ground in shallow streams. A swarm of prostitutes who had waited at one side of the square as the sacrifice was prepared now advanced in a surge of incense and clinking jewellery, trying to entice the men to honour the Gods in another way. Children dipped their hands deep in the blood and tore off through the streets, chasing each other and tagging every wall and doorway with tiny bloody hand prints, spreading the mark of the Gods to every corner of the city.

Inside the palace, Croesus pursued his wife.

Like a figure in a dream, her pace seemed to slow and hasten along with his. At any moment that he seemed on the verge of reaching her, she somehow drew further away from him. He almost called out to her, but realized that he had no confidence that she would respond to command.

Finally, after following her through the rooms and corridors of the palace, he found her waiting for him at the entrance to the women's quarters.

'Well?' he said. 'What is it?'

She looked at him, her eyes disbelieving, and under her gaze, he felt a sudden shame. 'I am sorry,' he said. 'I have not been kind to you.'

'You haven't been anything to me,' she said. 'A husband, or a king. Ever since—'

Croesus bowed his head and raised a hand, palm forward. He gestured to a cushioned couch in the corner of the room. 'Sit with me. Please,' he said.

They sat together in silence, and as they did, Croesus tried to remember how to speak to his wife. Once he could have said anything to her. He thought back, tried to think of the last time they had spoken that had not been at some official function, a private conversation that had not been merely an empty exchange of pleasantries. He could not. He had let her become a stranger to him.

She broke the silence. 'Why are you doing this?' she said.

'Doing what?'

'Fighting this war. And don't speak as you do to the others. Of glory or honour or necessity. They may believe it, but I don't. It's about you. It's always been about you.'

'I considered peace,' he said. 'I knew it is what you would wish for. But I realized that it might never come again. That I might pass my whole life without another chance.'

She shook her head. 'For what?'

'What is more real than this? What matters more than a war?' He paused. 'I wish there could be something else. But there is not.'

'My father once told me that only a fool chooses war,' she said. 'He said that in peace, sons bury fathers, but in war, fathers bury sons.'

'We buried our son in peacetime.'

'And now you ask others to bury theirs.'

'Perhaps you are right,' he said quietly. Then: 'I wish I still had a son.'

'You have a son.'

'But not an heir. I want to make a mark on this world, before I leave it.' She opened her mouth to speak, but he continued: 'Lesser men can be content with . . . I don't know . . . I honestly don't know how a slave or a common man can look back on his life and feel it worth anything. Fifty years of scratching at a field, haggling in the market. But I can do something remarkable.'

'We could be happy,' she said. 'Did you think of that? We have all the wealth of the world. You could spend it on anything you like. Why spend it on a war?'

'What could we buy that we do not have already? Spend it on the people? The greatest festivals are soon forgotten, and even if I were to make the streets of Sardis run with gold, what difference would it make? There's no glory in throwing money to the poor.'

'And there is in this?'

'People remember wars, don't they?'

'A name on a map, Croesus. That's all you're fighting for.'

No,' he said. 'It is a signature written on history. It lasts for ever. Atys should have been my legacy. I shall leave an empire behind instead.'

She sat in silence. At last, very quietly, she said, 'Do as you please.

When this war is over, if you are still unhappy, come to me again. Perhaps then you will see how wrong you are. Perhaps it is only then that you will try and find a way to be happy with me. And your son.'

She stood, and before he could find another word to say, she walked away into the women's quarters, the one place in the palace where he could not follow her. He listened, and thought he heard laughter from somewhere within, before all sound of her was lost.

He waited on the couch for a time, to see if she would return. When she did not, he rose and walked back out onto the balcony.

The sun was low in the sky, the red light echoing the carnage of the sacrifice. The stone floor of the balcony had been scrubbed clean and no trace of death remained, but when he looked down at his hands he found blood dried beneath his fingernails. He picked at it and rolled it to powder between his fingers, and then looked down on the streets below.

He saw a fire burning in the centre of the square, ringed by a dozen priests in heavy white robes. Piled beside them were the fat and bones of the twelve thousand dead – a mountain of offerings over which the flies swarmed in a cloud of black motion. All around the square, the people of Sardis had returned to the rooftops, having shed their bloody tunics for their finest clothing, ready to observe the next stage of the sacrifice.

For over an hour, the priests fed the offerings to the Gods. The unburned bones piled thickly around the fire, and it came to resemble one of the mass funeral pyres that are to be found at the end of a great battle. The crowd watched in respectful silence as each sacrifice was offered, though here and there he saw mothers hushing bored children with sharp warnings and slaps. The only other sounds were the roar and crackle of the fire, and the deep, throaty chants of the supplication the priests made to the Gods.

When all of the meat had been offered up to the fire, the time came for the second sacrifice: the gift of gold.

Croesus watched as the gates of the palace opened beneath him, and a convoy of a dozen carts rolled out, each one piled high with wealth from the heart of the palace, much of it from his own private quarters. Gold cups and silver-edged plates, elaborately crafted wooden chairs, heavy weaves of rare fabrics that had travelled from half the world, gilded couches studded with jewels. Each cart held more wealth than most of the people of Sardis would have seen in a lifetime.

The priests cleared a path for the carts, until the convoy was at the edge of the fire. The men with the first cart crouched down and laid their hands upon it, rocking it back and forth on its axles once, twice, three times. The third time, they gave a wordless cry and thrust it forward, their legs pushing hard against the stone and driving the cart towards the fire. They released it a few feet from the edge and skidded to a stop as the cart plunged forward, rocked up over the wood at the edge, tipped to one side and fell into the heart of the fire.

One by one, the remaining eleven carts followed, and the fire flared up, brighter than before. Soon, the cushions of the couches were blackening in the heat, the wood popping and cracking, the inlaid gold melting and running in priceless rivulets down to the bloody ground. Golden goblets warped and melted, finely worked leather belts cracked and disintegrated into ash.

Croesus watched as each family came forward in turn to make an offering of its own. The poor could offer only the crude clay pots and bowls that they had used for decades of simple meals, an old blanket for the cold winter months, the small, crude smock intended for a child that had been stillborn. Merchants offered the fine wines that they had hoarded for a day of celebration or for the bribery of a stubborn official, pulled the gold rings from their fingers and hurled them into the hungry, wasteful flames. Old men threw in the iron spears they had kept to remember their glorious, younger days, and children were encouraged to donate the toys and trinkets that were their own personal treasures. Many of the people burned too much, burned away their legacies of golden cups or silver jewellery that they had spent a lifetime trying to acquire and pass on to their children. Dozens of families ruined themselves for generations, infected by the sacred destruction of so much wealth. Within an hour, a tenth of the wealth of the city had been burned as an offering to the Gods.

After it was done, the people of the city returned to their homes, moving slowly through the crowded streets. Croesus waited, and soon pale smoke began to rise as they lit thousands of fires. The rich scent of cooking meat clung to the smoke, and the separate tendrils intertwined and thickened in the air until a single cloud hung over the entire city. A traveller viewing Sardis from a distance would have thought that it must have been burning under the torches of a foreign invader. The city had never known a festival like it.

Croesus waited on the balcony, until the stars were clustered thick in the clear sky, and he could identify the constellations of the Gods whose favour he sought to buy with blood and gold. After a time, he became aware of another presence behind him. He turned quickly, hoping that it would be his wife come to ask forgiveness.

But it was Isocrates. The slave looked weary, and had permitted himself the luxury of leaning against a wall as he waited. He gazed at his master with attentive eyes, ready to serve.

'Of course,' Croesus said. 'Everywhere I turn, there you are.'

'Would you like me to leave you alone, master?'

'No. Please, stay.'

Croesus looked down on the square, empty of people, filled with ashes and blood. 'Can a god be bought?' he said. 'Or is it men that I buy with this sacrifice?'

'Does it matter?'

'Quite.' Croesus hesitated. 'My wife hates me, I think.'

Isocrates said nothing. A moment later, Croesus continued.

'No, she doesn't hate me,' he said. 'But she has closed herself to me.' He leaned forward slowly, rested his forehead against the stone lip of the balcony. He straightened up a moment later, as the weakness passed.

'You are well, Isocrates?'

'I have no complaints, master.'

'You never do. It is remarkable. And your wife?'

'She is well, master.' The slave paused for a moment. 'She says she has not seen you for some time.'

'I have no time for Gyges,' Croesus said. 'Not now, in any case. But I am sorry not to have seen Maia. You heard about the statue?'

'I did, master. You honour us too greatly.'

'No, I don't think that I do.' The king turned to face his slave. 'I trust no one but you now. Isn't that strange?' Without waiting for a reply, he brushed past his slave and disappeared into the darkness of the palace.

Isocrates waited until his master's echoing footsteps had fallen silent. Satisfied that he was alone, he walked forward and looked out over the balcony, resting his elbows on the edge where his master's arms had rested only moments before. Had any citizen been gazing up from the streets below and seen the distant figure looking down over the city, they would have thought Isocrates was the king, watching over the people he ruled and weighing the fates of nations. Not a slave whose life depended on the whims of the man who owned him.

He looked down, and watched another convoy leave the gates of the palace. The third sacrifice, the gifts that had taken months to produce, taking their first steps towards the oracle at Delphi. The sacrifice of the animals and the burning of the people's treasures had been but a prelude to this, the great gift to the Gods.

The darkness was almost impenetrable, and the convoy had lit no torches to illuminate their way, but Isocrates thought that he could identify the glinting outline of a golden statue of his wife in one of the carts below.

He imagined the journey that the gifts would take. He thought of the carts rolling along the clear, wide merchant's road along the banks of the Hermus to Phocaea. They would spend at least a night there, the convoy guards drinking and whoring in the port taverns, brawling with sailors who had come from half a world away to trade for the golden coins of Lydia. Then they would roll onto a ship and sail out upon the deep Aegean, its colour that of the sky in another, perfect world. They would travel past the islands that loomed in the distance like mountain peaks above a sea of clouds, past solitary merchant vessels and the pirate ships that hunted them, until they made landfall at Phaleron and continued to Athens. The excisemen of Athens would extract double the usual levy from the foreigners, and the Lydians would pay gladly, the bribe a mere fraction of the riches they carried with them.

On dry land once more, the convoy would pass along the good, clear path to Thebes, the soldiers doubling their sentries at night to guard against the bandits who were always watching the road. Then it would ascend the steep mountain paths, to Delphi itself. The Lydian offering would join a gallery of riches, the only place in the world that could perhaps overshadow Croesus's treasuries. There were gifts from Croesus's father there, and from the kings that had ruled Sardis before him, four generations of Lydian kings who had sought to buy favour at a temple that none of them had ever seen. Their offerings joined gifts from dozens of kings, given over centuries, each ruler seeking the favour of the Gods.

Isocrates had never seen these places. He imagined the journey through lands that he knew only from travellers' tales. Perhaps along the way, he thought, they would have reason to put in at one of the islands as they crossed the Aegean. Bad weather, or sickness amongst the crew might lead them to a friendly harbour. Perhaps the winds would drive them far, far south, like wandering Odysseus, and of all the places they might put in, they might find themselves landing on the island of Thera – the one place, apart from Sardis, that Isocrates had seen with his own eyes. Dimly, he remembered red cliffs and black beaches, the songs his father sang as he laid out the fishing nets, the smell as his mother baked bread. It was the land he had been taken from as a boy, could now no longer clearly recollect, and would never see again.

Isocrates yawned and pinched the bridge of his nose. He went inside to find his master.

6

The answer from Delphi came swiftly.

With hesitant hands, like a shy lover, Croesus unrolled the parchment. On it were written four simple lines of prophecy:

> *If you wage war against Persia, mighty Croesus,*
> *Then know this: you will destroy a great empire.*
> *You must ally yourself with the strongest Hellenes*
> *To earn the favour of the Gods.*

Croesus thought of the wealth that had bought each stroke of every letter. The hundred gold ingots that had acquired the first letters of *Persia*, the colossal golden lion that had perhaps been enough to purchase the words *great empire*. He wondered which stroke his wife's necklaces and girdles had earned. What power there is in words, he thought. The force of these words is enough to win me an empire.

He turned to the messenger. 'This oracle, she is remarkable. Do you think that she would answer another question of mine?'

'Such was the generosity of your gifts, I cannot think that she would refuse you.'

'Good. Ask her for how long I will reign.'

The messenger nodded. 'It shall be done. Is that all, my lord?'

Croesus hesitated, and Isocrates, who stood at the king's side, looked at his master closely. It was the first time in months that he had seen Croesus show anything approaching doubt.

'Ask her one more favour for me,' Croesus said. 'If the oracle will permit it.'

'What should I ask?'

Croesus turned his head, and looked into the corner of the room. On the floor sat Gyges, idly running a piece of embroidered cloth through his hands. Since the day of the sacrifice, he had spent much of every day in Croesus's company. He followed the king silently but paid no apparent attention to him, retreating to some isolated corner of the room, toying with some piece of jewellery or fabric, and plunging deeper into whatever world his mind inhabited. Croesus could not imagine what prompted this behaviour, what it might mean. Occasionally he wondered if it amounted to some kind of reprimand, or warning. But for the most part, he thought it signified nothing.

The king turned back to the messenger, licked his lips, then spoke again. 'Ask her if my son will ever speak to me.' With that, he rose from his throne and walked away, his head low, declining to meet the gaze of any other in the room. He beckoned to Isocrates to follow him.

'Tell me about Athens and Sparta.'

'Athens and Sparta?'

'You heard the prophecy,' Croesus said, reclining on a couch in his private chambers. 'We must have allies for this war. Which is the stronger?'

'Athens is divided,' Isocrates said, after a moment's thought. 'They threw out their tyrant Pisistratus some years ago. But I've heard rebellion is coming. Pisistratus may return to power.'

'So Athens is in chaos?' Croesus said. He thought of Solon's love for his city, and felt a stabbing, guilty pleasure. 'What of Sparta?'

'Not as wealthy as some nations, but they are great warriors. I can't imagine you will find a more valuable ally, especially since their war against Tegea.'

'Strong and stable? Men like you, Isocrates.'

'Perhaps, master.'

'You do not like the comparison?'

'They worship war more than any other people I know. I do not think that is something to be proud of.'

'That makes them ideal for our purpose.'

'True, master. Shall I dispatch the emissaries?'

'Yes, yes. Immediately.' Croesus turned from Isocrates but the slave felt that he had not yet been dismissed. 'What a slow business this is,' the king said. 'I think I might spend a lifetime at this. Sacrificing to oracles. Sending emissaries. Haggling with my nobles. Assembling the army. I am not sure I have the patience. Then again, Solon . . .' He hesitated, like a superstitious man who utters an unintended blasphemy.

'Yes, master?'

'Solon told me that he spent a lifetime trying to pass a dozen laws. Laws that were repealed a decade after he left his city. I suppose I should be grateful if I can build an empire in a few years.' He stared out of a window, towards the east. 'Still, I wish I could begin my work.'

'Where you lead, we will follow,' the Spartan ambassador said. 'We have not forgotten your gift of gold for our temple. All we ask is that our sacrifices are not forgotten. Perhaps the wealth and strength of Lydia may come to the assistance of Sparta at some time in the future, when we have need of your help.'

'Of course,' Croesus responded lightly. The alliance between Sparta and Lydia had been sealed in writing a month before. The appearance of Lakrines, a flint-faced ambassador with close-cropped hair, clad in the red cloak of the Spartan nobility, was a mere formality, a ritual to be concluded. 'Your two kings send a gift, I presume?' Croesus said.

'They do. But, there is a greater offering that our craftsmen are working on. A great bronze bowl – we have heard that you love bronze.' Croesus flinched at this. He had forgotten how far that rumour had spread.

Lakrines bowed, and continued: 'But we hope this small token will suffice for now.' He gestured to one of his helots, who came forward, his eyes down, and presented a small wooden casket to Croesus.

The king opened the casket and surveyed its contents with little interest. Rough coins of gold and silver that, compared to the craftsmanship he was used to, were like the work of children. Paltry treasures that would occupy only a small shelf in one of Croesus's treasuries, but he knew that they represented a small fortune to the Spartans. He flipped the lid of the casket shut and smiled politely at his visitor.

'The king of Lydia thanks the kings of Sparta for their gifts, and expects that this is the beginning of a long and mutually prosperous alliance.' He stifled a yawn with his hand. 'You may leave us.'

The emissary bowed again, and Croesus waited until he had reached the entrance of the throne room before he spoke again. 'Stop,' the king said. 'There is one last thing I wish to ask.'

The Spartan turned back. 'Yes, King Croesus?'

Croesus steepled his fingers. 'Would you mind explaining your insult to me?'

'Insult?'

'You had your helot present your gift to me, rather than offering it with your own hands.' Croesus smiled thinly, and spread his hands wide. 'I'm sure there is a reason for this. I just can't think what it might be.'

'Ah.' Lakrines bowed low. 'Forgive me. We misunderstand each other. I may not touch these coins.'

'Some religious precept?'

'Something like that. No citizen of Sparta values such things.'

'Ah.' Croesus smiled in amusement. 'Interesting. Satisfy my curiosity. What is it you do value?'

The Spartan nodded. The question had been asked of him and answered many times. 'We value the man to our right,' he said. 'That is all.' He bowed again, and turned away before Croesus could question him further.

The king drummed his fingers together. 'Isocrates?' he said after a time.

'Yes, master?'

'Find out what he meant by that.'

In the days that followed, Isocrates immersed himself in the world of hoplites, shield walls and long spears. He learned about the great and weak kings of Sparta, the teachings of their renowned lawgiver, Lycurgus. He examined the tales that had made their way across land and over sea from Sparta to Lydia, each rumour growing and evolving along the way: stories of feral children who murdered slaves and stole their food, invincible warriors who stood ten feet tall, young women who had their hair cut off on the nights of their weddings. He had become expert at judging the tales of distant peoples, handling them the way a dealer in metals might approach a dubious piece of ore; weighing it, testing it, melting away impurities and discovering what value lay at its core.

Like a patient, studious child, the king sat quietly as Isocrates explained the phalanx, the rigid square that the Spartan warriors formed when they took to the battlefield, in which each man used his shield to protect the man who stood to his left. It was a battle formation dependent on the individual's subsuming of himself into the whole, each man placing his life in the hands of the man on his right.

'So that is the way wars are fought these days?' Croesus said. 'How disappointing.'

'You prefer the old stories of single combat?'

'Perhaps.'

'I always wondered what the rest of the army was doing while the two heroes spent hours battling each other.'

'Standing around and cheering, I suppose. I think I find it more heroic than standing in a square and hiding behind another man's shield. Still, victory is better than heroic defeat, don't you agree?'

'I prefer to be on the winning side.'

'Very sensible. So in this phalanx, the man on the far right has no protection?'

'No. That's the weakness of the formation.'

Croesus smiled. 'It's more than that. It's the flaw in their thinking. Who ends up on the right do you think?'

'I think—'

'I will tell you,' Croesus continued, gesturing his slave into silence. 'Sometimes it will be the unwanted, the weak. They will be pushed to the right and left to die by the others. But it won't just be them. It will be the powerful and ambitious men as well. There's no room for the great man in their world, or the wretched one either. Mediocrity is what they aspire to. Distinguish yourself in any way, for good or ill, and soon enough you will find yourself out there without protection, and you'll feel that spear in your ribs.'

Isocrates said nothing, and Croesus gave him a knowing glance. 'You have many different kinds of silences, you know,' the king said. 'An entire language of taciturnity. I recognise this particular silence. You have something more to say?'

'Just another possibility that you might not have considered.'

'Which is?'

'They might consider it an honour to be the man on the right. To be the one who is sacrificed so that the battle may be won.'

'You may be right. Still, I wouldn't want to be that man – would you?' Croesus leaned back in his chair and rubbed his eyes.

'You are tired, master.'

'Yes. Tired but content. This war will change the world. That's something, isn't it?'

'Of course, master.'

Croesus nodded slowly. 'Leave me. No, wait. Isocrates?'

'Yes, master?'

'Will you send for my wife?'

Isocrates clasped his hands behind his back, and looked away from his king. 'I should think she will be in the women's quarters, master.'

'How I hate that place being out of bounds to me. This ridiculous charade.' He shook his head. 'You can send your wife in to find her, can't you?'

'Yes, master.'

'And Isocrates, there's something I have been meaning to discuss with you. About Maia.'

'Master?'

Croesus said nothing for a time. 'Do you beat your wife?' he said at last, speaking quietly.

Isocrates went quite still. 'Master?'

'I have seen her several times with bruises on her face. She has told me that Gyges is not responsible, and I believe her.' He paused. 'It is your work, I take it?'

The slave stood in silence for a time. 'She is beaten, master,' Isocrates said eventually.

Croesus looked away. Such behaviour was hardly unusual, but he found himself disappointed. 'It is a husband's right, I suppose,'

Croesus said, 'But it does not please me. If I ask you to restrain your-self, will you?'

'I will try, master,' Isocrates said softly.

There was something strange in the slave's tone, and it did not sound like the anger or shame of a guilty man. For a moment, Croesus pondered whether or not to question his slave further, but decided against it. He would get the answer to this some other time.

'Go and send for my wife,' he said.

'Yes, master.'

Croesus waited alone, listening to the sound of the torches that lit the room. He blinked away his tiredness and tried to order his thoughts.

After a space of time that could have been a moment or could have been hours, he looked up, and saw his wife standing in the doorway.

'Please. Sit down.'

'I asked you not to come to me,' she said as she approached him.

'I didn't, did I? You came to me.'

'You are the king. I cannot refuse your requests.'

'Yes, I know. But I wanted to see you.'

She said nothing.

'I had a response from the oracle, you know,' Croesus said after a moment's silence.

'A blessing for your war. The whole city knows that. I do hear things, you know.'

'But did you know the oracle had answered two more of my ques-tions? The responses reached me yesterday. No one knows of them but me. And now, I would like to share them with you.'

She sighed. 'And what did the oracle tell you?'

'I asked for how long my line would rule.' She shook her head. 'You think me vain,' he said. 'But listen to her reply. She said that my people would rule until a mule sat on the throne of the Medes.'

'What does that mean?'

'Exactly. It's nonsense. My line will rule for ever.' Hesitant, he took her hand and cradled it his palms. 'Do you know what that means?'

'I suppose you will tell me.'

'It means we will have another child. Another son. And our son will have sons. That is wonderful, don't you think?'

She smiled sadly, but kept her head low. 'I am glad you have hope.'

'You will believe in it too. When I come back, after the war, all things will be different.' He leaned forward and kissed her softly on the forehead.

She looked up at him. 'You mentioned two more questions, Croesus. That is only one answer.'

'I asked if Gyges would ever speak.' He paused. 'But it doesn't matter now, knowing that we will have other sons.'

'What did she say?'

'She said that if Gyges ever spoke, I would regret it.' Croesus hesitated, then shrugged. 'I don't know what that means.'

She nodded to herself, then left to return to her chambers. He watched her, and did not try to stop her. He waited until he was certain that she had returned to the sanctuary of the women's quarters and would not return. He stood, and made his way down to the lower treasury.

The room was not as impressive as it had been. The gifts to Delphi had cost him greatly, and the fortress of his wealth had lost some of its former grandeur.

A part of him wished that the room could have remained as it was before: a place of glorious, unspoiled potential. Once he had seen a different vision each time he descended into the treasury. He had seen enormous theatres, vast temples and funerary mounds, fleets of trading ships that would map out every corner of the unknown world. He had dreamed an infinity of forms that his wealth might take.

Now, he saw only an army. An army of flesh and leather and iron and bronze that would spread the kingdom of Lydia across half the world. An army whose marching feet would write his name into history for ever.

He would have to be content with that.

7

Far to the east of Sardis, a village lay on the banks of the Halys river. Its clustered huts were of many different kinds, relics of all the tribes who had lived here at one time or another. Some were made from river reeds lashed together, others had been fashioned from mud or clay, others were wooden frames covered with animal hides. The fishing was good enough to support a few families, the soil too poor to allow the village to grow beyond that, and so the settlement never became larger than a village. None of the people who had ever lived in this place felt a need to give it a name, and so it did not have one.

There was only one thing that distinguished it from the many other villages by the Halys – the bridge that passed over the deep river a short distance from the huts, the bridge that at this time corresponded to a line inked on to a map. It marked the border between Lydia and Cappadocia, the easternmost point of Croesus's empire.

It was still early in the morning, while the fishermen were beginning to lay out their nets, that the first signs came. The observant noted the birds that flocked overhead in larger numbers than usual, all of them flying from west to east. Soon after, to the west they saw a dust cloud rising as though a tornado were making its way towards them. Then, confirming what they all knew by then, they heard the steady, thudding sound of an army on the move.

The villagers acted quickly. The young men and women hid in dark corners of the huts, or in the undergrowth near the village. They pulled aside piles of rushes that concealed small buried chambers, and they secreted there all the grain, bread, and salted fish that they had. The children hid as well, and soon only the old men and women remained outside, watching the army approach.

The villagers neither knew nor cared who ruled over them. On occasion, two elders might choose to argue over whether they thought it was the Cappadocians or the Galatians to whom they might owe their loyalty. It was a debate with no consequence, to pass the long hours when there was nothing else to do. The rumour had come to the village many years before, that it was now the Lydian king who ruled them. It had been dismissed as preposterous. No one in the village could imagine that the power of that distant kingdom could ever reach so far as to affect them, yet now the forces of the Lydian king marched towards them.

The old villagers stood and stared as the army approached, waiting to see if the men would slow for a moment, if a squadron of cavalry would peel away from the main column and ride towards them. It would be the work of a moment for some squadron of the marching horde to turn aside and burn the village to the ground.

The army did not slow. They had marched past dozens of villages like this one, and each one seemed to be on the verge of starvation, populated entirely by old men and women. There seemed not a single piece of bread that could be spared, not a single young man to join the army or a young woman to entertain the spearmen, not in the entire kingdom of Lydia.

The soldiers were aware of the deceptions of the villagers, but they were well provisioned and under strict orders not to ravage the countryside. Not yet. All knew that once they crossed the river into lands that were not ruled by their king, the rules would change. Life would be worth less beyond the Halys.

The old men and women watched as tens of thousands of warriors crossed the bridge into foreign land. Armoured infantry, their faces dripping sweat beneath their heavy bronze helmets, marched beside archers and slingers who wore little apart from their weapons; Thracian mercenaries cursed thickly in their own language at the Lydian cavalry who rode beside them. Following them all, in the train of the army, rags wrapped around their faces against the thick clouds of dust stirred up by fifty thousand men, came the slaves and the supply wagons, driving vast flocks of sheep and goats with them as a living larder, the animals almost outnumbering the men who had marched before them. The people of the village, who had been unmoved by the passage of the warriors, nudged each other and stared wistfully at the passing animals, and wondered at the power of a chieftain who had so many cattle at his disposal. Here was wealth they could understand.

They watched the horde of men and animals go by and disappear over the horizon, marching towards the low-hanging sun as though that was what they sought to conquer. When the army had gone, and had been reduced to nothing but dust and sound on the horizon, the young men, women and children emerged from their hiding places, and gave thanks that they had been spared. Then they gathered up their nets and hurried to the river, competing, as they did every morning, to see who would earn the Gods' favour by landing the first fish of the day.

They camped a day's march beyond the Halys, sleeping on alien earth for the first time. Most men lay on the ground rolled in their cloaks, piled together around campfires in great packs to share warmth. There was only one tent at the very centre – small and simple, but a palace for this wandering band of men. Inside, next to a single brazier casting warmth and light erratically, Croesus held a council of war with his general, Sandanis.

'Any word yet on the Persians?' the king said.

'Not yet, my lord.'

'But they know we are coming?'

'Yes,' the general answered. 'They have been preparing for it.'

Croesus nodded slowly. 'And they will bring their army out to meet us in battle?'

'Yes, my lord.'

Croesus gazed for a time at the ornate patterns of the tent wall and tried to summon some order to his thoughts. It was a strange thing, to be occupying land belonging to another. He found that he liked this sensation of gradual ownership, of conquest by possession. If he could only enjoy this feeling without the battles and the killing to come, that would have been better. But such a thing was impossible.

He turned back to his general. 'It all seems strangely consensual, Sandanis.'

The general frowned. 'I don't understand.'

'It is very accommodating, that they will bring their army all the way across the kingdom to fight us.'

'It is the custom,' Sandanis said bluntly. Croesus sighed, and wished again that he had brought Isocrates with the army. For all his skills as a general, Sandanis was not a thoughtful man.

'I would have thought,' Croesus said, 'that when some foreigner marches an army on to your land, custom would be the last thing on your mind. Why not wait, make us pursue him?'

'He wants this settled as much as you do. It shames him to have us on his land.'

'Yes, I suppose it does.' The king rubbed his jaw. 'What do you know about this Cyrus?'

'I know much about his army. Little about him.'

'A pity. Everyone has a different story. They are good ones, too. Raised by wolves, some say, others say by farmers. I wonder how that confusion began. There were half a dozen prophecies foretelling his birth and it is said his line will rule for nine generations. Do you believe any of that?'

'I could not say, my lord.'

'Well, I would like to know the truth of it. I wish they told such stories about me,' Croesus said. 'I suppose it does not matter. What happens now?'

'We make the men eager to fight.'

'And how do we do that?'

Over the weeks that followed, Croesus watched his army pass over the land like a walking catastrophe, an earthquake of a hundred thousand feet.

The land alone could not sustain them, so unnaturally large was the gathering of men, and they descended on every farm, village and town and took the food that they needed. They were, Croesus thought, as capricious as the Gods. One family of farmers would be greeted kindly by the passing soldiers. The fighting men would play with the children, and their officers would communicate, by gesture and the odd word of common language, their needs to the farmers. Sometimes they would leave gifts in compensation for food and wine. At the next farm, the same men would take the crops by force, carry off the women and young boys and torture the men to death for sport. There was no pattern to it.

Croesus understood that they took crops and cattle because they would starve if they did not. Why they murdered men and raped women was more mysterious to him. Perhaps, he thought, it was because they had to learn that they were powerful in this foreign land, that they were not bound by the laws that had ruled them before. Perhaps even as they fed themselves and learned how to kill, they knew that there was something else expected of them soon, that their killings were but rehearsals for a greater slaughter. No one would remember the villages and small towns that they destroyed. Through the thousands of little murders the army committed, there grew a desire to do something unforgettable; something that would mark the conquered land as theirs.

This collective dream grew strong and yet remained unfulfilled until they came at last to the city of Pteria.

They destroyed the army that guarded the city. They broke open the gates and tore holes in the walls. Then that night, for the very first time, Croesus watched a city being razed to the ground.

Now that darkness had fallen, he could not see the people running in the streets, nor the soldiers who pursued them. He only saw fire – enormous, angry lakes of flame where palaces, temples, and entire districts of houses had once stood – and the tiny, moving points of light of men with torches. It was as though he observed a city from another world, where flames had become sentient and built a city of their own.

'What do you think they are doing over there?' he asked his general.

'They are doing what I ordered them to do,' Sandanis replied.

'Which was?'

'Enjoy themselves.' Croesus winced, and the general smiled patiently. 'It needn't concern you,' Sandanis said. 'It is what happens.'

'It makes me think of my home. Don't you?'

'Yes, of course.'

'How does that make you feel?'

'I'm glad it is happening to their home and not to mine.'

'Nothing more than that?'

The general shrugged. 'They had bad fortune. The Gods didn't favour them. They were weak. That is what I think.'

The king nodded, but did not reply. He looked back on the city of fire.

He imagined what was being done in the distant streets. The men tortured and killed, the women raped. The elderly and the children put to death, there being no value in their capture. Everything of value taken, every sacred building put to the torch.

In the morning, there would be a great gathering at the blackened gates of the city. The healthy men and women, roped together like unruly cattle, would be marched back west and sold. All that would remain of Pteria was in their memories and in the stories they would tell. He wondered how many generations would pass until the memory of the place faded entirely.

He could feel, somewhere half hidden within his mind, a sense of shame. The emotion was close but could not reach him, as if it did not belong to him at all and merely lurked in his mind, misplaced by some other, more feeling man. He wondered where it came from, this barricade in his mind that meant he felt nothing, and whether it was the mark of a strong, ruthless king, or of some kind of monster.

'It doesn't make me feel anything, you know,' Croesus said. 'Isn't that strange?'

'Why should it?'

Croesus shook his head. 'You are lacking in imagination, Sandanis.'

'That may be so, my lord.'

'You may leave.'

The general bowed.

'The reports are confirmed. The Persian army is coming. They will be here in ten days.'

'Good. How do we respond?'

'We wait, and we meet them here. It is as good a place as any to fight a battle. The sight of the city will act in our favour.'

'I knew we destroyed it for some reason.' He tried a smile, but the general did not respond. 'Will the Ionians remain loyal?'

'Yes. My people tell us that they refused Cyrus's offer last night.'

'Very well. I am glad the waiting is over, at least.'

'Yes, my lord.'

Croesus hesitated. 'These things are necessary in war, you said?'

'Inevitable, my lord.'

'Very well. Let the men do what they will tonight. But tomorrow, you will get them ready to meet the Persians. I would rather see a battle than butchery.'

Sandanis raised an eyebrow. 'Say that again after you have seen battle.' He bowed again. 'Goodnight, my lord. Sleep well.'

It was on the tenth day of waiting, sometime after midday, that the Persian army came into view.

Croesus's scouts had kept careful track of its progress, and so when the Persians arrived, they found the Lydian army arrayed to meet them. Each army was a reflection of the other, and for hours, they shifted across the plains like mirror images. The two armies shuffled from side to side, moving from one place to another, each army taking it in turns to offer a position to its opponent that was declined. After a time, seeing that their opponents would not be deceived into assuming a weak position on the battlefield, both armies gave up trying to gain an advantage. They simply tried to settle on a part of the plain where they could face each other, a place where a hundred thousand men could line up in order and kill one another.

At last, after hours of manoeuvring, they reached a position with which both were satisfied. Having negotiated silently, they were ready to exchange words, and Croesus's emissary came to him to request his final instructions.

'If they want us to return to Lydia,' Croesus told him, 'they must disband their army immediately, reinstate the royal family of the Medes, and Cyrus must surrender himself personally to me.' He turned to Sandanis. 'Will that be enough?'

'I should think each one of those demands unacceptable enough on its own.'

'Let us see how they respond to three impossibilities. Oh,' he said, turning back to the emissary. 'One more thing.'

'Yes, my lord?'

'After their man refuses and offers up some insulting demands of his own, ask him if his master will meet with me, face to face. That is all.'

Croesus watched his emissary gallop out, and saw his Persian counterpart match his trajectory until they converged at the very middle of the field.

'Why meet with him?' Sandanis asked.

'As I said, I am curious to meet the man. I would like to settle some of these rumours. Besides, isn't this what kings do before great battles?'

'You are enjoying yourself, I see.'

'It was my will that brought all these men here,' Croesus said. 'Today, we will play our part in reshaping the world. That is remarkable, don't you think?'

The general pointed to the centre of the plain. 'He's coming back.'

'That was quick.'

The emissary rode back through the Lydian lines, and bowed from the saddle to his king.

'They refuse our demands, and insist that you send your army back across the Halys river and surrender yourself to the king of Persia.'

'That is two impossible demands to our three. Did he consent to a meeting?'

'No, my lord.'

'A shame.' Croesus paused. 'Did he give a reason? I assume his refusal came with an insult?'

'There was no reason, my lord.'

'Very well.' Croesus breathed in deeply, once. He felt no doubt, for it was too late for such things. He felt the easy courage of a man liberated from choice. 'Let it be done,' he said softly.

Sandanis turned and nodded to the man at his side. The soldier lifted the horn to his lips and blew, answered a moment later by a thousand horns in the Lydian army, then, like a reply or an echo, by the horns and drums of the Persians; a symphony of a single note played on ten thousand instruments.

The army advanced, the tips of their spears glittering in the clear light like waves under a low sun, the horses dancing nervously as they walked. The men were silent, a particular silence that has the quality of prayer, and the only sounds that Croesus heard were those of foot against earth, of metal against metal.

A line was crossed, some invisible threshold between the two forces. The first flight of Lydian arrows whispered into the air, and was met with an answering volley from the Persian archers. Both flights of arrows hung for a moment at the top of their arc. It seemed that they might remain there for ever. A cloud of wood and iron and feathers clustered thickly together in the middle of the sky, the weapons of two nations mingled so close together that it was impossible to tell them apart.

Then the arrows fell.

8

In the unnamed village on the edge of the Halys, the villagers watched the army return.

The Lydian army had first marched past in the height of summer. Now it was harvest season, and across the continent, towns and villages and farms waited to see what the soil and the Gods would consent to give them. A good harvest, and they could wait out the winter in some kind of comfort. A swarm of insects, a sudden flood, and thousands would starve. Everything depended on the gifts of the earth.

Beside the river, once again, the soil had reluctantly surrendered a small harvest of grain. Each year, as they gathered in their feeble crop, the villagers cursed the stubborn soil and promised themselves that the next year they would move on to a more fertile place. Every spring, they looked up at the sun and forgot their promise and again sowed their seeds with hope. They were gathering the last stalks from the fields when they heard and saw the familiar signs once more – the omens of an army on the move.

The young hid themselves once again, and the old men and women waited in the fields and watched the army pass.

It was much reduced, some said by a quarter, others by a third. The old men had lived long enough to see many armies pass over the river.

They had learned to read, in how the soldiers walked and in the tone of the songs they sang in languages that the villagers could not understand, whether the wars had been won or lost. Even the sound of the army as it moved, the rhythm and force of thousands of footfalls, could tell a story to those who knew how to listen.

The villagers saw that these soldiers did not march with pride, but neither did they have the hollow faces of men who have fought and been defeated. They marched with the exhausted air of men who had risked their lives, had seen their friends die, for the sake of a stalemate.

On the long journey back to the Halys, Croesus had fought the battle in his mind many times.

Everything, at first, had gone as Sandanis had said it would. When the first arrows fell, Croesus had looked from one army to another, wondering if by chance his eyes might alight on the first man to die that day, and realizing, with a kind of abstract horror, that there was a pleasure to be found in watching men die at his command.

The Persians planted their wicker shields on the earth and held their ground, and Croesus's spearmen swept forward, hoping to break the line. The sounds that filtered back to Croesus were not what he had expected. There were few war cries and little screaming. What Croesus heard more than anything else was the sound of thousands gasping, as though there were not air enough in the world to keep so many alive in one place, as if they had to kill each other in order to breathe.

He watched as the Persian cavalry circled his spearmen and felt a sudden surge of fear. Sandanis had told him it was necessary, but even so, he shut his eyes when he heard a wail of panic break out from the trapped Lydians.

At last, Sandanis gave a second signal, and as though summoned by the cries of their countrymen, the Lydian cavalry, the greatest in the world, came forward. They lowered their long spears, and charged.

That should have been the moment. The moment that he would remember for the rest of his life, the moment when the Persians broke and ran, and he won himself a new empire.

But neither side broke. The horseman charged, but did not push through, and all movement ceased on the battlefield. The two armies fixed their positions against one another, and the killing began in earnest.

Hours passed. Each hour brought another ten thousand dead, but the two armies did not move more than a hundred yards. The excitement Croesus had felt when the first men fell had long faded. He sat on his horse, watching and wishing nothing more than for the battle to be over.

Suddenly, as if they had heard his thought, the armies moved apart. The hours of killing had erased the thought of retreat from their minds, until one man had rediscovered the ability to step backwards, and shared this gift with his companions. The two armies separated, a few wary paces at a time. The captains yelled at their men to advance, to attack again, but the men would not listen. Persians and Lydians had struck a silent truce. They had had enough of killing.

At last, the generals sounded the retreat. The battle was a stalemate. Croesus had not known such a thing was possible, that tens of thousands of men could die, yet nothing change, the world unmoved by such a quantity of blood.

The king had said little since the battle. He had mechanically followed his general's advice in the aftermath without offering a word in response. Now, as his horse crossed the midpoint of the bridge over the Halys and he returned to the lands he ruled, he had found his voice again.

'Why did we lose, Sandanis?'

'We did not lose, my lord,' the general said. 'They retreated, and we retreated. There was no dishonour.'

'Then why didn't we win? We were better equipped. Better organized. That's what you told me.'

The general shrugged. 'There were more of them, and we were on their land. It evens out.'

'So why were you so eager to fight that battle?'

'I was confident that we would not lose. I was not sure that we would win.'

Croesus shook his head. 'We lost a quarter of the army—'

'They lost many more.'

'Do not interrupt me. We lost a quarter of the army, and we have nothing to show for it.'

'We will come back. Next year, we will have the Spartans with us. If you had waited for them—'

Croesus gave him a look of warning. The general bowed his head.

'Forgive me,' Sandanis said. After a moment he added, 'We will come back next year. If that is your wish.'

Croesus nodded, but in his mind he saw a war that could continue for decades. Brief, bloody summers, and long, tedious winters spent waiting for those summers. Waiting for the killing to start again; a war that he might watch over for the rest of his life, as though he were raising another child.

'I had hoped it would be over by now,' he said.

'Yes, my lord.'

'Was that naïve?'

'A little. But we will win. You need not worry.'

Croesus nodded again. After a moment, he said, 'I remember your words at the council. You think this is a pointless war, don't you?'

'It doesn't matter what I think,' Sandanis said. 'I live to serve you, my lord. I hope my loyalty is not in question.'

'Never, Sandanis,' Croesus said. 'You are a practical man. You and

Isocrates should spend more time together. Perhaps you will get the chance, this winter.' He turned to look back at the bridge that marked the edge of his lands. 'We will be back next year,' he said. 'We will keep coming back every year, if we have to. We will come back until we have won.'

The villagers watched the army pass into the distance, and gave it little thought. A few of the men exchanged bets on whether or not they would see the army return the following year, wagering leather belts, knives of flint, and tortoiseshell brooches, but that was the extent of their interest. They went back to gathering their crops and cursing the soil.

Some time after the army had passed, the villagers saw two more riders cross the bridge. Each man held the reins of another, riderless horse beside his own. The men had dark skin, and wore strange leather clothes of a kind that the villagers had never seen before. The horses were thin, tall and sleekly muscled, bred for speed rather than war.

The men crossed over the bridge in a moment, quite unaware of the significance of their passage. They were the first men of their nation ever to cross the Halys river. Then they too disappeared into the distance, pursuing the army as it retreated back west.

Cautious, they maintained the distance of a day's march from the Lydian army. For most of the journey, they never saw a single man from the army that they pursued. They followed a phantom across alien lands, a monster that marched with thousands of feet and left a long, unmistakable scar across the land.

The two scouts slept in copses and deserted farmhouses, drank from rivers and sucked dew from the grass. They ate small birds that they shot from the sky with curved bows. They sneaked into orchards at night like mischievous children and stole what fruit they could find.

At one lean time, as they passed through a land ruined by both a failed harvest and the passage of the hungry army that had preceded them, the two men each opened a vein in the neck of one of their horses and drank a little blood to sustain them.

They followed the army until it reached the walls of Sardis. There, at last, watching from the hills, they allowed themselves a long look at the monster they had been pursuing.

They watched as the mercenaries received their payment of slaves and gold at the gates of the city and left for their native lands. They watched as several thousand Lydian citizens were released from the army to begin their own long journeys back to their homes in the distant corners of the empire. They watched as layer after layer peeled away from the Lydian army, until its core, perhaps a third of the number that had first crossed the Halys all those months before, entered the city walls to wait out the winter.

Having seen enough, they turned around and began their own journey home. They lashed the reins and stirred their mounts. The two men would not sleep or eat on their return.

They rode east, back towards Persia.

9

It was winter in Sardis.

For the wealthy in the high city, the season was a passing inconvenience. Food was dull, with no fruits except those that had been preserved in honey. They conducted love affairs to pass the time, drank too much, and dreamed of the liberation of spring and summer, when their lives would begin again.

For the poor of the lower city, winter was a more serious matter. They spent the rest of the year planning for the cold months, saving up wood enough to last them through. Those who miscalculated, or had their stockpile spoiled or stolen, threw themselves on the charity of others, going from family to friend to acquaintance until they found someone to take them in and give them access to a fire. This was not usually difficult, for most were happy to crowd more bodies around the flames, aware that they themselves might have need of such a favour in a future lean year. But there were always those who did not have friends or relatives from whom they could beg for the charity of heat. Such people froze to death quietly in the poorest houses of the city, and were found only when the spring thaw opened up their tombs.

Not all in the palace were free from worry in winter. In an exposed courtyard, Maia clutched her cloak around her and shivered as she watched Gyges trudge through the snow. He looked more and more like a wild man in the winter since the royal barbers had given up their erratic attempts to attend on him, given his habit of wandering outside, and let his beard and hair grow long. Maia was not fond of treating him like an animal left to grow out its pelt, but there seemed no other way to keep him warm.

In the long winter months she had to watch him closely, as he felt neither cold nor pain. In years past, when she had been less familiar with his habits, he had come close to frostbite walking barefoot in the snow until his feet were hard and white. She remembered the hours he had screamed as the guards held his feet in warm water; he rebelled against their touch far more than the pain of his thawing skin. Now, she observed him carefully, always ready to coax him indoors to play by the fire when he had been outside for too long.

As she watched him pace around the courtyard, she heard footsteps approaching, an unfamiliar combination of weight and pace on the stones. In the long years of silence spent with Gyges, she thought she had become familiar with the footsteps of every inhabitant of the palace, but these were alien to her. She wondered if it were some new slave passing through, or visitors from a distant land who had been trapped in Sardis by the winter. But when the owner of the footsteps came into view, it was someone she recognized.

'My lady.' Maia bowed. 'How can I be of service?'

Danae looked at her in silence. 'I wanted to see my son,' the queen said eventually. 'It has been a very long time since I last saw him.'

'Of course. He will be glad to see you.'

'Will he?' she said absently. Maia could find no response to this, but the queen did not seem to expect one. She stepped through the snow until she stood by the slave, and watched her son in silence as he wandered aimlessly from one corner of the courtyard to another. Maia noted that Danae had no attendants with her, not a single slave or bodyguard. How the queen had managed to dispose of them and wander the palace alone, Maia did not know.

'Has he ever spoken to you?' The queen's words summoned Maia from her thoughts.

'No, my lady,' the slave said. 'He has never spoken to anyone.'

'You're sure of that?'

'As sure as I can be.'

'He is deaf, then?'

'No. He can hear. Those scholars that the king commissioned, they tested him; clapping their hands by his ear, knocking over a chair on the other side of the room. He responded to them. I wonder . . .' She trailed off.

'Please. Go on.'

'I sometimes think that he does understand us.'

'You think he chooses not to speak?'

'I don't know.'

Danae nodded absently. 'How do you stand it? Living with his silence.'

'It is not so difficult. It gives me time to think.'

'What does a slave think of?' Danae said, then put her hand to her face and turned away. 'What a foolish thing for me to say. I am sorry.'

'Not at all. Will the king be coming here as well?' Maia said. 'He used to see us often. Gyges misses him, I think. He would be glad to see you both.'

'My husband does not know I am here. I have no wish to see him.'

Maia said nothing.

'Do not worry, Maia. You do not have to say anything to that. What is there to say?'

They watched Gyges in silence. He gave no sign that he knew or cared that he was being observed. He ended his absent wanderings in the snow, and retreated to a corner of the courtyard that was covered by a small awning. A brazier burned there, and he sat on a pile of rugs and stared at the embers.

Looking at him, Maia wondered how long ago it must have been that a man first stared into a fire and sought to read his fortune in the reddish embers and turning flames. She wondered how much longer it would be before the last man, if there ever were such a thing, stared into a fire as the world broke apart, and thought of the countless people who would sit and consider the flames in the time between, connected across time only by a moment's peace, a point of heat. At least in this act of contemplation, if in so little else, Gyges seemed to belong in this world, and not another.

'Perhaps I could try with him,' Danae said.

'My lady?'

'Try and get him to speak, I mean.'

'Of course,' Maia said. 'If anyone could convince him to speak, surely it is you.'

She looked at the slave. 'If that were true he would have spoken by now. You are more of a mother to him than I am.'

Maia bowed her head to avoid the queen's gaze. 'Would you like me to go? Perhaps you would like to be alone with him?'

'No. Please stay.' Danae hesitated. 'I wish that I saw more of you. That I had you at my side, as the king has your husband. But I don't suppose my husband will ever release you from this duty.'

'That is true.' She smiled carefully. 'But if it pleases you, perhaps you may come here again, my lady.' She nodded to Gyges. 'He won't mind. I love your son, but I would welcome more talkative company.'

'Perhaps I will. My thanks.' Danae looked back to Gyges, and the smile slowly fell from her lips. Slow and hesitant, as if cornering a skittish animal that might startle and bolt, she approached her son.

He ignored her, staring into the fire like a priest seeking a sign

145

from the Gods. She sat down, waited beside him patiently, and then began to try and convince him to speak.

'There was no trouble settling our debts, Isocrates?'

'No, master. The allies are pleased. There was plenty to distribute from Pteria.'

'Good, good,' Croesus said. It was late, and most of courtiers had retired for the evening. Only Isocrates and a few guards remained. The throne room was dimly lit, and now Croesus wished he had commissioned more torches for it – it was hard to read the face of his slave in the shifting play of shadows. 'Will they all return next year?' Croesus continued.

'Who can tell what the Thracians will do from one year to the next, master?' Isocrates said. 'But I expect they will be back, for the gold if for nothing else. The others certainly have no cause to complain at their share.'

'Very good. Send some offerings to the Spartans as well. Enough to let them know we bear them no ill will. They did say that they could not join us this year. But enough to let them know we expect them promptly next spring.'

'I will see to it immediately, master. Is there anything else you wish me to do?'

'Send an emissary to Babylon. I have heard Nabonidus fears the Persian. Perhaps he will join us as well.'

'Yes, master.'

Croesus slipped one of his rings from his hand and rolled it between his fingers. 'When this business is finished,' he said, 'I will go to Babylon. We will go to Babylon, I mean. I shan't go travelling without you again. Wouldn't you like to see the city?'

'I will go where you will it, master.'

'They say it is the greatest city in the world. A city of marvels.' He thought for a time. 'I would like to see it,' he said quietly. 'They claim to have invented writing. We may have invented money, but to be the first people to write, that would have been remarkable.' He paused again. 'It is the oldest city I know of. Surely, if anyone has the answers, they must. Don't you think?'

'Answers to what?'

Croesus did not reply, and stared absently into space.

'Is there anything else, master?'

'No. Go.'

Isocrates bowed and went to the door, but as soon as he placed his hand on it, he heard the king speak again.

'Isocrates. Wait.' It was the tone that the slave feared from his master, more than any other. Doubt.

He turned back. 'Master?'

The king smiled at him hesitantly. 'Is it right that I do this?'

'Forgive me. I do not understand.'

'The war, I mean. What do you think?'

'You can do whatever you want, master,' Isocrates said. 'You are the most powerful man in the world. Doesn't that make you right, whatever you do?'

Croesus's mouth twisted, and he felt the blood rush into his cheeks. He beckoned Isocrates forward, and when the slave was before him, leaned in close until he was only a few inches from the other man's face.

'I wish you would not talk like that,' Croesus said. 'Do you not have a voice? A mind of your own? You offer me nothing but sycophancy? What use are you to me?'

'Master—'

Croesus hit him; the clumsy, open-handed slap of a man unused to violence. Isocrates took the blow without complaint, running his tongue over his lips to check for the taste of blood. Croesus slumped back and turned from his own action in disgust.

147

'Can I speak freely?' Isocrates said after a moment.

'I wish you would. Just for once.'

Even with this permission, it was a long time before the slave spoke again. 'I wish,' he said, 'that you had asked me that a long time ago. I wish I could have told you not to go to war.'

'But you could not speak without being asked.'

'No, master.'

'Perhaps you are right. Maybe we should not return.' He stared at Isocrates. 'And I think I may have to free you, if your slavery means that you must keep your thoughts from me. Would you still serve me, if I gave you the choice as a free man?'

Isocrates looked at the ground. 'I don't know, master.'

'Ah. An honest answer. Thank you.' Croesus paused. 'I am sorry I struck you. It was a mistake.'

'You never have to apologize to me.'

Croesus turned away. 'I wish the winter was over,' he said. 'I can't stand to be trapped in this city any longer.' He closed his eyes. 'You're still here?' He waved a hand at the slave. 'Go.'

10

Afterwards, as always, there would be stories of omens. Of horses consuming snakes in the fields, of sacrifices that went rotten in moments on the altars, and of predictions that had been made five generations before. But, in truth, there were no signs. When it came, it came as all true disasters do, with no warning at all.

A farmer beneath the walls of Sardis saw it first. He was cutting wood on the outskirts of the city, working fast to keep warm in the cold winter air, when the wind blew against his back and brought with it some strange fragment of sound. A distant voice in a foreign tongue, coupled with the sound of metal on metal.

He assumed at first that it was some trick of the wind, and continued cutting. The sound came again – stronger, more insistent, like the repeated calling of a name. He placed his axe to the ground, turned and looked to the east. It was there that he saw the unimaginable.

A numberless mass of men sprawled across the land to the east, consuming the horizon. Even then, confronted by the sight, he could not understand what he was seeing. His mind refuted it. It was not until he looked more closely, saw the horsemen whose steeds snorted frost, the spearmen with heavy sheepskins slung over their necks and rags wrapped around their hands, that he believed it.

The farmer looked on the legion who had done the unthinkable, marching for days and nights on end through a foreign land in winter, faster than any messengers who might have been sent riding ahead of them. Surely no army had ever achieved its like before. Even at this distance, he could see the alien banner under which they marched; the towering eagle that held a globe in each talon, as though even the conquest of one entire world would not be enough to satisfy the king who marched beneath that banner. It was the flag of Cyrus, and of Persia.

'No army marches in winter,' Sandanis said at last, to fill the terrible silence.

'What?' Croesus said.

'No army marches in winter.'

'Is that your excuse?'

'I was—'

'Why not? Custom again, I suppose?'

The general said nothing. Croesus looked away in disgust.

They were in the emerald throne room, its pillars studded with jade, green silks falling from the ceiling, and the king wished they had moved to some private meeting room when the news had come. It was no place for a council of war. Croesus felt like a man pretending to be a king.

He turned back to Sandanis. 'Can we defeat them?'

Sandanis hesitated. 'Perhaps.'

'That is all you can say?'

'Yes. That is all.'

Croesus looked around the room again, and the men and women of the court regarded him silently. Defeat hung heavy in the air around him.

'Gather the army,' he said at last.

Sandanis bowed, then looked up at the king again.

'There is something more?'

'You will have to come with us, sire.'

'You think I will inspire the men?' Croesus said bitterly.

'Yes, my lord.'

He stared into space. 'Isocrates?' he said.

The slave stepped forward. 'Yes, master?'

'I left you behind before, and it was a mistake. You must come as well.'

For a moment, Isocrates said nothing – a half-beat of disobedience. 'As you wish,' he said.

The Persians waited, with a strange courtesy, for what remained of the Lydian army to take up position. In spite of their winter march, it seemed that they still had some regard for the habits of war.

Croesus watched the Lydian cavalry move to the vanguard, and despite the great numbers that stood against them, he let himself feel some small hope. He told himself that the Persians must be exhausted by their forced march across the continent. Perhaps it was here, beneath the walls of Sardis, that he could win his greatest victory.

Before he could speak and order the attack, a series of horns sounded from the Persian army. Every other man on their front line stepped to the left, exposing a series of empty columns. Through these gaps, strange figures advanced, bulky creatures that seemed to have two heads and six legs. Croesus wondered if the rumours were true, that the Persians had tamed monsters as part of their army. Then his eyes began to make sense of what he saw and recognized the figures for what they were. They were camels, being led by servants to the front line.

The men walked forward hesitantly dressed in ragged clothes, their heads bowed. The ungainly pack animals, still heavily loaded, bleated stubbornly and spat at their handlers. They seemed to be aware that they were being taken somewhere they did not belong.

'What are they going to do,' Croesus said, 'charge us with their baggage train?'

There was no response from Sandanis. He saw the general's mouth open a bare fraction in disbelief. 'Sandanis?' Croesus said, suddenly afraid. He felt a wind blowing on his face from the east.

With that wind, a wave of madness passed through the front ranks of the Lydian cavalry. The horses reared and bolted, twisted and fell. He heard the animals cry out in fear and all Croesus could think, at that moment, was how human their screams sounded.

He saw riders falling from their saddles and kicked to death, saw others jumping clear and running, and soon every horse was free of its master. They broke in every direction at first, then gathered together, re-formed into a herd like wild horses in the plains. They galloped away to the north, and were lost from sight.

A thick, heavy stench came through the air, diluted by distance, but still powerful enough to make his own mount stamp and toss its head. Croesus looked up at the strange, humped animals, led by slaves and laden with supplies, that formed the unlikely vanguard of the Persian army. He closed his eyes.

'No,' he said.

'Their horses must travel with the pack animals,' the general said, his voice dull. 'They are used to the smell.' He shook his head. 'Quite brilliant.'

Croesus heard the horns sound, and saw the Persian army begin its advance.

'We have to retreat,' the king said.

'No, my lord.' Sandanis's voice was firm.

'Without the cavalry—'

'Yes. We will be defeated.'

'Then—'

'You must go back to the palace. The rest will stand here and fight.

It is too late to run. If we retreat now, our army will scatter and they will take the city.'

Croesus thought of the thousands of men who were about to die for him, of how their last thoughts would be of their king and how he had betrayed them. 'It isn't fair,' Croesus said, barely louder than a whisper. 'I won't do it.'

Sandanis leaned in towards the king, his voice close to anger. 'It is their fate to die. It is our fate to live, and rule over them.' He placed a hand on Croesus's shoulder. 'Go now. I will give the orders, and then I will follow you back to the palace.'

Croesus felt the touch of a hand on his arm. It was Isocrates. The slave said nothing, and his face gave no sense of what was in his mind, whether he wanted his king to retreat, to live, or to stay and die. But in the silence of his slave, as he had so many times before, Croesus let himself find some kind of forgiveness. Croesus bowed his head, and turned his horse back towards the city.

He heard the first screams behind him. He looked over his shoulder and saw the great Persian army spill forward like a flood. He watched the unhorsed Lydian cavalry, their lances gripped like spears, run out to meet them.

Then he turned away. He did not want to see any more.

11

Sardis waited.

On the fourteenth day of the siege, Croesus finally found the courage to go out on to the city walls and look down on what had once been his army.

He imagined that those more familiar with such matters could inspect the pattern of the dead and reconstruct the battle from it; where the first men had fallen, where the battle had turned, when the losing side had tried to run. He stared at the heaped mound of Lydian dead on the plains beneath Sardis, not a horse amongst them, and he wondered if they had tried to surrender and had been butchered even as they threw down their weapons, or if they had died fighting to the last man, waiting for a relief that was never going to arrive.

It seemed likely, he thought, that the city would now die too, just more slowly. A death by encirclement that would take months, rather than hours. On its sheer-sided hill, with only a single path leading up to it, Sardis looked like a city that could wait for a thousand years, if only it were manned by automata, and not by men. Without a harvest or foreign traders to supply it, Sardis was not a fortress. It was a tomb.

During the day, the Lydians assessed their dwindling supplies, and looked down at the Persians below. They did nothing else – there seemed little point in doing anything but waiting for each day to pass, both hoping, and fearing, that nothing would change. At night, Croesus imagined that everyone in Sardis must have dreamed the same dream, of exhausted Lydian messengers arriving in foreign courts, of allied armies hastily assembled that would march day and night to reach Sardis and rescue them. Every morning, the people of the city woke from these dreams, flocked to the walls and windows, and stared out to the horizon. But no army came.

He looked down the steep walls, and saw, far below the upper city, the waiting Persians. The scattered buildings of lower Sardis were not sufficient to contain them, and so they had built a new city of their own, a city of tents and animals, an echo of the first settlement that had sprung up in that place centuries before, when a gathering of nomad tribes, tired of wandering and hunting, looked up at the steep hill and imagined a fortress to call their home.

Already, he saw, their encampment bore the marks of civilization. Clear paths had been traced through the tents and masses of waiting soldiers, the grass worn down into roads by thousands of marching feet. Commerce did not take long to establish itself. Even from above, Croesus could see the large clearing on the northern side of the camp that had become the centre of a black market trade, where the soldiers gathered to trade their weapons for food, their food for slaves, then their slaves for weapons again whenever rumours came that an attack was imminent.

From every corner of the waiting army, he could hear music echoing. Men gathered around fires, playing drums edged with metal rings, singing to drive away the cold and the boredom. Every day, Croesus listened to this music as though he were listening to the heart-beat of some great monster. When the music faded away entirely, it would be because the men were too starved to play, and it would be time for them to retreat back to the east.

He turned away from the Persians, and back to Sardis. It was a silent city. In the streets, people tried to talk, but their conversations would soon falter and fade, sometimes even mid sentence. It was the silence of those who are afraid to speak, as though the safe deadlock of the siege were a spell that could be broken by a single misplaced word. The Lydians waited behind their walls, and the Persians in their tents, two cities facing each other, and waited for something to change.

As Croesus began his slow walk back to the palace, to the endless councils of war and meetings that awaited him, a movement caught his eye. It was a young Lydian soldier rushing along the south wall, his helmet in his hand. He was late for his post, no doubt. The king turned away, and gave no further thought to what he had seen.

As this soldier ran along the south wall of Sardis, he tripped on a loose stone and reached out his hands for balance. His helmet slipped from fingers that were still numb with sleep, bounced once on the parapet and tumbled far below.

His name was Ardys. He had overslept, and was going to be late to his post for the second day in a row. Despite the cold air his helmet had stifled him, and he had taken it off as he ran. Now, he would be punished for something much worse than a moment's lateness.

He saw, by some miracle, that it hadn't fallen all the way to the ground. It had caught on a tough old bush, its bark gnarled and whorled like ancient skin, that clung to the cliff just as it clung stubbornly to life. One of the branches of this bush had hooked the helmet as it fell, and now it hung there sixty feet beneath him, the bronze giving him a mocking wink of reflected sunlight when the wind stirred the branch.

There was no great reason to go down after it. If he didn't, his captain would scream abuse at him and shame him in front of the others. He would be assigned the worst duties for a week or so, and be the victim of jokes for somewhat longer than that, but that was all.

He looked down the wall for one last time. Before he knew what he was doing he had slipped off his boots, had hooked his fingers on top of the wall and was gently lowering himself down, searching for a place to put his feet.

On the day of the great sacrifice to Delphi, a year before, one of his fellow soldiers had made a bet that no one would ever climb the south cliff. It was an idle gamble, not meant as a challenge. But Ardys had spent his youth in the mountains, learning the secrets of weight and motion that blank faces of rock reveal to their followers. He had taken the wager, gone to the base of the wall, and begun to climb.

After he had climbed ten feet, they were still yelling insults at him. Once he had climbed thirty feet, they were shouting at him to come back down. By the time he was fifty feet off the ground they had all fallen silent, like men in a temple observing a sacrifice. That silence held until he made it all the way to the very top. He remembered that silence, afterwards, above all else.

There was no one to watch him now as he reversed the climb he had made many years before. With his face so close against the rock, the sound of his breathing was like a hard wind in his ears. At each sharp intake of breath, he felt himself on the edge of panic. On each slow breath out, the fear receded just sufficiently for him to make one more move. Slowly, carefully, he felt his way down the cliff, feeling the grain of the rock beneath his fingertips. A single misplaced hand or foot would be enough to send him down onto the boulders below. He pressed his feet flat against the rock when he could not find an edge, pinching at the tiny holds until his fingers were white with pressure. The more he climbed, the more he became convinced that he could not fall.

Even as he focused almost entirely on the climb, a small part of his mind was free to wonder why he was doing it. Perhaps, he thought, it was to answer a challenge from the Gods, who had placed his helmet there, in the exact place he had climbed once before, as a test of his courage. Perhaps there was no good reason at all.

It seemed as though only a few moments had passed, and suddenly he could feel his left foot brush against the branches. The wind grew strong, the breath of an angry God, and he felt his fear return. He was almost equidistant from safety in either direction. His hands began to shake, and his feet felt as though they were balanced on nothing at all. His weight tugged him back into the empty air. He began to fall.

His eyes found a hidden pocket in the rock just as his feet slid away from him. He jammed three fingers deep into the cliff face, and for one moment he hung there, his hand and arm sharp with pain. Then his right foot found a dent in the rock. Barely an inch wide, yet it felt like a ledge ten times that size. He patted his other hand over the rock face until it found a hold. He was safe once more.

He worked his way down a little further, then reached down tentatively, until his fingers hooked under metal. He placed the helmet back on his head, and breathed easy again.

He looked below him, and for a moment he hesitated, tempted to continue his climb to the bottom. It seemed a shame to go only halfway down the cliff and not to finish it. But he had been foolish enough for one day.

He looked back up at the rock he had to reclimb, but felt no fear. He knew that he would not fall. He closed his eyes and breathed out once. Then he began to climb again.

He did not climb unobserved.

The Persians watched the south wall as infrequently as the Lydians patrolled it. Why waste time staring at the impossible? But, quite by chance, Ardys was spotted by a single Persian soldier, a man called Hyroeades.

Hyroeades had been a shepherd with a love for the mountains. But he had a tendency to daydream and his flock had a tendency to wander, so he had been sent to the city by a disappointed father. When the Persians conquered that city only a few days after his arrival and forced him to join their army, he did not try to escape. He was a man who always accepted fate with indifference.

Since the siege had begun, to get away from the others, he had taken to walking the deserted parts of the besieging line. The slack discipline of the army at siege suited him well – none knew or cared if he stole away for a few hours each day.

On the fourteenth day of the siege, as he was walking alone by the south wall, he mistook the sound of the falling helmet for that of an arrowhead glancing off stone. He ducked into cover by instinct, and lay still against the ground. He watched Ardys climb.

From a distance, Hyroeades felt none of the fear that Ardys struggled against, observed none of the moments where the Lydian came close to misplacing a foot, saved at the last moment by instinct or judgement. To Hyroeades, even Ardys's momentary slip onto one hand looked graceful, almost predestined. After Ardys had climbed back up, Hyroeades headed, almost shyly, towards the foot of the cliff. He placed a palm flat against it and looked straight up.

At first he saw nothing but a blank rockface, and he wondered whether it was a man or a god that he had seen on the wall. But then, even as he stared at it, he saw a vertical path appear out of the blank stone, that same path that Ardys had identified years before. Like Ardys, his first thought on seeing it was one of simple delight – the impossible made possible, a blank wall of stone transforming into a causeway to the city. A shy smile played on his lips. Then he thought about the consequences of his discovery, and the smile faded.

Perhaps he would say nothing. Unlike many, he was enjoying the siege; the long, slow days without responsibility, where nothing was expected of him but waiting. He would have been happy, he thought, to wait a hundred years beneath those walls.

But he was a man who was obedient to authority, who feared the consequences of disobedience above all else. Suddenly fearful, he looked around to see if anyone was watching him, and might attest to his hesitation. He saw no one, but the fear remained.

He turned and began the long walk back towards the encampment, to go and tell his captain what he had seen.

12

Rough hands shook the king awake.

'Master?'

'What is it?'

'They are in the city.'

'What?'

'The Persians are over the wall.'

Croesus said nothing for a time. He stared at Isocrates, uncomprehending. 'How?' he said at last.

'They climbed the south wall.'

The king shook his head. 'That's—'

'They found a way up. I don't know how.'

Croesus seemed not to hear for a moment, one hand plucking absently at his blankets. Then he let out a single sharp sob, and pressed his fingers to his eyes. Isocrates looked away.

'Is there any hope?' the king said.

'No, master.'

Croesus took his fingers from his eyes, and nodded slowly. 'Where is Sandanis?'

'He is dead.'

'What?'

'He took poison. When he heard the news.'

Croesus nodded dully. 'He should have fallen on his sword. It would have been more fitting.'

'Master, I need to go and find my wife.'

Croesus looked up at him. 'How dare—' he began. Then he hesitated, seeing the expression on the slave's face. He doesn't need to obey me any more, Croesus thought. He is doing this as a last courtesy.

'Of course,' the king said. Isocrates turned to go, but Croesus spoke again. 'Is there . . . Is there anything you think I should do, Isocrates?' the king said.

'No.' The slave shook his head. 'There is nothing left to do.'

Sardis burned.

For the Persians, the city was a monster to be slain – every temple, house and statue an appendage to be cut away and burned, every man and woman of the city a drop of blood to be bled.

The people of Sardis knew that there was no hope for them. Some knelt and prayed openly in the streets, others gathered and barricaded themselves into temples that would soon become charnel houses. Others tried to buy their way out, offering gold and slaves, their daughters and wives, in a bid to escape the slaughter. Many rushed to hurl themselves from the high cliffs rather than die at the hands of the Persians.

The Lydian soldiers, for the most part, threw down their weapons and moved amongst the people. Some tried to maintain a sense of martial order, and here and there a group of soldiers would assemble together and make a futile stand at a corner of a street where they had once played as children, or at a statue that one of them had worshipped every day of his life – anywhere they could find that was of significance to them. One wild-looking soldier died after challenging a series of Persians to single combat on the steps of his favourite brothel, as though he were defending a temple or the house of a king.

The people of Sardis knew that they would not survive the night. They each tried to find the right place, the right way, to die.

It was quiet in the throne room.

The marble room was located near the heart of the palace, and the Persians had yet to enter the grounds. Occasionally, he heard the solitary, panicked footsteps of someone running in a corridor nearby, feet beating louder and louder against the stone floor, then fading back to silence. He tensed each time he heard someone approach, praying that they would not enter, hoping that they would. So long as he was alone, he felt safe. So long as he was alone, he felt himself edging one step closer to madness. He wondered how long it would take them to find him.

He thought about how he used to play at being a king. Back then he had been forced to make do with a dusty room, a shattered chest for a throne, a host of imaginary courtiers for company. Now, he saw that without others to serve him he was no longer a king. He was a man sitting alone in an empty room, waiting to die. He couldn't even bring himself to occupy the throne itself, and he squatted at its foot like a dog or a slave, his back resting against it.

After a time, he heard something different. A pair of familiar slow, scraping footsteps approaching the throne room, inch by inch. At first they were so faint, and paused so often, that he was certain he imagined them. Soon there was no doubting that the footsteps were real, no question whom they belonged to. Croesus sat still at the foot of his throne and waited for his son.

It had been many months since his son had permitted anyone to bathe him. He had a long beard and dirt-matted hair, and even from a distance the air was thick with the stink of him. He looked

163

like a wild man, a mad prophet. He looked like anything but a prince.

'Gyges,' Croesus said softly.

The king watched as his son slowly made his way to the exact centre of room and then stopped, perhaps compelled by some unspoken, geometric command. He looked up at his father with the unchanged, blank eyes with which he had looked upon the whole world since was born.

Croesus rose from the steps of the throne, walked down, and gathered his son into his arms. Gyges did not acknowledge Croesus's embrace, but he stood still to accept it. It was the first time he had allowed his father to touch him.

Croesus released his son, and smiled at him. He placed a guiding hand on the young man's back, and led him from the throne room.

'Come with me, Gyges. Let us go and see the city.'

In the women's quarters, a battle raged.

It was not a battle against foreign invaders. It was Lydians, not Persians, who sought to enter the women's sanctuary, and the men who beat at the doors were brothers and cousins of the women who battled to keep them out. As soon as they knew Sardis was lost, and that they would all be dead in a matter of hours, men from all over the city had swarmed to this forbidden place. Soon, they would roam freely in a place where no man had set foot in generations.

The women fought against them, slaves and noblewomen united in barricading the doorways and using whatever weapons they could find, but they were outnumbered. The doors were splintering, and would soon collapse entirely. The sanctuary would become a place of nightmares.

In a secluded corner of the women's chambers, Danae sat alone.

She did not help the others who struggled to keep the doors closed, did not think of what would happen when the Lydians broke through. She thought only of what would happen when the Persians finally took the palace.

She knew what happened to the queens of conquered cities. She thought of the women in the stories she knew who had been taken as trophies, the countless tales of gods and heroes and princes who celebrated their triumph with the capture of a wife or a daughter or a queen. She wondered if history could be reduced entirely to the endless kidnap and exchange of stolen women from one country to another. She tried to imagine what favour the king of Persia would seek to buy with her.

She stood, and walked to a window. She stepped up, and looked out at the burning city.

With the same slow, careful step as his wife, Croesus stepped out into the streets of Sardis.

For a moment, he could pretend that nothing had changed in his city. The smoke in the air could have risen from the sacrificial fires of a festival, like the great sacrifice that had sent the gifts to Delphi years before and filled the sky with sacred ash. The still bodies on the street could be beggars, or revellers in a wine-soaked stupor. The large fires were still distant, working their way to the heart of the city, lighting the sky like a dawn come too early.

He let Gyges lead him through the city, the way a man in strong water might stop fighting and let the currents be his guide. His son moved quickly and confidently, in contrast to the slow, dragging steps with which he had walked his entire life. Gyges recoiled from a marble statue of a goddess as though it were a monster, but smiled as he crouched down beside the corpse that lay beside it. Perhaps, Croesus thought, he has always lived in a mirrored world. All the beauty and wealth of my city were a vision of horrors. Now on this last day, he sees the things that are beautiful to him.

No one else would have dared to chance her life on the crumbling stone ledge barely half a hand wide, but Danae moved across it with ease, calm and fearless, and left the women's quarters behind. At the next opening she stepped back inside the palace again. She moved through the deserted corridors, searching for her husband and her son.

As she explored the palace, she stayed away from the treasuries. Even at a distance, she could hear the cacophony of another battle being fought, as slaves and citizens killed each other for riches that they would never get the chance to enjoy, just to possess them for a moment before they died.

Away from the treasuries and the women's quarters, the palace was at peace. She did not see many others – mostly single figures running down the corridors, or cowering in isolated hiding places. The epidemic of rape did not seem to have spread beyond the women's quarters.

She searched for Croesus and Gyges in bedchambers and dining halls, kitchens and armouries. Emptied of people, and with much of the furniture and decorations already taken or destroyed, the palace was like a place half remembered and recreated dimly in a dream. She fancied that if she pushed her hand up against one of the walls her flesh would penetrate it, like a hand pressed into water.

Eventually, she found her way to her husband's deserted bedroom. She sat on the bed for a time. As she waited there, wondering where she should go next, a man came into the room. She looked up hopefully, but it was not her husband or her son. It was a nobleman whose name she should have remembered.

He started in surprise to see her there, then grabbed a handful of the jewels and rings that lay openly on a table. He backed out of the room, his eyes still on her.

As soon as she heard the door close, Danae realized where her husband must have gone. She left the bedroom, and moving at a half-run, as though afraid she would forget the sudden insight that had come to her, she went to the stairs and began to ascend to the upper levels of the palace.

'Danae?'

The queen started and turned, hoping to find her husband, but Isocrates and Maia stood a short distance away. 'What are you doing here?' the queen asked them. 'This part of the palace is forbidden to slaves.'

Maia tried to smile at her. 'Come with us. We're going to—'

'Have you seen my husband?' Danae interrupted.

'No,' said Isocrates. 'Please, you have to come with us.'

'Don't worry, I know where I can find him. Him and my son,' the queen said.

Isocrates exchanged a look with his wife. 'Come with us,' Maia said again, 'please. We can keep you safe, but you have to do as we say.'

Isocrates began to walk slowly towards Danae. 'The king asked us to find you. We are glad to see you. Please,' he said, offering her his hand.

She smiled at him, and began to reach out to him. As she did so, she saw him tense his body. Only a shiver of tension, but enough to let her know what he intended to do.

She turned from him, and began to run. Behind her, she could hear the shouts of Isocrates and Maia, imploring her to wait. Husband and wife together, she thought, and she knew where to find her family. They had bled into the ruins of the city to escape the Persians. They would live there for ever, in dream, myth and memory. She had to find a way to join them.

167

Passing through the dark rooms of the upper palace, she thought she would never escape the labyrinth of bedrooms and antechambers that seemed to continue without end. But then she saw a glimpse of the fire on the horizon, caught sight of the open air, and she went towards it.

She came out on to the balcony overlooking the city, where her husband had spoken with a philosopher all those years before. She wished that Croesus could have been there with her.

Danae stepped up onto the ledge, and looked down on Sardis one last time.

Most of the Persians passed straight by Croesus. Perhaps, caught up as they were in the slaughter, where all that was forbidden was permitted and encouraged for a single night, there was no pleasure in taking life from a man who wished for death.

At last, a warrior stopped and looked at the king. The Persian, a heavy-set man with a thin beard, was tiring of the killing, and was now more interested in gold than in blood. He would have passed Croesus by like the others, but his eye was caught by a gemstone brooch that the king wore.

Their eyes met, and Croesus saw that the man would give him what he was after. He turned to Gyges. 'Go, now,' he said, but his son gave no sign of understanding. Croesus placed his hands on his son's chest and pushed him. Gyges tottered a few steps backwards, but did not turn away or leave.

Croesus felt a heavy sense of despair. He had brought his son with him, this man who didn't even know him as a father, because he was afraid of dying alone. What few extra minutes or hours might his idiot son have lived if he hadn't taken him from the palace. Perhaps it might even have been years – the Persians might think it a bad omen to kill a madman.

It doesn't matter, Croesus thought. There is nothing I can do to save him now. He won't understand what's happening, anyway. I can be thankful for that, at least.

He turned back, and watched the warrior come forward, slow and cautious, unable to understand why Croesus did not run or beg or fight. He reached forward with his left hand and grasped the king's tunic. Still, the king did not move. Satisfied with Croesus's inaction, no longer suspecting a trap, the soldier raised his sword and aimed the blade at the king's throat.

'Do not kill Croesus.'

Croesus and the soldier both flinched at the words, and turned to face the speaker.

'Do not kill Croesus,' Gyges said again, in the same soft, clear voice.

The Persian soldier understood only one word. The name. He stared at Croesus, but the king ignored the soldier. He looked only at his son.

Gyges stared back at him, and for the first time his eyes seemed to look upon the same world that Croesus saw. If his son could teach him to look on the world with those eyes, the king thought, perhaps he might be able to salvage something from the ruins of his life. He could find his wife, and together before the end, they might have a chance to learn from their son.

For a moment, standing on the narrow ledge of stone high above the dying city, Danae hesitated.

She thought of the past, of all the ways that she could have acted differently. Those moments when she could have changed the course of her life, changed the destiny of this city, her family, and her husband. The hundred things that she should have done or said in order not to have found herself here, at this worst of all possible endings.

She heard the pursuing footsteps behind her, and she knew she had no time left to think.

She stepped into the air, and the ground reached up to embrace her.

13

Cyrus woke.

From the fields beneath Sardis, he could not hear the cries that echoed through the broken city. He had retired to his tent as the attack on the wall began and told his commanders to wake him if he were needed. They had not woken him, and the silent air was rich with victory.

The king of Persia, Media, and now of Lydia cast off his blankets and rose naked from the pallet. He moved with an almost artificial grace, like a rehearsed dance that gives the illusion of perfect spontaneity, and his face was ageless. He could have been younger or much older than his thirty-three years; it was as if he had decided, through sheer force of will, to refuse to accede to ageing, as if it were merely a convention.

He glanced at the half-dozen bodyguards in the tent, and they nodded silently back to him, their eyes bright from the herbs that they chewed to ward off sleep. Even when he made love to one of his wives, they never let him out of their sight. Occasionally, in an idle moment, Cyrus would try to remember the last time he had been entirely alone, but he could never recall it.

He let his servants dress him in his ceremonial armour, raised the flap of the tent, and stepped into the cool dawn air.

The city on the cliffs cast its shadow over the western part of the camp. Looking on Sardis, he took as much pleasure in the sight as another man might take in a beautiful sculpture, admiring every curl of smoke, every fiery point of light, each hint of distant movement from the dying city. For a few moments, he stood in the quiet and enjoyed his victory.

The silence was broken. He heard a barked curse, followed by two shouting, familiar voices. He turned and entered the tent next to his.

'Our warriors have ended their war,' Cyrus said as he entered, 'but I see that between both of you the battle continues.'

The two men turned to face their king. The first bowed awkwardly, with the slow and heavy movements of an old man. His name was Cyraxes, a Persian courtier and counsellor who had served Cyrus's family for decades. Now in his sixtieth year, he moved stiffly, but his mind showed no sign of following his body into decay. The other man, a Mede general called Harpagus, dipped his body sharply and briefly, the action of a man more used to receiving such gestures than performing them.

Cyrus nodded to them then sat cross-legged on the ground. 'What matter requires my attention?' he said.

'We were debating what to do with Croesus,' said Cyraxes.

'Ah. Debating. So that's what the shouting was.'

'Forgive us.'

'No forgiveness is needed. I appointed you both to argue with each other. The attack was a success, I see?'

Harpagus nodded slowly. He was younger than Cyraxes by a decade, and, looking at him, few would have thought that he was much older than Cyrus. Only his eyes, deep and blank, like the eyes of a dead man, revealed that he had lived to see half a century of war and politics. 'Yes. Our scouts took the wall, and by the time the Lydians were alerted, we already had enough men over the wall to hold the battlements.'

'And they took Croesus alive?'

'Yes. They found him with his son.'

'His son? Is he a threat to us?'

'Hardly. The man is an imbecile. Almost mute.'

'That is for the best. Reward the man who captured Croesus, as I promised.' Cyrus covered a small yawn with his hand. 'Now, back to your debate. Tell me what I should do with him. Cyraxes?'

'His people love him,' the old man said. 'He knows the region, knows its politics. He will be the perfect satrap for Lydia. Under our close supervision, of course. With his army destroyed, he poses no threat. Why not let him continue to play as a king?'

Cyrus nodded. 'Very well. And Harpagus? You disagree?'

The general shrugged. 'People like strong kings.'

'And?'

'I don't think they'll forgive him for losing a war that he began. These people have no reason to obey us unless they fear us. I can't see that we will be safe until Croesus is dead.'

Cyrus nodded again. 'Thank you both.' He thought to himself for a time, and his advisors waited silently. Finally, he said, 'The Cappadocian prince. Harpagus, you said you weren't sure of his loyalty?'

Harpagus showed no surprise at the change of subject, for he was used to the lateral shifts of the king's conversation. 'Cappadocia is a burned-out wasteland,' he said. 'My spies tell me the people feel they have received little reward from being under our protection, after what the Lydians did to them.'

'I don't want to deal with a rebellion there. We have more important things to do than put down the Cappadocians. Let them have some compensation.'

'If I can say—'

'Yes, Cyraxes, I have heard what you've had to say. Let Croesus live, and I could be facing two rebellions. Cooperative governors are easy enough to find. Rebellions cost much to put down. I have made my decision.'

The older man bowed again deeply. 'Your will be done. When?'

'Let's get it over with. At dawn tomorrow.'

Cyrus spent the night in what had been Croesus's bedchamber, more out of curiosity than as a symbolic conquest. He knew almost everything about his enemies long before his armies marched to war. His spies reported on the strength and composition of their armies, his emissaries calculated a nation's wealth, almost down to the last head of grain and talent of gold. He learned everything he could about their weaknesses and fears, their sexual desires and taste in food. Every piece of information mattered, anything that could give Cyrus the measure of his opponent. No detail was too intimate to be found out, except for where the king slept – the only secret that a ruler could maintain.

Cyrus had expected much from Croesus's bedchamber, the private sanctuary of a man who had almost made a religion of his wealth. Here, where no one else could see them, Cyrus had imagined that Croesus would keep his most beautiful artefacts, but there was something half-hearted about the priceless ornaments that decorated the room, as though they had been placed out of obligation, rather than true desire.

The morning of the execution, Cyrus rose long before dawn. The servants who came hesitantly to wake him found him waiting for them, fully dressed and reading by torchlight to pass the time. He accompanied them down staircases that had been scrubbed clean of blood just hours before. At the same moment, somewhere far below, he knew that Croesus was being woken and led to the place of his death.

Cyrus reached the entrance to the atrium in good time, and waited for the sun to rise. One by one, his advisors appeared and came to wait with him, their faces long with exhaustion. Cyraxes looked especially tired; grey faced and stooped. Cyrus leaned forward and clapped his hands by the old man's right ear. Cyraxes jumped in surprise, and the other men laughed, grateful for the break in tension, before they lapsed back into silence.

The moment came at last, and Cyrus pushed open the double doors, and entered with the sun.

He looked at the pyre, the wood heaped at its base, the high stake and wooden throne, the pale figure tied to it with a single iron chain. A wooden colossus, built to consume itself. He glanced at Croesus for only a moment before he sat down at the table.

He waited for his taster to sample the food, but when he was at last allowed to eat, he ate lightly – a few pieces of bread, some dates and olives. He took a single sip of wine and gazed at the prisoner on the pyre.

Cyrus had looked into the eyes of many condemned men. Kings he had conquered, traitors he had executed. criminals on whom he had been asked to give final judgement. He knew that all of them, as they met his gaze, believed that they were showing him something unique. They were not. There were only a few ways for a man to meet his death, and Cyrus had seen them all many times over. In Croesus's eyes, the king saw something familiar. Acceptance.

Cyrus leaned back in his chair, and gestured to the servants around the pyre. He beckoned to another man on the balcony to bring him his parchments. He heard but did not see the fire being lit. and at the same moment acrid incense filled his nostrils. Cyrus sniffed in distaste, and bent over the table to busy himself in the affairs of state.

Some of the messages he reviewed had travelled merely hours to reach him. Questions about supplying the army that now occupied Sardis, or the appointments of new local rulers for the conquered towns and cities of the Lydian empire. Others were messages from the far side of his kingdom, which had taken weeks to arrive over mountains and seas, passing through a dozen hands before they reached the attention of the king.

For these delayed messages, he gave commands in response to events that had yet to occur: on receiving news of a food shortage in Ecbatana, he sent an order to put down the riot that he knew would have broken out by the time the message arrived in the east; learning that a fleet of merchant vessels was a day late in reaching Suhar, he sent his scouts to scour the coast for the shipwreck he was certain had occurred. Ruling the future, Cyrus was fond of saying, was the last great skill for a king to master.

He had dispatched only a few messages when he heard a low groan from the pyre. Cyrus looked up in surprise; perhaps wood burned quicker in the west, he thought. But the fire had not yet reached the prisoner. Cyrus saw Croesus's lips move twice, but he spoke too softly for the Persian king to hear. Then he said the same word a third time, just loud enough to be audible.

'Solon.'

Cyrus frowned. 'What does that mean?' he said to his interpreter.

'I do not know.'

'Ask him.'

'My lord?'

Cyrus nodded towards the pyre. The interpreter bowed, and asked the question in Lydian.

Croesus raised his head and looked at Cyrus. 'He is a man all kings should speak to,' the prisoner said, his eyes streaming from the smoke.

'Oh?' Cyrus said, after the interpreter relayed this to him. 'And why is that?'

'He taught me that the Gods hate the fortunate,' Croesus shouted over the rising roar of the fire, 'and that I would die unhappy!'

Cyrus watched as Croesus threw his head back against the stake and bared his teeth. The fire had yet to touch him, but it would not be long before some straying lick of flame touched off the oil on his robe. The smoke grew heavier and hid Croesus from view. Occasionally, Cyrus still caught a glimpse of movement through the thickening air, as Croesus writhed against the stake. Cyrus sat, his chin resting against the palm of his hand, and listened to the hoarse screams of the dying king.

Cyrus had sat through many executions. Some swift, most slow. He knew the worst was about to come, the point at which the condemned man was beyond all chance of reprieve, was certain to die but not yet dead. It was a terrible thing, to watch a man in those last moments, when there truly was no hope.

'Put it out,' he said.

Six men stepped forward, pouring sand and water. The fire, which had seemed so powerful and irresistible, was extinguished in a matter of moments. The guards came forward to free the prisoner, but were driven back by the heat of the embers. They waited, their cloaks wrapped across their faces.

Eventually, one of the soldiers leaned forward and poked at the ashes with the shaft of his spear. Seeing the embers fade to red and grey, he stepped carefully over the pyre, the half-burned logs breaking underfoot. Seeing Croesus slumped forward, he raised the prisoner's head and rolled open his eyes. The soldier nodded, as if in satisfaction, and unlocked the chain that held Croesus to the stake.

Croesus cried out as his weight came down on his feet, and curled up against the wooden chair. He looked up at the soldier who had freed him. 'I can't walk,' he said. The guard frowned. Irritably, Croesus jabbed at his feet with a finger. The soldier nodded in understanding, and, passing his spear to one of his companions, he knelt and picked Croesus up, one arm under the crook of his legs, the other around his back. The Lydian closed his eyes against the shame of it, and put his arms around the Persian's neck, letting himself be carried down and placed on the cold ground.

Cyrus walked down the stairs and across the courtyard towards his defeated enemy. His pace was unhurried, like a man taking an idle stroll at dusk to enjoy the last of the daylight. He stood over Croesus for a time, his entourage of advisors, slaves and bodyguards gathered behind him. The two kings looked at each other in silence.

'So,' Cyrus eventually said, in gently accented Lydian, 'tell me about Solon.'

Croesus stared at Cyrus and then at his interpreter. Then he shook his head. 'Why?'

'Because I am curious.' Cyrus glanced at the pyre, still pouring smoke into the air. 'When they first lit the pyre, you had the face of a man hurrying towards death. When you said that name, it seemed to me that you changed your mind.'

Croesus looked at the ground. He spoke slowly. 'He was an Athenian who came to my court. I had been on the throne a year. I had my wealth, and my family. So I asked him if I was the happiest man he had ever met.'

'And?'

'He said no one was happy until they were dead. Until then, you are just lucky. He claimed that it was only when he had seen a man's entire life, and the way he met his death, that he could say whether or not that man had lived a happy life.' Croesus shrugged. 'I thought he was a fool.'

'I see,' said Cyrus. 'That is all?'

'Yes. I thought of him, up there. I thought of what he had said to me, and thought what an awful thing it was to die, having wasted your life.'

'Your life has been a waste, then?'

'Yes.'

There was silence for a time. Behind him, Cyrus's entourage began to fidget and shiver in the cold. The general, Harpagus, tried to catch his king's eye, to seek some direction or order, but Cyrus seemed to be in no hurry to do or say anything.

Eventually, Croesus looked up and asked 'What are your men doing in the city?'

'I should think they are taking everything you own.'

'No. I own nothing now,' Croesus said, absently. 'They are robbing you.'

Cyrus laughed. 'True enough. I hadn't thought of that. What should I do?'

Croesus looked up at the king, expecting to see a mocking smile on the other man's face, but Cyrus seemed quite serious. 'You cannot simply take it from them,' Croesus said. 'They might rebel against you. And you can't let them pillage as they please. One of them might grow rich and powerful enough to be dangerous to you.'

'A conundrum.'

'Yes. So put some men you trust at each gate of the city, and as your men leave with their treasure, demand that they donate a tenth to the Gods who have given them victory. That is what I would do. They can't argue with giving a share to the Gods.'

'And should I take this gold that they surrender at the gates for myself?'

'That is your decision. I don't know how pious you are.'

Cyrus smiled, a fractional lift of one corner of his mouth. 'You chose poorly in going to war against me,' he said. 'But, still, I think you are wise.'

Croesus shook his head. 'You are wrong No wise man chooses war.' He looked away. 'In times of peace, sons bury their fathers. In times of war, fathers bury their sons.'

'Perhaps your war has taught you something, then. You could be of use to me.'

'As a slave?'

'We Persians aren't as fond as you are of taking slaves. But there are exceptions. You are a danger to me as a free man.' The Persian paused. 'Perhaps one day you will earn your freedom again.'

Croesus said nothing in response. Cyrus continued: 'I will grant you a boon of your choosing.'

'Why?'

'It is the custom. I even granted Astyages a boon when he entered my service.'

Croesus looked up sharply, and Cyrus nodded to him. 'Yes, when I overthrew your brother king, I spared his life, despite all he had done to my people. He too became my slave.'

'I don't see him with you today. Did he displease you? I don't think I will last long in this court of yours. I would rather die now, than have you keep me like a dog and murder me on a whim.'

'You are mistaken. He did not die by my hand, but by his own.' Cyrus shrugged. 'I gave him no reason. So long as you are loyal to me, Croesus, you shall live. Come, what favour can I grant you?'

Croesus thought. He thought of his treasury, that all those years before had once contained an infinity of desires. He had never thought he would be reduced to one command, to have the power to perform just a single action before his freedom was taken. And yet, now it was offered to him, there was only one thing he found that he wanted.

'Let my wife be spared slavery,' he said eventually. 'And take good care of my son.'

'You would like her by your side, I presume?'

'No. Let her go to the temples, or marry again if that is what she wants. I want her to be free. That is all I ask.'

Cyrus nodded, and conferred with his advisors. One of them glanced uneasily at Croesus, shook his head, and leaned in to whisper a message to the Persian king. Croesus watched, and covered his face with his hands.

'I will take care of your son, Croesus. Your wife is dead,' Cyrus said.

'How?' Croesus said, without raising his head.

'She jumped from the palace walls as the city was being taken.'

'Yes,' said Croesus slowly. 'She would choose that.' He shut his eyes against the tears, but they still flowed through.

Cyrus paused. 'Have an hour. Then you may request another boon.' The Persian king looked Croesus over. 'Did the fire hurt you?

Croesus reached a hand towards his burned feet. 'Yes, a little,' he said.

'Who was your personal slave?'

'He is called Isocrates. I don't know if he survived the fighting.'

Cyrus smiled. 'Slaves are great survivors; they tend to outlive their masters in a time of war. That is how they became slaves in the first place – by living when they should have died. I shall see if he can be found.'

Cyrus turned and spoke to his servants in Persian. One of them bowed, and pointed to the other side of the courtyard. Cyrus laughed, and turned back to Croesus.

'He is here. You see? Already he is making himself useful to me. A clever slave indeed.' He glanced over his shoulder. 'Isocrates!'

Croesus watched the slave come forward and bow at another man's command. 'How can I serve, master?'

'Tend his wounds.'

Isocrates bowed again. 'Yes, master.'

Cyrus turned to go, but looked back, snapped his fingers to one of his guards and beckoned him forward. He took the man's cloak from him, tossed it to Croesus, and began to walk away.

'Cyrus?'

The Persian king turned back. 'Yes?'

'What will you tell them? The people, I mean. As to why you put out the pyre. Won't they take your change of heart as weakness?'

'You are correct.' Cyrus looked up at the clear sky and smiled. 'We shall say a god put the fire out. Who could argue with that? I think it might even be true.'

Croesus wrapped the cloak tightly around him, for the comfort as much as for the warmth, and watched his new master walk away.

'I shall not dress your feet for you,' Isocrates said after the king had gone, 'because I'm not your slave any more. Do you understand?' Croesus stared sightlessly at the smouldering pyre, and nodded.

'You must learn to understand and to act quickly,' Isocrates continued. 'Things will not be repeated for you. If you make the wrong choice, or you don't understand, you will die.'

'You make it sound like being a hunted animal.'

'That is not far from the truth.'

'What were you doing here, when Cyrus called for you?'

'Pouring sand on that fire.'

'So you saved my life?' Croesus shook his head. 'How touching.'

'I also helped stack the wood this morning to burn you. So don't be sentimental.'

Croesus looked down at the marks the heated chains had left on his arms. 'Will I always be marked like this?' he said.

Isocrates looked briefly, with little interest. 'No. They will heal.'

'But I will always be a slave.'

'Yes. You serve at the pleasure of your master, now. Don't forget it.' Another man came with a poultice and bandages, and Isocrates took them from him. 'Now,' he said to Croesus, 'watch what I do.'

Croesus watched as Isocrates demonstrated how to apply the poultice and the bandage, listened as the slave described what herbs went into the wrapping and what they did. When the other man had finished, he made a passable effort at wrapping his feet himself. The bandages were clumsy, but they did not unravel, and he repeated the effects of the herbs first time. He winced at the pain as he wrapped his feet, but did not cry out.

Isocrates nodded in approval. 'Not bad. And that is good enough. For now, at least.'

'Cyrus thinks I am a wise man,' Croesus said. 'That is why he is keeping me alive.'

Isocrates said nothing.

'I am not a wise man, am I?'

'No, Croesus. You are not.'

'What do I do?'

Isocrates stared at him, and shrugged.

'Learn quickly,' he said.

The Slave
545 BC

I

The Persian army slept.

From a distance, the torchlit gathering of men could be mistaken for a city. Eyes would play tricks, connecting the disparate points of fire to form impossible architectures, conjuring a city of the mind out of nothing. It was only on drawing closer that one could see past the fires to the outlines of tents and sleeping pallets stretched out in every direction. A hundred thousand souls, sleeping and dreaming in a land that was not theirs. Small fires ringed the edges of the encampment where sentries fought to stay awake, watching the stars and counting away the time until they were relieved, and could rejoin the dreaming army.

At the heart of this gathering, this temporary city of the plains, Croesus, a torch dripping sparks in his hand, moved through the tents and sleeping men towards the place where Cyrus held court that night. He looked warily into corners where men might be hiding in ambush, watchful of figures that might lurk in the darkness. In his first few months in service to the Persian king, some of the servants had found pleasure in beating this slave who had once been a king. They called him to some quiet corner on a false errand, knocked him to the ground, and whipped him with their belts until his tunic was stuck to his back with blood. He had learned to be cautious.

No one stopped him on his journey across the camp, the few sentries he passed nodding to him without interest. They were used to the king's slave being summoned at all hours, day and night. Distant at first, then drawing closer, he saw the ring of torches that identified the king's open-air council for that night.

Cyrus ruled a nomad's court, and whether it was in a forest clearing or the burned-out palace of a conquered king, he did not seem to care. He had spent his life as a king travelling at the head of an army, never remaining in the same place for more than a few days, for Cyrus was the only centre the kingdom had, his army its capital city. Not content with the half-dozen throne rooms that Croesus enjoyed in Sardis, he travelled through his empire scattering thousands of them, seeding the earth with ghostly courts that were used once and never again, marking his kingdom like an animal.

Cyrus's court that night was bounded by a circle of tall torches thrust into the ground. At the edge of this circle, his bodyguards slouched on the ground like idle dogs, as if mocking the rigid attention of the ordinary soldiers. Croesus had seen them move fast enough to know that their indolence was merely an act. In the centre, a leaning stone the height of a small child served as a throne: the only feature that marked this circle out from the arid plains that stretched out in every direction.

When Croesus had left the court a few hours before, dismissed by the king to go and sleep, the gathering had been relaxed. A few issues of future strategy lightly discussed, without any sense of impending catastrophe. But there was now an air of near panic. The men of the court spoke over and across each other all at once. Some shouted each other down, others gathered at the edge of the circle and whispered to one another. Only Cyrus was calm, waiting patiently and silently in the middle of the circle like a man waiting for a storm to blow itself out. He alone noted Croesus's arrival.

'Ah, Croesus,' he said, his slightly raised voice a sign for the others to fall silent. 'How good of you to join us.'

All eyes turned to Croesus. He dropped his eyes to the ground. 'You sent for me?'

'Yes I did. Cyraxes? Tell him.'

The old man cleared his throat. 'An emissary from Sparta has reached the camp,' he said. 'We didn't know he was in the country, let alone this close to us.' He shot a glance at Harpagus. 'Our spies, it seems, are not as infallible as some have claimed.'

Harpagus ignored him. 'I still think we should dispose of him. We have nothing to fear if he doesn't report back to his master.'

'Kill an emissary? Can you think of a more foolish idea?'

'He knows too much.'

'And whose fault is that?'

'You don't have to repeat what we all know,' Harpagus said. 'If you have nothing else to say, keep quiet.'

'It is your failing that—'

'Enough.' Cyrus did not raise his voice, but the word cut through the air and brought silence with it. The king turned to Croesus and smiled thinly. 'So. The Spartans are considering an expedition across the sea.'

'What happens if they do?'

'They will join with the Ionians, and we cannot stand against such an alliance. If they come, I expect we will fight a bloody war and be destroyed, Croesus. More fathers burying sons, as you once said.'

'What can I do?'

Cyrus pointed to a place beside his throne. 'Kneel at my side, and don't speak unless I tell you to.'

Slowly, his body still unused to responding to such commands, Croesus did as he was told.

'Good.' Cyrus looked at Harpagus. 'Admit him to our presence.' He looked around the circle. 'And the rest of you, be quiet. You stink of fear. If you can't control yourselves, then leave.'

The court settled, and a single figure approached from the

darkness. The bodyguards gave him the briefest of glances as he passed them, but Croesus saw them tense, their hands disappearing into the folds of their robes.

Croesus looked at the emissary, and recognized the man. It was Lakrines, the Spartan who had come to his court, many years before, when he was a king who could still dream of empires. The Spartan's hard face had not changed, though now he wore his hair long, down far past his shoulders, and Croesus wondered what strange new custom had prompted the change. He dropped his head and studied the ground, but Lakrines paid no attention to a slave. He had eyes only for Cyrus.

The Persian king looked at the emissary and said nothing, stretching out the silence at his leisure. 'You bring a message?' he said at last.

'I do.'

'And what is it?'

'The kings of Sparta command you to withdraw from these lands, and return to the east, Cyrus. That is all.'

Cyrus stared at him blankly for a moment. Then he asked, 'Who are the Spartans?'

The emissary must have anticipated many responses, but not this one. Eventually, he smiled thinly. 'You are joking, I think.'

'I have never heard of you.'

'We are the greatest warriors in the world, Cyrus. The most powerful of the Hellenes. You would do well to listen to us.'

'Your fame, I'm afraid, has not crossed the sea to reach me. I think you are a long way from Sparta, to be giving commands to a king.'

'I have seen your army. We have little to fear from you.'

'Perhaps you should speak more carefully.'

'We both know you won't harm me, Cyrus.'

'Do we?' Cyrus looked off into the distance and said nothing for a time. Without looking back at the emissary, he said, 'Tell me, what lies at the centre of your city?'

The Spartan narrowed his eyes. 'A market square, where the trades-men gather. What does that matter?'

'I thought so. You see, in Persia, we have no such thing. We do our business behind closed doors. We do not make a god of trade. You claim to be great warriors. I do not know your people, but I have no fear of a nation of men who have a place to meet, swear this and that and spend all day cheating one another. Yours is a nation of mer-chants, not warriors.'

'You cannot frighten me with insults, Cyrus. We have the blessing of the Gods. Our oracle says that we will win a great victory if we fight against Persia.'

'Really?' Cyrus said. 'Tell me, did they say *when* you would achieve this great victory?'

The Spartan hesitated. 'No.'

'Croesus, look up,' Cyrus said. 'You recognize this man, Spartan?'

'Yes.' Lakrines inclined his head slightly. 'I am sorry to see you this way, Croesus.' He looked back to the king. 'I suppose it is true what they say, if you would treat Croesus like this.'

'And what do they say?'

'That every man in Persia is a slave to the king.'

Cyrus laughed. 'Tell this man of prophecies, Croesus,' he said. 'Tell him about the favour you asked from me, two years ago, when I made you my slave.'

Croesus swallowed, and let his eyes drop back to the ground. 'For the boon you granted me, I asked you to send my chains to Delphi,' he said slowly. 'I had made many sacrifices to them. They told me if I went to war I would destroy a great empire, and that my people would rule Lydia until a mule sat on the throne of Media.' He shook his head. 'I wanted to know why their God had betrayed me.'

'And what did they tell you?' Cyrus said.

He closed his eyes against the memory. 'They told me that the great empire I was to destroy was my own. And that you, the child of a

Mede mother and a Persian father, were the mule that the prophecy described.'

Cyrus looked back at the emissary. 'Your prophecies are no use against me,' he said. 'Look what your Oracle did for Croesus. You think that you can travel across the sea, and wage a war against me without consequence. Have an adventure in the East. If you win, you can take my empire. If you lose, why, then you may retreat, and come back another time. Croesus thought the same. You think I am too far away to come and wage war against you. You are wrong. Cross the sea to face me, and after I have broken your army, I will travel halfway across the world to find your cities and burn them to the ground. That is my promise to you.'

'Cyrus—'

'You may tell your kings,' Cyrus continued, 'that if they come here, I will put a collar on them both and have them kneeling at my side, like this slave who was once a king. Tell them I am a king who makes slaves of kings. Perhaps, one day, your people will win a great victory against mine. But not yet.' He made a small gesture with his hand. 'You may go.'

The Spartan opened his mouth to speak, but, looking once again at Croesus, he hesitated, and remained silent. He bowed, looked for one last time at the man who had been king of Lydia, then turned and marched out of the circle and into the darkness. There was silence in the court.

'Do you think that will succeed?' Cyrus said to Harpagus, when the emissary was out of sight.

Croesus had never seen Harpagus smile. His lips seemed to twitch; perhaps this was as close as he got to a true smile. 'I think it will,' the general said.

'A fine performance, my lord,' Cyraxes said. Others began to speak in praise, but Cyrus waved off the compliments.

'We shall see what comes of it. It pains me to play the ignorant

Eastern king. But a man who has never heard of the Spartans will have no fear of going to war against them.' He yawned. 'Have our people watch him until he has left the country, and send word to our contacts in Sparta. If they are going to come, we must know of it. Send for that man Tabulus as well. It is about time we gave him his orders. We're going to put him in charge of your old kingdom, Croesus.'

Croesus did not reply. Cyrus looked at him, and for the first time Croesus saw hesitancy on the king's face, something close to regret. Or perhaps he only imagined that he saw it.

Croesus bowed deeply, to hide his shame. 'I am here to serve, master,' he said.

Later, Croesus returned to the tent, stumbling with exhaustion as the first sign of dawn appeared on the horizon. He entered carefully. He did not want to wake the others.

When Cyrus had told him that the Persians did not like to keep slaves, he had thought it a piece of empty rhetoric. Yet he had spoken truthfully, for in Persia it was only those who were most unfortunate, those cursed by the Gods, who found themselves the property of other men.

Half a dozen slaves shared the tent with him. They were the favourites of the court, each with his own particular function, some quality that made him too valuable to set free. One young man was the lover of a Persian nobleman, pampered and spoiled by his infatuated master. A few years of beauty were left to him before he would be discarded for another and cast out to be a catamite for the soldiers; he spent his days staring at his reflection in pools of water and polished stones, watching for the slightest sign of ageing. Another of the slaves had been a poet as a free man, and was lucky that Cyraxes had a weakness for the epic. But the old man never liked to hear the same poem twice, and so the poet chased around the camp searching for a poem he did not know, or spent hours in the tent in a fever of forced composition. Each of them, like Croesus, was a plaything of one nobleman or another. Existing to entertain, and surviving on a whim. A single mistake would be enough for them to be cast out.

Of the six, only one was awake, his eyes like two small white stones in the darkness.

'What happened?' Isocrates said.

Croesus hesitated. 'Go back to sleep,' he said. 'I am sorry that I woke you.'

'You didn't wake me. That idiot stepped on me when he came to wake you up. What happened?'

Croesus looked at the others. 'Don't worry about them,' Isocrates said. 'Nothing disturbs the sleep of a slave.'

'Cyrus wanted to show me off to an ambassador,' Croesus said. 'A Spartan.' He smiled bitterly. 'Lakrines. The same one who came to see me, when I was king. You remember? The Gods have a cruel sense of humour.'

'I remember him. What was that like?'

'Humiliating.' Croesus sat down and shook his head. 'Every day, I think there is not another shame to endure. Now I am to be paraded. An exemplar of foolishness.'

'Well, at least it is easy work.'

'You think so?'

'Ask the slaves in the mines, or the helots of Sparta. I'm sure one of them would be delighted to change places for a lifetime of humiliation.'

'It might have stopped a war; at least that is what Cyrus said. I don't think the Spartans will come now. That is something.'

'Don't be naïve. It might have stopped war with the Spartans. The wars in the north will come soon enough. Cyrus just wants them to be massacres, rather than battles.'

Croesus said nothing. Isocrates yawned. 'What do you dream of, Croesus?' he said.

'What?'

'I know you dream of something. Sometimes you cry out.'

'Why do you want to know?

Isocrates thought for a moment. 'I think I dreamed when I was younger. I don't remember. I grew out of it, I suppose. I don't think slaves dream much, as a rule.' He paused, then added, 'I am curious as to what it is like.'

Croesus lay down, and curled his arms beneath his head. 'It is usually the same dream,' he said, speaking slowly and softly.

'Not always?'

'No. I dream of many things. But usually, when I dream, I see a palace of fire.'

'There's nothing but fire?'

'No. Everything else is dark. Like the sky without stars.'

'You are in pain, I take it.'

'No. Not at first. I can reach out to the walls, and they are quite cool to touch. The air is cold, like standing under trees in winter. I feel quite calm. There is no rush to move on. No fear.' He paused, then said, 'Perhaps it is worth what comes after in the dream, just to enjoy those moments of peace.' He stopped again, expecting some sharp comment from Isocrates, but there was silence. 'Are you still awake?' he said.

'Go on, I'm listening.'

'I walk through the palace. It is like a labyrinth, and I take a different route each night. There must be thousands of paths through the maze. Ten thousand different combinations of turnings that I can take. I go a different way each time. I am nowhere near to exploring them all. But it doesn't matter. Whichever way I go, I always reach the centre.'

'What is there?'

Croesus shrugged. 'People. They change every night.'

'Am I ever there?'

'No. Only the dead. My father. Sometimes I see Atys. Sometimes . . .' His voice trailed off.

'Danae?'

'Yes,' he said. 'I try to speak to them, but they never respond. They look behind me, and I know there is something terrible there. I don't want to look, but I can't help myself. I turn and see the pyre, and I know then that I have been a fool. That I never had a choice, and it was always going to end this way.' He licked his lips, suddenly dry. 'I can feel the heat then. All at once, from nothing. I try to cry out, but I feel the fire roar down my throat, burning away my voice.' He paused. 'That's when I wake up.'

They lay in silence for a time.

'You are not in danger of the pyre any more, you know,' Isocrates said eventually.

'Thank you.'

'You misunderstand,' Isocrates said. 'Slaves aren't worth the spectacle. Or the wood.' He yawned again. 'If you ever displease Cyrus, he'll have you strangled instead.' And with that, Isocrates rolled over and went back to sleep.

Croesus stretched out a hand and opened the tent flap slightly. He could see the first fringes of light in the east, the pale blue of the sky promising dawn. The next day would come soon. Another day of wondering if this was the day when Cyrus would grow bored or displeased. Another day of slavery, to add to the hundreds he had collected already. Perhaps, he thought, I will live long enough to have been a slave longer than I was a king. Thirteen more years, that is all it would take. I would rather die before that can happen.

He lay down to get what sleep he could before the new day came, and returned to his dreams of fire.

2

The first year had been the hardest.

After they had taken him down from the pyre and assigned him to the slaves' quarters, Croesus was certain that this was some kind of a cruel joke, that Cyrus would keep him alive for a week, a month, before taking him back to the pyre, and that the other men of the court would laugh and wonder how Croesus could have been so foolish as to think he would be allowed to live. But after a time, just as the pure fear of death was fading, the second horror came to him; the humiliation of being at another man's command, with less freedom than a dog. He thought of all the things that he could never do again, about how he would continue like this for months, years and decades. Forty years, perhaps, spent looking back at the wreckage of a ruined life. Living in fear was a terrible thing. Living without hope was something else entirely.

Isocrates had not spoken to him much in those first months. Perhaps it had been some kind of a test, to see whether Croesus would survive alone in his new way of life. Perhaps he had simply been too busy with his other duties. Whatever the reason, one day, Croesus came back to the slave quarters to find Isocrates waiting for him.

'Sit down, Croesus,' the other man had said. 'I am here to teach you.'

'To teach me what?'

'To teach you how to live, of course. Now sit. We have much to discuss.'

Croesus had sat cross-legged on the ground. 'You think I need your help?'

'Yes, I do. And I think you are too proud to ask.'

'Very well. And where do we begin?' Croesus said, imagining Isocrates would start with some abstract principle.

'We begin with your feet.'

Croesus had thought it a poor joke, but Isocrates was quite serious. He told Croesus that a slave's death always began at the feet. Rushing around on one errand or another, wearing thin sandals or boots that were always on the verge of disintegration. Then came the blisters, which slowed you down. Beatings would follow, and the slave would become slower still, and never be able to rest. Blisters became open wounds. Then followed infection, exhaustion, and death.

Isocrates then spoke of the value of things. Where once Croesus had lived in a sea of coins and a labyrinth of rare artefacts, now he would learn to treasure a small piece of sharp flint, a good pair of boots, a handful of coins, a flask of good wine.

They spoke of much else that night, and gradually Croesus saw how he could survive in this new world. A world that lay alongside that of kings and courtiers, which he had lived in for most of his life. A world that ran parallel, but separate, as though he really had died on that pyre in Sardis, and had been condemned to wander the courts of kings as a ghost. A world in which he was invisible, unless he made a mistake.

After they had finished, and Isocrates rose to leave, Croesus found himself asking one last question. 'Why did you come?' he said.

Isocrates turned back, and gave a slight smile. 'Maia sent me. Why else?' Then the slave was gone, and Croesus was left to consider what he had been told.

He did not find the next day better than the one before it, but nor did he find it worse. The decline had been halted, for a time at least, and his mind had remained in this uneasy truce with itself for over a year now.

It was remarkable, he thought, that one could transform a king into a slave so quickly. He was even ashamed to find that there was now some comfort in the numbing simplicity of his life, the freedom from any kind of choice. But occasionally, at the edge of his mind, the feeling came that he was only buying time. He knew that there was no happiness in this way of life, and that life without happiness was no life at all. He took care not to follow that line of thought too far. When the army left Sardis and went in search of other lands to conquer, Croesus began to lose himself in repetition.

Each morning, waking with the dawn, he would at first lie still, enjoying a rare waking moment when his time was his own, waiting for the fear of being punished to outweigh the rebellious pleasure of stillness. He would listen to the muted, familiar sounds of the army waking around him, the soldiers and slaves readying themselves for a day's back-breaking labour so that the army could drag itself forward just a few *parasangs*, could crawl its way across the land, heading to the west.

He would rise and check his feet as Isocrates had taught him, then unroll the small piece of cloth that served as his treasury, taking an inventory of the coins and tools and small luxuries that were all he owned. After accounting for all his possessions, he secreted them one by one into the hidden pockets he had stitched into his tunic. The servants stole from their masters when they were certain they could get away with it, and they stole from one another as a matter of habit.

Before he left the tent, he would look enviously at the other slaves. They had learned to sleep until the very last moment, in order to take as much rest as they could, rising just in time to hurry to their tasks.

Perhaps, untroubled by dreams, it was easier for them to sleep that way. He wondered if he would ever manage to forget his dreams and sleep as they did.

Then he parted the cloth of the tent and emerged to another day of servitude.

He had lived this peripheral life, numb and inconsequential, for the better part of two years. He thought that twenty more might pass in such a way, until news came from the east that would place him at the centre of things once again.

Lydia had rebelled.

Croesus saw that Cyrus was not angry at the news. He had never seen the Persian king in a rage, and even now, a faint sense of frustration was all that was apparent, the frustration of a man facing a problem that was well within his powers, almost insultingly so, but that would take time and precious energy to solve.

'Now,' said the king, 'explain to me again what has happened, Cyraxes. And perhaps, more importantly, how we have allowed it to happen.'

'Pactyes—'

'A man you recommended to me.'

'Yes. He has declared himself ruler of Lydia, and bought himself an army. He is besieging our regent—'

'Tabulus.'

'Yes. He is under siege in Sardis.'

'What did Pactyes use to buy his army?'

'Gold.'

'The gold that we gave him.'

Cyraxes bowed his head. 'Yes.'

'You see, Croesus? Your riches haunt me still.' Cyrus looked back at his courtiers. 'How did this happen?'

No one answered, and Cyrus divided his gaze equally between Harpagus and Cyraxes. 'I should have known that there was something wrong,' the king said eventually, 'when you both agreed that he was the man to trust. It was unprecedented – an appointment without an argument. Now I see there is much to be said for precedent. But what is to be done now? Harpagus?'

'His army won't be able to resist ours. A single battle is all it will take to rout them.'

'You are certain?'

'Quite certain. A man like Pactyes assumes that loyalty can be bought.'

'And it cannot?'

'It can for a battle. Not for a war. His mercenaries cannot compare to our soldiers.'

'Why?'

'Your men don't follow you for the gold,' Harpagus said matter of factly. 'They follow you because they love you.'

'How kind of you to say so,' Cyrus said. 'Very well. Take half the army. You will travel faster that way.' Cyrus held out a hand, and a servant handed him a skin of wine. He drank, and passed it back. 'So, what do we do afterwards?'

Harpagus frowned. 'What do you mean, sire?'

'For such a practical man, Harpagus, you surprise me. What do we do about Lydia?'

Silence fell, and every one of the courtiers turned to look at Croesus, kneeling at the king's side. Cyrus did not. 'If they can rebel so soon after we have conquered them,' he continued, 'they will rise again. Unless we can discourage them in some way.'

Harpagus nodded. 'I see. After we have defeated them, I would suggest we enslave them. We can repopulate the cities and towns with migrants from the east. Let the Lydians become a race of slaves.'

'I have no love for slavery, Harpagus.'

The general looked pointedly at Croesus. 'The Lydians do. Doesn't that make it a fitting punishment?'

Cyrus nodded slowly. 'Well, Croesus?' he said.

'Master?'

'You have raised a proud people in a rich land, Croesus. That presents me with a problem.'

Croesus took a deep breath. 'Master. I ask you not to do this.'

'You can beg all you like, it won't—'

'Harpagus, quiet,' Cyrus said. He turned back to Croesus. 'I'm afraid he is right. Begging won't do any good. I am open to an alternative, if you can convince me. But I don't see one.'

Croesus opened his mouth to speak again. He hesitated. It had been so long since he had any influence over a life other than his own. He had forgotten what it was to have the fate of a nation depend on his words, and he found he no longer had a taste for it.

He must have been the greatest murderer that Lydia had ever seen. Tens of thousands killed in the war to the east, thousands more dead at the fall of Sardis. Who was he to plead for mercy, or restraint?

He thought of the generations who would be born and live in the country that had been his. Sons and daughters who would haggle and trade in the markets of Sardis, raise crops and hunt for gold on the banks of the Pactolus, playing in the water and dreaming of oceans that they would never see. Hearing stories of the Lydian kings, and above all of the fool Croesus, who had gambled their freedom for his vanity and lost. It was not the future he had wanted for his people, but it was a future, nonetheless. A future that was about to be taken from them.

He had been the last king of Lydia. Perhaps now his country would die with him, its people taken as slaves, taken to serve wherever their masters sent them, their stories forgotten, their language lost, their history turned into myth. An entire civilization conquered, and destroyed.

This was a last service he could perform for them – he could ensure that they might live free from kings and wars and slavery, for one more generation.

He looked up again, and began to speak.

3

'What did you tell him?' Maia asked.

Croesus smiled, and looked at her thoughtfully.

He wondered how many words he had spoken to her when she served him as a slave. He did not think they would number much more than a hundred, as if his son's mute nature were somehow infectious. Then, she had been an invisible convenience. Now, on the rare occasions when they were both free from responsibility, they gathered to share their stories. She would recount the intricate politics of the field kitchens and supply wagons, he the petty debates of the court. They could not decide which of them lived in a more tangled network of alliance and betrayal.

She alone of all the slaves and servants seemed to wish to speak with him, and one night he had asked Isocrates why this might be. Isocrates had muttered something to the effect that she had always been fascinated by unusual creatures, and that a slave who was once a king certainly qualified as such. That was the only answer he would offer.

'Well?' Maia's voice brought him back. 'What did you say?'

'I told him to send his people around Lydia. To encourage the playing of musical instruments, promote trade, and encourage them to long for fine fabrics and jewels. Make them wear long tunics and high boots, like musicians and catamites. Turn them into a nation of poets and merchants, not warriors.'

She raised an eyebrow. Croesus continued, 'I told him that if he did this, through edicts and rewards and threats, he would see them turn into women, not men, and they would never rebel against him.'

She laughed. 'I was thinking quickly,' he said. 'They were about to put my people in chains.'

'What did he say?'

'He was silent for a long time. Eventually he said, "Soft lands breed soft men." That's when I knew that he would try.' Croesus remembered the quiet smile of the Persian king, his eyes alight with possibility. 'I can't believe that he agreed, but he did. We are to go on a campaign of change. Spreading harps and drums, encouraging new fashions, subsidizing trade and making the owning of weapons unfashionable. Turning men into women.'

'What did Harpagus say to that?'

'He swore in some language I didn't understand. Then he walked away. I don't think I have ever seen him so angry.'

'All the servants are scared of him. They say Death took him over a long time ago. When you look into his eyes, you see Death looking back at you. Not a man.'

'He scares me too. Sometimes I see him watching me at court. I asked Isocrates if I should be concerned, but he said there was no danger there.' This was, in fact, only a partial truth. Isocrates had told him not to be concerned, but there had been a doubt in his voice. When Croesus pressed him, he had said nothing more.

'I feel ashamed at what I have done to my home,' Croesus continued. 'But they will survive as free people. That is something.'

'Why be ashamed?' She smiled archly. 'I think it will be an improvement. The world would be a better place if it were filled with soft men.'

'That's not the world we live in.'

'So men like you always say. Are you to be rewarded for your work?'

'I am. I can't stay long. Cyrus has invited me to his private quarters tonight.'

'Such an honour!' she said. 'You have done well. I don't recall that Isocrates ever received such an invitation from you.'

Croesus shook his head. 'That is more a reflection of my ingratitude than his lack of service.'

She laughed, and they fell together into a comfortable silence. He found that this love of silent company was shared by both Isocrates and Maia, and he wondered if they spent what little time they had alone together in wordless communion. It was alien to him, and at first he had always tried to fill such silences with idle talk. Now he let them continue unbroken.

He remembered the first time he had spoken to her as a slave, not long after Isocrates had come to give him his lesson in servitude. She too had taught him much, though not in the direct and practical fashion of her husband. She led by example, teaching him to take rest and pause whenever he could, to rediscover the value of laughter, for a slave a more unusual treasure than any other. The first time they had spoken he had asked her about Danae. Afterwards, when she had told him what she had seen, he wished he had not asked, that he did not know of the chase through the palace, the desperate plunge from its highest point on to the rocks below. He could have imagined a better end for her. Now, when he did not dream of fire, he dreamed of his wife, falling away from him.

He looked at the sky, and saw that the moon was up. 'I must go. The king expects me.'

She nodded. 'If you have a favour to ask him,' she said, 'will you—'

'I know what you are going to ask.' He paused. 'If the king permits me, I will go to see him.'

'It has been so long. They won't allow me to go. I worry about him.'

'I know, Maia. I will ask. I am sure Cyrus will let me. He is a good man, I think.'

She rolled her eyes. 'Well, you know my thoughts. I don't trust any king. He should spend some time in the kitchens or the fields, to teach him the meaning of hard work.'

'He did, when he was younger. He was raised by farmers, or so the story goes.'

'A story he cultivates to win favour. I don't imagine that pampered man has worked a single day in his life.'

Croesus winced. 'I don't suppose I would want to know the kind of things you said behind my back, when I was still a king.'

'No. You wouldn't,' she said.

He rose to go, but hesitated. He could see, though he did not want to, a fresh bruise on her cheek.

He remembered that he had spoken to Isocrates about those marks, when he was still a king. He had not found the courage to do so again as a slave.

He turned away from Maia, and tried to forget his cowardice.

When Croesus stepped into Cyrus's tent, he crossed the threshold by only a few feet before he stopped and stared at the ground, awaiting instruction.

'Relax,' he heard Cyrus say. 'You are here to be rewarded. Look around you.'

Croesus looked at the walls of the tent. Each was divided into dozens of panels, each panel embroidered with a different image. Cities, seas, farms, deserts, castles and temples. Some of them he recognized – the city of Pteria, now destroyed, living on only in this image. The sea view from Phocaea. He felt a coldness settle on

him when he saw Sardis on its steep-sided hill, its buildings a mixture of Lydian and Persian design: the city as it would be rebuilt
in a generation's time. In this tent, Cyrus could look on his whole
empire.

Half the panels were still blank.

'Much work to be done,' Cyrus said. 'With your help, of course.
Come.' He beckoned Croesus into the next chamber.

The king's personal tent, a vast construction when viewed from the
outside, seemed even larger from within, a honeycomb of fabric chambers, a palace that was built anew every night.

The next chamber was a small one. In an ornate wooden chair,
studded with precious gemstones, a woman sat, two children at her
feet.

Croesus recognized Cassandane, one of Cyrus's wives, and as
beautiful as they all were, with golden eyes set high on a heart-shaped
face, silver bracelets moving against dark, delicate wrists. Beside her,
the two young boys knelt on the floor playing knucklebones. The
younger played with a carefree ease, whilst the elder was hunched
over, his eyes intent, the way children see significance in a game that
no adult can understand. By them, a wax tablet lay untouched. A
lesson ignored for a game.

Cyrus cupped his wife's face in his hands and kissed her. 'I have
missed you,' he said.

She accepted the kiss, then looked at him archly. 'It would have
been better if you paid more attention to me than to that Egyptian
who shares your bed at night,' she said.

He shrugged. 'She pleases me.'

'And I?'

'You please me also.'

She shook her head, and her smile lay somewhere between anger
and tolerance.

The older boy glanced up. 'An Egyptian has hurt you, Mother?'

'No, Cambyses,' she said, 'it isn't like—'

The boy reached out and put a finger to her lips. He nodded gravely. 'Don't worry. When I am king, I shall destroy Egypt for you. Would you like that?'

'You are your father's son, you bloodthirsty beast,' she said, laughing. She examined her visitor. 'Cambyses, Bardiya. This man serves your father.'

'You mean he is a slave?' said Bardiya.

'Yes. But an important one.'

'There are important slaves?' Cambyses said dubiously.

She looked Croesus over. 'So some say.'

Croesus knelt down beside the boys. He remembered what it was he had loved about his own children when they were small. Like a coin, a child was all possibility. He smiled at Cambyses, the heir to the empire, charmed by the boy's bright eyes. He stretched out a hand to touch the child on the head.

The boy bit him.

Croesus yelped and stood, shaking his hand. Cyrus laughed, and reached for his son. Cambyses tried to bite him too, and Cyrus slapped him for it. The king pointed a warning finger at his son, leaving it a testing distance away from the boy's mouth. Cambyses did not move, standing in silence, the red weal rising on his face.

'Good,' Cyrus said. He turned to Croesus. 'He has spirit. He will make a good king, don't you think?'

Croesus stared at the boy for a time, and Cambyses gazed back, undaunted. 'Yes,' he said.

'Come, there is one more thing that I want to show you. Your reward.'

They moved into the depths of the tent, passing through a dozen different chambers. Croesus saw a map room, and then an exotic armoury, filled with strange weaponry from distant lands that the empire had yet to conquer. They passed through one chamber that was thick with a bitter smoke that made Croesus feel light-headed after a single breath. Another was unlit, filled with the scent of musky perfume. Reaching out to guide himself in the dark his hands touched naked flesh.

Finally, they arrived at their destination – a treasury. Candlelight danced on golden cloth walls that were stitched with pearls, and fell on the tables topped with rare artefacts from across the Persian empire. Croesus recognized a few choice items taken from his own treasuries.

'You have good taste,' he said.

'I envied you your treasures, Croesus. They were quite remarkable. It is a shame I cannot take more with me. It would take another army to carry it all.'

'They were always for show,' Croesus said, running his fingers over the familiar, useless relics that decorated the room, the crowns of forgotten kings, the sculptures of fallen cities. He turned back to his king. 'I always preferred the coins, myself.'

'I know,' Cyrus said. The king's palm opened, and a flash of light against metal passed through the air. Croesus caught it and looked down.

From the face of the coin the Lydian lion looked back at him. He ran his thumb over its surface, a single touch enough for him to know if one or a thousand hands had held the coin before him then cocked his head, confused.

'This is new,' he said. 'Newly minted. I don't understand.'

'I considered having the new coins marked with the emblem of my empire,' Cyrus said. 'But I think I'll keep them as they are.' He smiled at Croesus. 'What do you think of that?

Croesus studied the coin, sitting heavy in his palm as if he were a god holding the entirety of the cosmos in his hand. Perhaps this was what he had sought before, when he stood and dreamed in his treasury all those years ago. The dream of an empire that lived only in the mind, that had no borders or boundaries or kings to rule over it. A kingdom of wealth, unconquerable and eternal. The ultimate ruler of men.

'Thank you,' Croesus said.

Later, they sat at a table, deep within the world of the palace tent. Cyrus clapped his hands, and attendants pulled on the ropes that were coiled in the corners of the chamber. The roof of cloth rolled back, and the stars shone above them, distant and inviting, like the lights of an unconquered city.

Servants brought wine, and the two men sat and drank in silence for a time. Cyrus stared into the distance. Croesus sent the coin dancing over his knuckles like a street performer.

'Isocrates . . . he is a good slave, isn't he?' Cyrus said at last.

'Yes, he is. Worth more to you than I am.'

'You value yourself too lightly, Croesus.'

'I don't think I'm worth much as your advisor.'

'No?'

Croesus shook his head. 'I think I am here to remind you what a king must not do. A lesson in hubris.'

Cyrus laughed. 'But you have some interesting thoughts. Your answer for Lydia, for instance.'

'I am still surprised you agreed so easily.'

'To your unlikely plan?'

'Yes.'

'I lose nothing if it fails. We will do as Harpagus wants. But to pacify a nation with music and fine fabrics? It has never been done before. That is something, don't you think?'

'Ah. Now I do understand you. At least in part.'

'What understanding do you lack?'

'Why a man as happy as you wants to build an empire.'

'A king must have his mysteries.' He smiled. 'Perhaps I will tell you some day.'

'Perhaps.' Croesus drank. 'Your wife is very beautiful.'

'She is my favourite.'

Croesus ran his thumb over the edge of the cup, letting the red drops soak into the whorls of his skin. 'How many do you have?'

'Only three so far.'

'It never felt right to me, taking more than one wife at a time.'

'If I can love more than one woman, why not marry more than one? Desire is not a limited resource, Croesus.'

'Not for you, perhaps. The rest of us hoard what we can, and dole out our love piecemeal, like stingy merchants. It seems Cassandane would rather you loved a little less broadly.'

'I will not be possessed by anyone, Croesus, least of all a woman. Isocrates has a wife, doesn't he?'

'Yes. Maia. She has been a good friend to me.'

'Beautiful?' Cyrus said.

'No. Homely. A peasant. She smells of rosemary and mint.'

'I see. The smell of the kitchens is off-putting to you?'

'No. The smell of the dead,' Croesus said, thinking of Atys.

'The smell of the dead?'

'They wrap the dead in rosemary and mint. You do not know this?'

'You have buried more family than I have, Croesus.'

'That is true.'

They shared a silence.

'Would you like a woman, Croesus?'

'What?'

'A woman. Or a boy, if that is your taste. I could arrange it for you. As a reward, for your good service.'

Croesus hesitated. 'No,' he said.

'No? How old are you, Croesus?'

'Fifty. An old man.'

212

'Not old enough to forgo the pleasures of a woman. I don't understand.'

He thought for a time. 'What have I to give to a woman?' he said.

Cyrus tilted his cup and turned it slowly, watching the last drops of wine circle their way around the bottom. 'Do you have a favour that I *can* grant, Croesus?'

'Yes,' Croesus said. 'Will you let me see my son?'

Cyrus paused and looked at him. His face was unreadable.

'Of course,' the king said. 'And I will ensure that you can see him when you want, from now on. Will you accept that, as a reward for two years' service?'

Croesus blinked at his tears, sharp and sudden. 'Thank you,' he said.

He looked away, and listened to Cyrus disappear to his bedchamber, somewhere even deeper within the labyrinth of cloth that few were permitted to see. Then he stood and followed a guard out of the maze, and towards a place where no other man would wish to go.

It was a small gathering of pale-coloured tents, ringed round with rows of black cloth staked to the ground, and separated from the main encampment by a clear expanse of unoccupied land. Every man who walked past did so quickly, head down, muttering a prayer and reaching for any personal charm he carried. None wanted to linger near the place where the sick were taken, and the wounded went to die.

Some had been dragged there from the battlefield, hacked and bleeding from a dozen wounds, and later recovered, knotted with scars like blessings from the Gods. Others would arrive with the slightest of wounds, a puncture from a nail or a bite from a dog, laughing at their clumsiness. They would burn with fever and die in days. The surgeons who worked in these tents were all too aware of the uncertain science they practised. Shunned by the rest of the camp as traders in death, they were solitary, and darkly superstitious.

Croesus felt a quickening fear as he approached that place where death stood close by, capricious and unpredictable. He made his way past the tents that held the sick and the wounded, to the place that was looked on with fear even by those who lived and worked there. It was a single white tent, set apart from the others: the home of the insane.

There were not many, only a few dozen. Some had survived wounds to the head on the battlefield, others had been struck down by apoplexy or fever, and had awoken with half their minds gone. There were others who had suffered no injury at all, but the slightest sound of war – the creaking of leather armour, the thud of a spear against the ground or a bowstring pulling taut – would send them into a shaking panic that took hours to coax them from. Perhaps there were, hidden amongst them, some who merely feigned madness, preferring to be imprisoned than to chance their lives in war, seeking to grow old amongst the insane.

It had been many months since Croesus had seen Gyges. He could visit only when he had coin with which to bribe the guards, or when some other favour or opportunity presented itself. He made his way past the slow, shuffling figures of the men whose minds had been broken by war, and sat down beside his son.

Gyges had changed little. Croesus did not understand how it was that his son, who had resisted any attempt to restrict his movements in the palace, was able to stand being confined to this tent, and yet somehow Gyges seemed more content here than ever he had in Sardis. He sat next to his son in silence for a time, struggling, as always, to know how to begin.

'Cyrus will let me visit as often as I like now,' he said at last. 'How often should I come, do you think?'

Gyges did not respond.

'I have pleased the king,' Croesus said slowly. 'Though I think I made an enemy of Harpagus. He is angry that the king took my advice and not his. But what can he do while I have the king's favour?'

Beside him, Gyges shifted a little, as though in discomfort. 'Perhaps this talk of politics bores you. I am sorry.' He hesitated. 'Maia wishes she could see you,' he said. 'They still won't permit it. They say they won't allow a woman amongst the mad, some foolish custom of theirs. She misses you.' He paused. Gyges was staring ahead into thin air, giving no sign he had heard anything that his father had said.

Croesus shook his head. 'You won't talk to me. I still sometimes wonder if you talk to the Gods, you know,' he said. 'If you are a prophet.'

'I am no prophet.'

Croesus started, feeling the shock of the words pass through him. Gyges had spoken ever since the fall of Sardis, but his words came rarely, as if he had only a limited number to use, like an archer in a siege who must make his dwindling ammunition count. 'What are you then?' he said.

Gyges shrugged, and looked away.

'Are you happy?'

Gyges hissed in irritation.

'You think it is a foolish question,' Croesus said. Then he paused. 'I can be content at least, serving this king,' he said. 'If things do not change.'

'They will change,' Gyges said, almost absently. Then he turned away, and looked at the grass, like a king dismissing an out of favour courtier. The conversation was over.

Croesus stood and brushed the dried grass from his knees. He hesitated before going. In two years, he had teased out perhaps twenty sentences from Gyges. Each time he had seen his son, the encounter had been as inconsequential as this one, and yet he was still possessed by the same sensation that had taken hold of him at the fall of Sardis, when Gyges had spoken for the very first time, the sense that there was some mystery that his son understood that he did not.

Perhaps, he thought to himself, it would be revealed in action, in touch, not in words. He hesitantly reached a hand out towards his son.

Gyges flinched away. He had once permitted his father to touch him, when Sardis fell and death appeared certain for both of them. But it seemed it had been a single gift, and Croesus made a promise to himself there, before he left Gyges to the company of madmen, that he would not try to embrace his son again.

4

His son had denied he possessed any gift of prophecy, yet the change he spoke of followed his words.

News soon came of the collapse of the Lydian insurrection. Of armies that had disappeared overnight, their thousands of men melting back to towns and farms and burying their weapons in the forest; of rebel counsels that had preached independence and patriotism, now dissolved into desperate denunciations and pleas of loyalty to the Persian king. The usurper Pactyes had fled with his gold to some foreign haven, to live out his life in dreams of what might have been. The rebellion was over.

With this news, the Persian army divided, like some wandering tribe grown large and cumbersome, in which the young break away, restless and dissatisfied, to build a new world of their own. Half were to go to the western coast, to conquer the scattered cities of the Ionians. The others, to the east, to see what other lands Cyrus might add to his empire.

When the break was announced, Croesus had thought that he would go with the king. And yet when the names were read, of who in the court would go east and who would go west, he was told that he would now serve Harpagus.

He looked around at the men of the Persian court, seeking some explanation, but no one looked back at him. What interest would they have in the comings and goings of a slave? Then Harpagus caught his eye. The general looked at the slave, and, for the first time, Croesus saw him smile.

'He requested me,' Croesus said. 'That's what I was told. What can that mean?'

Isocrates did not reply.

'I would understand if it was Cyrus's command. But why would Harpagus ask for me?'

'You ruled over the Ionians. Perhaps he thinks you can be of use to him.'

'No. He thinks I am a fool. I cannot make sense of it.' Croesus hesitated. Even in the darkness of their tent, Isocrates would not look at him. 'You know something, don't you?'

'Yes.' But it took him a long time to speak again. 'They say he murdered Astyages.'

'What do you mean?' he said.

Isocrates shrugged and looked away 'That is what I have heard. It is what the other slaves say, anyway.'

'Gossip. Idle talk.'

'Slaves know more about what really happens than anyone, Croesus.'

'Why would he kill him? Tell me that.'

'Astyages became the king's closest advisor, after being taken as a slave. Closer even than Harpagus, or so they say. Then Astyages killed himself, just as he was beginning to win the king's favour. It makes no sense.'

Croesus thought on this, seeking some way out of the trap. He found none. 'What should I do?'

'I don't know. How much time do you have?'

'We leave tomorrow.'

Isocrates said nothing.

'How did he do it?' Croesus said.

'Poison. That's what they think, at least.'

Croesus nodded slowly. 'That's good.'

'That's good?'

'If poison is the method he favours, he will have a hard time getting it to me.'

Isocrates shook his head. 'I wish you had made an enemy of any other man. He is cleverer than you, Croesus.'

'Yes, I know. But he has something to lose. Unlike me. That's something.' Croesus hesitated. 'I don't suppose I shall see you again, after tomorrow.'

Isocrates said nothing. Croesus rose, turned, and walked out into the night.

He passed through the tents of the army, watched the flickering of firelight on the bored young faces at the sentry fires, kept to the shadows and listened to the talk of soldiers fighting sleep, passing the time until dawn.

He could not believe that he had grown attached to this army, that he almost considered it a home. An army at peace could be mistaken for a gathering of nomads, wanting nothing but to travel and be free. An army at war he knew to be something else entirely.

He thought of escape. Of slipping past the fires and out into the wilderness, and finding a new life in a place where they had never heard of Croesus and the mistakes that he had made. But even if he could have made his way past the soldiers on watch and out of the camp, he knew nothing of how to live off the land, and he had no allies to run to. No man would take in a runaway slave, unless they wanted a slave for themselves, and he had no value as a worker in a house or in the fields. He knew only kingship, and war.

He thought of Harpagus, his little smile of triumph. Then he tried to think of nothing at all.

When Croesus woke in the morning, the patch of ground beside him was empty and cold. Isocrates had gone. Croesus could not blame him. Amongst the slaves, it was understood that one's own life was always more valuable than that of a friend. There was no shame in leaving a doomed man to die.

But when he walked towards the southern edge of the camp, where half the army was preparing to leave and ride west, he discovered that he was wrong. Isocrates and Maia were both waiting for him on the main path that ran through the encampment.

'You shouldn't be here,' Croesus said. 'There will be trouble for you.'

Isocrates waved off his concerns. He took Croesus's hand, and Croesus felt the familiar metallic shapes settling into his palm. He looked down on a scattering of gold and silver coins. A pittance for a king. A small fortune for a slave.

'Use them carefully. I am sorry I couldn't get more,' Isocrates said. 'There are few who will lend to a slave.'

'Thank you, Isocrates.' He bowed his head, and tried to smile. 'I will have lived a few years longer than I should have, anyway. I suppose that's something.'

'Self-pity doesn't become anyone, least of all you, Croesus.' Isocrates placed both hands on the other man's shoulders. 'He will have to catch you first. Stay alive until the wars end. That is all you have to do.'

Croesus turned to Maia, but before he could speak, she embraced him and kissed him on the forehead. 'Take care,' she said. 'We will see you again in a few years.'

He opened his mouth to reply, but found nothing to say. A heavy hand closed over his shoulder. He turned and saw a soldier behind him. The Persian was barely awake, rubbing sleep from his eyes with his free hand and resting his spear in the crock of his neck.

'Come on,' he said. 'We are late.'

As they passed through the encampment, they came within a hundred paces of the tents of the sick and the mad. Some way distant he saw Gyges wandering aimlessly; a guard followed him closely, escorting him. Croesus raised his hand, in greeting and in farewell. Gyges looked up and saw him, but did not respond. There was a moment when their eyes met, and then his son returned to the tent of the madmen.

It could be that he did not care that his father was going to his death, but Croesus tried to believe that there was another reason for his son's indifference. He wanted to think that Gyges knew something that he did not. That Croesus would live, and that they would see each other again.

Half of the Persian army broke away, with Harpagus at its head. They rode west, back towards the country where, once already, Croesus had cheated death.

5

The army drew up on the hills overlooking the coast, above the paired harbours of Phocaea.

It was the first of the cities that Harpagus intended to conquer, the most northerly of that cluster of Ionian settlements. Their inhabitants' ancestors had fled wars in Attica and the Peloponnese, and had travelled to make new homes by the sea, wanting no more than to live in peace.

There must have been some reason, Croesus thought, why he had brought war to this place when he was a king, had sought to tame this poor and divided people. He could not think of it, and did not know what it was that now drew Cyrus and Harpagus to the place, to put the Ionians to the sword once again, other than some kind of historic inevitability, the way that kings always seem drawn to repeat what has been done before.

Croesus saw the people of Phocaea gathered on the walls, staring up at the Persian army. They must have lived their lives in fear of the sea, he thought, in fear of a towering wave, sent by some angry god, that would drag their city beneath the water. Now here was a wave that came from the land, a sea of spears and men and horses that would sweep over them and drown them all.

He looked across at Harpagus. 'Fine walls,' was the general's only observation, delivered with grudging respect. He dispatched his emissary to deliver the terms of surrender. They stood silently on the hill, and waited for the Phocaeans to say no.

'Well?' Harpagus, when his man returned.

'They ask for a day to consider our terms.'

Harpagus grunted in surprise. 'What do you think, Croesus?' There was a taunting edge to his voice. 'I don't see any reason to wait. We can take the city in a day.'

'Do you care what I think?'

'Let us pretend that I do.'

Croesus looked out at the harbour, and remembered what little he knew of the Phocaeans.

'Wait,' he said. 'Where is the harm in that? It is only a single day. The army can rest. And the Phocaeans might change their minds.'

'They won't,' Harpagus said. He shrugged. 'But as you wish.'

Long before dawn, Croesus made his way through the sleeping army, and returned to the hill that overlooked the city and the sea. There was no moon, and he could see almost nothing of the settlement below. There were just a few points of light, where a torch had been lit or a fire still burned, as though the night sky had laid a part of itself over the city like a veil, covering it with darkness and a scattering of stars.

Croesus sat and wrapped his arms around his knees. He shivered, and waited for the dawn.

When the wind blew towards him, Croesus could hear the sounds of the city. Ropes drawing taut, water lapping against hollow wood, the creak of carts through the streets, arguments between families in an unfamiliar language, orders given in hard whispers.

The sun finally rose behind him, and it broke over a vision from a myth. A city on the water.

The sea was filled by a fleet of fifty oared ships. They rode low in the water, weighed down by huge sacks of grain and jars of water wrapped in fishing nets and lashed to the sides, their decks packed to overflowing with women and children. The entire city of Phocaea, its people and its treasures, were safe inside the wooden hulls and launched onto the ocean. The oars struck the water and drove the ships to the west, in search of a new world where war could not touch them.

Croesus thought of what might lie in those ships. Parchments that would be ruined by salt water, deciphered and copied and guessed at until they said something quite different. Heirlooms and treasures with stories that would be half-forgotten and misremembered, until their owners had invented a new past for themselves, better than the one they had left behind. Perhaps they had even taken with them a few chipped fragments of the statues that were too heavy for the boats, fragments that would inspire the next generation of Phocaean sculptors to recreate their lost artworks. A civilization that would be reborn when the ships again touched land.

Croesus sat and watched the fleet for a long time. Long enough for the ships to blur into each other on the horizon, as if they had been transformed into earth and stone and turned into a new island by the Gods.

When he finally looked away from the sea, he found Harpagus standing beside him.

'You knew they would sail away, didn't you?' said Harpagus eventually.

'Yes.'

Harpagus nodded. 'As did I. Don't think that you tricked me.'

'You let them go? Why?'

'Cyrus wants the port,' he said, looking out over the sea. 'I don't believe he cares much what happens to the people.'

'And you?'

'I don't care either.' He looked back at Croesus. 'The Phocaeans are my gift to you, Croesus.' He gestured towards the fleet, the new city on the sea. 'Remember this sight. There will not be much mercy after this.'

After that, the wars in the north passed like a nightmare remembered in fragments. Scattered sensations and scenes of chaos that were vivid to him when remembered individually, but made no sense when he tried to piece them together.

Nations he had himself conquered, years before, were enslaved once more. Cities that had been lain beneath the bull and lion were marked now with Cyrus's gold eagle. Teos, Myrus, Priene, Colophon, Erythrae, and all the others. A thousand dead for each city taken.

As a king, he had seen nothing of the places he had defeated. The arrival of a messenger, an unrolled scroll, a single inked line, was all he had seen of conquest. Now, as a slave, he saw everything. Burned cities where the bodies of the dead melted and fused with the buildings, creating monsters of flesh and masonry. Temples stripped of their treasures and used as burial chambers, the flies teeming above the altars. The tiny armies that lined up before the Persian forces, armies which had no chance of victory, cobblers and bakers with rusty armour and the shields and spears of their fathers. They fought and died, and were forgotten, heaped together by slaves into huge piles that burned for days when the torches were put to them, sending towering pillars of smoke up into the sky. Offerings to the Gods, a warning to the men who watched from neighbouring cities, waiting for the Persians to come for them.

Croesus fought a war of his own. He had as many enemies as Harpagus had cities to conquer. Routine, complacency, betrayal, exhaustion and fear were what conspired against him, and he spent each day resisting them.

He barely slept, finding a different hiding place each night to close his eyes for a short time, never sleeping in the tent he was assigned to. When he did sleep, he dreamed only of wars and conquered cities. His dreaming life and waking life were the same, to the point that in the small hours of the morning, or deep in the night, one mirrored the other so well that it was impossible to tell them apart.

When they passed through burning cities, Croesus would steal from the ruins, from the dying and the wounded, gathering gold to bribe others for information about Harpagus, or to buy a night's protection from one of the soldiers. Gold could buy anything. Even a longer life, if one spent it wisely enough.

Each morning, Harpagus summoned him, and questioned him about the city they were marching against, asking about water and fortifications, religious customs and superstitions, spearmen and gold. Croesus gave his knowledge, yet he always held something back, only hinting at what he knew of the next city they were to conquer, hoping that his usefulness might keep him alive. Harpagus was a practical man, after all.

He remembered when he was a boy, sitting on his mother's lap and enjoying the spicy smell of her hair, as she laid out samples of poison for him to taste and learn. He tried to remember those tastes again, and wondered which one Harpagus preferred. He was always watchful for a knife in the darkness, the bowl of food that had been prepared especially for him, the wineskin that was offered to him first with a smile.

To his eyes, the encampment resembled the labyrinths of legend, with one exception: there was no path by which he might escape. The only way out was the passage of time. Each day that passed was another step towards the ending of the wars, and their return to the east, to the safety of Cyrus's court. But with every city that they conquered, his knowledge became a little less valuable. He imagined his life weighed on the scales; the satisfaction of his death placed against the value of keeping him alive. As he woke each morning, he wondered if this would be the day when the scales would finally tip.

6

They came, at last, to Pedasus. It fell just like the others that had fallen before it, its secrets betrayed, its army destroyed, its fortifications breached, its people butchered.

Croesus gave it no thought. He could think only of sleep.

He could not remember when he had last been able to buy a safe night's rest. The world, washed out and grey, like a landscape in a half-forgotten memory, no longer made sense to him. People had to repeat themselves many times before he could understand them. Mundane objects became fascinating to him – he could spend hours staring at a candle flame as it shuddered in the air, or running his fingers one way and then another through tall grass, or watching the motion of water over stone. He had taken to keeping a thorn in his hand, so that he could close a fist and force himself awake with the pain.

He sometimes wondered, in the dull way of someone too ex-hausted to care, if he might have died weeks before and passed on without noticing. The next world might be a mirror of this one, a world that slowly disintegrated one sense at a time, that rotted like a body, until one was left with only an incomprehensible blankness. Or perhaps he had simply gone mad, and no amount of sleep would return the world to sense. He would be trapped in this half-life for ever.

He could focus only on knowing where Harpagus was, hoping to retain some illusion of control, but Harpagus had the general's gift of being everywhere and nowhere at once. Ask half a dozen different people where he was, and you would receive twice as many answers. He was consulting an oracle in the hills, was in a whorehouse in the city, inspecting the cavalry, overseeing an execution and arguing with an emissary, seemingly all at once. Still Croesus continued to ask, like a man picking at a wound, even when he knows it will not bring him peace.

The night that Pedasus fell, he received, for once, a clear answer. Looking out of his tent towards the end of the day, he asked a passing soldier where the general was.

'The general has gone on already,' the other man replied. 'Through the woods with some of the men. We are to follow him in the morning.'

'He's not here in the camp? You are sure?'

'Yes.' The soldier smiled dryly at him. 'Glad to be away from the master's gaze?'

'More than you can know.'

The soldier laughed. 'Sleep well, mighty king, sleep well,' he said, and walked away.

Croesus watched him go. He began to think about where he might snatch a few hours of sleep that night. He sat down on the ground inside the tent to rest his legs and eyes for a short time before he went out again. His mind occupied by other things, he leaned back and lay flat on his back.

He was asleep within moments.

'Croesus!'

The torch was in his face again, the fire curling towards his mouth. He flinched from it, and woke, his mouth thick with the taste of sleep.

A soldier stood over Croesus, looking down on him, his eyes two dark voids in the shadow of the torchlight. 'Get up,' he said. 'Harpagus wants you. He doesn't sleep. That means neither do you tonight. Come on.'

At his touch, Croesus woke up fully for the first time in months. The world came back into focus, and he understood what was happening to him.

'Wait,' he said, 'just one moment.'

He reached towards the bundle of cloth that held his possessions together. He groped at it, hoping to feel the hard shape of a statue, the thin metal strands of a golden necklace, the round weight of coins, something with which he could buy his life. But there was only worthless fabric beneath his fingers.

He looked up at the soldier. 'It must be now?' he said slowly.

'Yes, of course. Come on.'

Croesus remembered the morning they came to take him to the pyre in Sardis. He wondered at how calm he felt, now as then. The strange lack of urgency that came from being locked into an unfamiliar sequence of events, shaped by another's hands and quite out of his control.

He could not truly believe that he was being led to his death. He kept imagining that each moment might bring a chance for escape or reprieve. His mind would continue to fabricate these impossible escapes, he thought, even as the sword was being drawn, or the noose fastened around his neck. Perhaps, in the final instant, just for a moment, he would truly understand that he was about to die.

They passed out of the camp, and into the surrounding woods. This will be the place, Croesus thought. Each time he saw the captain rein in his horse, his heart shook. But it was always for some trivial reason – a debate over the route with one of the scouts, uncertain ground that the horses needed to pass over slowly, a brief wait for some lagging member of the column to catch up. A mad desire grew within him to yell at them to get on with it. Anything was better than this, waiting for them to choose a place at random where he might be put to death.

He heard something. A soft rattle in the woods. The sound of wood against wood. A sound that was almost natural, but not quite; this was wood guided by human fingers, not by the wind or by the passage of an animal. It was a familiar sound, and he tried to remember what it was.

The first arrows came so fast that it was as though they grew from the things they struck. Cancerous, murderous eruptions, sprouting from the thick earth at his feet, from the flanks of suddenly screaming horses, and from the throats and eyes of the men ahead of him.

A heavy weight fell against his back and pinned him to the ground. He felt a warmth soaking through his tunic, then hot against his skin. He felt a shudder pass through him as another arrow struck, and the man on his back lay still. He watched as some of the soldiers broke and ran, and others charged into the woods, screaming war cries. He lay against the ground, shaking and weeping in fear. He had never wanted to live more than in that moment.

Croesus felt the weight lift off his back. He covered his face with his hands, but it was a Persian soldier who pulled him to his feet, and told him to run.

They ran together, half tripping with every step, barely able to see in the darkness. Behind and around him, Croesus heard the dull sound of arrows striking wood, the skipping rattle as they bounced and spun through the undergrowth. His chest burned, as though he had swallowed the fire of his dreams, and the strength went from his legs. 'Don't leave me,' he said, but the Persian soldier ran on ahead, leaving him alone in the darkness.

Croesus leaned against the closest tree, his breath rasping like that of a dying man, his eyes tight shut, as though he could wish the waking nightmare away. He heard the sound again behind him, of arrows in the quiver. He forced himself to keep moving, waiting to feel the arrow bite into his back.

He broke out of the woods, stumbling in an exhausted half-run, and saw the lights of the camp ahead. Now would be the time, he thought. With sanctuary in sight, now was the time for the arrow to find him, but still it did not come.

Staggering now on aching feet, driven forward by empty lungs, he made it to the picket line. The Persian sentry yelled at him to stop, seeing only a bloody foreigner charging towards the camp, but Croesus ran on, sinking to the ground before the man who stood over him, spear raised.

'Please,' he said, clasping his shaking hands together around the man's knees. 'Please.'

7

Harpagus sat by torchlight. On the heavy table in front of him, parchments concealed a stained, yellowing map so that it could barely be
seen at all. A fragment of Egypt, a scattering of Hellenic islands, were
all that remained uncovered. He preferred it this way. Soldiers and
servants speculated over the contents of the three deep chests that
Harpagus kept closely guarded in his tent. They would have been
disappointed to discover that they were filled only with paper.

His captains complained incessantly (behind his back, thinking
that he did not know) about the reports they had to deliver almost
every day. Exact inventories of weapons, food stocks, the condition of
armour, state of morale, reports on praiseworthy soldiers and troublesome individuals. His spies were instructed to produce reports with the
same precision. The exact height of walls, depth of wells, consistency
of soil. Here in his tent, with the army itemized and inventoried, the
next city reduced to a few sheets of parchment, he could create a
world on paper. A world that he could conquer.

He heard footsteps approach, fast and hard. He expected a messenger or a scout, but when Croesus entered, unannounced and
unescorted, he did not react. He took in the blood and dirt on
Croesus's clothes, the angry, fearful look in his eyes. He laid down on
the desk the paper in his hand, and waited for the other man to speak.

'I am here now, if you want me dead,' Croesus said. He felt tears fill his eyes, and angrily blinked them away. When his vision cleared, Harpagus still gazed at him impassively.

'Not that you will believe me,' the general said, 'but I really don't understand.'

'Who were the archers in the forest?'

'Archers?'

'They killed most of your men. They almost killed me.'

Harpagus paused. 'Bandits,' he said after a moment. 'Or men from Pedasus, looking for revenge.' He smiled thinly. 'No doubt they saw you being escorted by the soldiers and mistook you for someone important.'

'Stop treating me like a fool!' Croesus shouted. The sound seemed to hang in the air like a living thing.

'You have come close to death,' the general said slowly. 'You have forgotten yourself. I forgive you for it. Come back tomorrow. We will talk then.'

'No. We will talk now.'

'As you wish.' Harpagus turned away and picked up a wineskin. With his back still to Croesus, he poured out a cup.

'Here,' he said, turning around and offering the cup. 'Take some wine. It might calm you down.'

Croesus looked at the wine and hesitated. Harpagus's smile widened, and he drank deeply. 'I see,' he said. 'So you believe the stories.'

'Shouldn't I?'

Harpagus shrugged, and gestured to a chair by the table. 'Sit down.' Croesus didn't move. 'Come on, don't be a fool. Sit.'

Croesus followed this command. They stared at each other in silence. A pair of flies wound in spirals through the air, trying to alight on Croesus's bloody clothes. Each time he twitched them off with a shrug of his shoulders, like a beast in a field. He did not take his eyes from Harpagus.

'Have you heard about how I came to serve Cyrus?' the general said suddenly, breaking the silence.

'What?'

'Cyrus. How I came to serve him.'

'I don't see how—'

'Just listen, will you, Croesus? You talk too much for a slave. The story may give you a little understanding.'

Croesus nodded slowly. 'Very well.'

'I served Astyages, when he was king of the Medes. Did you know that?' Croesus shook his head. 'Your brother-in-law trusted me more than any. One day he complained about a dream to me. The soothsayers and prophets were consulted, and they all agreed. His daughter's child would take his kingdom from him. She was married to a Persian nobleman, and she had just given birth to a son. Astyages asked me to kill the child. I agreed, of course. I had no choice. The Spartans expose hundreds of children each year, I thought, those who are weak or malformed. I was sure that I could manage to let one child die for the good of the kingdom.'

'Why didn't you?'

'I don't know. I am not a sentimental man.'

'I would not have guessed.'

'Perhaps it wasn't anything to do with the child. Perhaps I did it just for myself, to spite Astyages. He was a cruel man, you know. Ruthless and stupid.'

Croesus nodded. 'Yes, I know. I always pitied my sister, having to marry him.'

'And yet you went to war to recover his empire for him.'

'I think we both know that isn't why I went to war. Come on, finish your story.'

'Well, in any case, I thought it over some more. In the end, I found that I didn't want to murder a child because Astyages had overeaten at the dining table and given himself nightmares. I gave the boy to some shepherds to raise, and talked to the cooks about reducing the richness of the king's diet. I tried to forget any of it ever happened.

'Well, he found out, many years later, when Cyrus was a boy. It was obvious to anyone with eyes in his head that he was not a peasant's son. He resembled his father a little too well.

'Astyages summoned me and asked me if I really had let Cyrus die all those years before. I could see that he already knew the truth and so I confessed. I hoped that if I did so, he would at least spare my wife and son. I expected him to order my immediate execution, but he smiled at me, and told me that he was glad to hear it. That he had always regretted giving that order, and it had been preying on his mind for years. He clapped me on the shoulder and asked if I would come and have dinner with him.

'I ate with him that night. I wondered if the meal would be poisoned. But after a time, when there was no apparent taste of poison on my lips, I began to think that he really had forgiven me. So I tried to enjoy the meal, which wasn't hard. It was a good meal. But he didn't touch any of it. Just sat there, drinking wine and talking and watching me. I asked him why he didn't eat. He laughed, and reminded me that I had told him to be more careful about what he ate.' Harpagus paused, remembering. 'It was a rich stew.

'When I was finished, he asked me if I would like some sweetmeats. He always laid a good table, so I said yes. They brought in a covered platter, and he reached to lift the lid himself as soon as it touched the table. That is when I knew that something was wrong. Astyages never did anything that a servant could do for him. Not even wiping his mouth at the dinner table. He reached over so fast, setting his hand to the lid, that I knew that something terrible lay under it. Do you know what was there, Croesus?'

Croesus shook his head.

'He raised the lid, and underneath was the head of my son.'

Croesus stared at him. 'It is quite true,' Harpagus said. 'Astyages

asked me if I had lost my appetite. I told him that I had. He asked
me if I knew what I had just eaten. I said that I did. He asked if I
had learned my lesson. "Yes," I told him.' Harpagus fell silent.

'Astyages always liked that story,' Croesus said.

'What?'

'The story of Tereus. One of the old kings of Thrace. His wife
did that to him, after he betrayed her for another woman. Astyages
was always asking the poets to recite it. That is where he got the idea.'

Harpagus nodded. 'What does he say?'

'What?'

'What does Tereus say in the story, when he discovers what he has
done?'

Croesus thought for a moment. '"I am the tomb of my boy."'

'Yes,' Harpagus said. 'That sounds right.' He gave a ghost of a
smile. 'Never make an enemy of an educated man, Croesus. History is
a fine teacher of cruelty.'

'What happened then?'

'He let me live. I suppose he expected me to kill myself, after that.
My wife did, when I told her.' Croesus winced at this. Harpagus
continued, 'But I knew that I had to live for as long as I could, in the
hope that I would have my chance at revenge.'

'And Cyrus was that chance?'

'Yes. Astyages spared him too – apparently the soothsayers decided
the boy was no threat, having been raised as a peasant. He even let
him return to his real parents, and take his place as a Persian nobleman. I encouraged Cyrus to lead his people in rebellion, and I
betrayed the army of the Medes when it marched out to meet him.'

'And how did you feel, when he took Astyages as his advisor?

'How do you think?'

'So you had him killed.'

Harpagus shrugged. 'Perhaps.'

Croesus shook his head. 'You said this story would reassure me.'

Harpagus leaned forward. 'If I told you I didn't kill him, would you believe me? No? So why bother saying either way? But if I did kill him, it wasn't because he was my rival. I killed him because he was a murderer of children. Of my child. You are safe from me, Croesus. Surely, that is what you really care about. What does it matter if I killed him or not?'

The silence grew heavy between them. Croesus reached forward and took the wineskin, then poured himself a drink.

'What is the worst thing you ever did to someone?' Harpagus said after a time. 'When you were a king, I mean.'

Croesus looked away.

'Something bad, I take it?' Harpagus said. 'Come on, tell me. I cannot think it could be as terrible as what Astyages did to me.'

'There was a plot to put my half-brother on the throne,' Croesus said. 'One man . . . I cannot even remember his name . . . he was of my household, and he was passing information to the conspirators. I had him tortured. I promised him that I would execute him quickly if he talked, and so eventually he told me everything.'

'What did you do to him?'

'I was advised just to execute him and be done with it. To keep my word. But I thought that a king had to set an example. No, that's not it.' He curled his lip in disgust. 'I wanted to give him a death that no one would forget. I suppose I was already looking to be remembered, even for something like that. Unique achievements are always remembered, aren't they? So I gave him a unique death.'

'So?'

'I had him dragged over a carding comb.'

Harpagus shrugged. 'What is that?'

'Weavers use it for separating thick strands of wool. A large metal comb.' He held up two fingers pressed together. 'Spikes on it that thick. Very sharp.'

'How long did it take him to die?'

238

'I don't know. I didn't watch. I heard it took a long time though. They had to . . .' He swallowed and licked his lips. 'They had to weight him down. In the end. They dragged him over it five or six times, until his skin was hanging in ribbons. But he wouldn't die. They tied weights to him and did it a few more times, and at last they managed to finish him off.'

'You did not watch?'

'I was going to. It was a public execution,' Croesus said. 'I was inside the palace, about to go out. I could hear the sound of the crowd. I could hear how eager they were for it to begin. I knew his family would be there to watch. I had insisted on that. But I found I could not stand to watch. I told my steward to inform the crowd that something had happened – some important matter of state. That was my excuse. I heard . . .'

Croesus trailed off, and stared into the empty air. Harpagus said nothing, and waited for him to continue.

'Sometimes I would see people talking about it,' Croesus said. 'Months afterwards. But they fell silent when I came near. The way they looked at me. I wish I had seen it. I am sure it can't have been as bad as I imagine it to be.'

'You are wrong there. I don't think you have the courage to really imagine what it would be like, to die like that.' Harpagus toyed with an empty bowl on the table in front of him. After a moment, he looked back up at Croesus. 'Have you ever seen a man burned?'

'No.'

'A worse death than your carding comb, I should think. They bleed, you know. The skin cracks and the blood pours out of them. But they do not die quickly.'

'Why are you telling me this?'

'I am trying to help you, in my own way. Cyrus would have had you burned to death. Does that make him a cruel man? Surely crueller than you, if burning is a worse death than flaying?'

Croesus hesitated. 'I don't know.'

Harpagus leaned forward. 'Cruelty doesn't matter. It is how you face it that makes you strong or weak. Cyrus would have watched you burn. He wouldn't have taken any pleasure in it. He would never forget it. But he would have watched. That is the difference, between you and him. That is what makes him a great king. And what makes you a coward.'

'You think I am a coward?'

'I know you are a coward. How you managed to keep hold of your kingdom for so long, I really don't know. You are quite clever, I suppose. But you haven't the heart to do the hard thing. If I were going to kill you, that is why I would do it.' He leaned back and smiled thinly. 'Fortunately, I am not weak. I can protect Cyrus from your cowardice. So there is no need to kill you.'

'That is supposed to comfort me?'

'It is the best that you'll get from me,' Harpagus said. 'You are fortunate to be serving such a king. We both are.'

Croesus shook his head. 'You know that I hate war. And you dragged me out here to help you fight a dozen of them.'

'I didn't know that, actually. And I wouldn't have cared one way or the other if I had known. You serve Cyrus. You had better get used to wars. You will be part of them for the rest of your life.'

'Will he ever stop?'

'No.'

'Why?'

'It is a king's duty. Cyrus rules well. He is a better king than those he conquers. We have to teach others how to live like us.' He took another drink. 'It is too late to stop now, anyway.'

'What do you mean?'

'If he were to stop now, it would be a sign of weakness. Some other king would try and take his kingdom from him. Strength is nothing if it is not demonstrated.'

'How am I supposed to make my peace with that?'

'However you please. Manufacture a few acts of mercy. As you did with the Phocaeans. Pretend that it means something.' Harpagus exclaimed suddenly, 'Oh Gods. You must have had a miserable life these past years,' he said. 'Thinking I wished you dead. I did wonder why you always seemed so nervous.'

'I am glad I amuse you.'

'You must feel quite the fool.'

Croesus said nothing.

'It made you feel important again, didn't it? That you were so significant that I would do anything to get rid of you? That is why you believed it. I am sorry to offend your vanity. But your life has no value. Not any more.'

'That's enough,' Croesus said softly.

Harpagus shrugged. 'Well, it doesn't much matter.' He lifted a scroll from the table. 'A messenger came in today with this. You have been recalled to the king's service.'

'What?'

'Our campaign is almost done here, and Cyrus desires your counsel. There is something that he would like your help with. So, whether or not you believe me, you will be out of my reach soon enough.'

'When do I leave?'

'Tomorrow. Go and sleep, Croesus. You will have to leave just after dawn, and you have a long journey ahead of you.'

Croesus nodded. He stood, and walked to the entrance. He paused there, and looked back over his shoulder at Harpagus.

'Did you kill him?' Croesus said.

'Astyages?'

'Yes.'

'It does not matter, does it?'

Croesus opened his mouth to reply, hesitated, and swallowed

what he had been about to say. Instead he said, 'What is it, by the way?'

'What is what?'

'This project that Cyrus wants my help with?'

'Oh. That. Nothing of consequence,' Harpagus said. He looked again at the parchment, and then back at Croesus. 'He's invading Babylon. That's all.'

8

Babylon.

As a king, he had listened to every story of Babylon that travellers and merchants brought back from the East. It was the largest city that would ever be built, they said. There was a sacred tower, ramped with steps that went above the clouds; one could climb to the top and speak to the Gods, and priestesses would remain at night to lie with them. The Ishtar Gate was so beautiful that men had torn out their eyes at the sight of it, so that it would be the last thing they ever saw. And the gardens were the greatest treasure of all, where water ran uphill, where delicate flowers and thirsty trees flourished impossibly in the desert city. It was a place where the rule of nature had been suspended.

Croesus discovered later that, as it was known that news of Babylon was a sure way into his presence, half of what he had been told was pure fantasy spun by those who had never been near the city. But this only added to the mystery of Babylon; a city that existed half in myth.

The city rarely left his thoughts as he travelled east along the Royal Road with a company of soldiers, winding along the old trading paths, bearing messages and treasures for the king. They met many merchant caravans heading in the opposite direction on these gold roads, traders from a dozen different nations drawn west, for commerce always followed in the wake of war.

At the forts and cities and way stations on the road, Croesus sat each night and listened to the travellers exchanging stories. Of Cyrus in the east with his invincible army; of Harpagus in the west, conquering city after city, becoming a figure of almost legendary terror to the Ionians; of the Hellenes across the sea, poor, backward cities that thought too highly of themselves; of the decadent Egyptians to the south and east, the ancient people whose civilization had existed long enough to witness the rise and fall of great mountain ranges, let alone the hundred human kingdoms that had faded to memory and dust. They traded stories about the Scythians and Massagetae to the north, nomads who drank blood from skulls and slept in the open like dogs. Once, they spoke of the fall of Sardis, a traveller telling the tale he had heard that a man called Hyroades had scaled the impossible south wall and let the army in. The others dismissed it as impossible.

Sometimes his own name was mentioned in these stories. None of the travellers would have thought that the grey-haired slave who sat silent in the corner, his skin like that of an old drum, off-white and taut against the bone, his eyes deep and weary, could once have been a king. If he ever was asked his name, he said he was Solon, Tellus, or Isocrates. The Persian soldiers exchanged knowing glances, but never gave him away. They let Croesus listen to the tales that were told of him.

Some travellers said Croesus was a wise man, and had engineered the irresistible Persian advance. Others countered that Croesus had lost his kingdom through foolishness, and was hardly a man to turn to for counsel (Croesus, listening silently, could not fault this logic). There were those who insisted that he had died in Sardis, that the stories of his service to the Persian king were just that, stories spun for fools to listen to.

These nights of storytelling were more than just a way to pass the evenings in company. For the Persians, they were a way home. They hunted the army as though it were a colossus that wandered the continent, following its rumours like a spoor. The closer they approached, the more stories of the army multiplied and contradicted each other. Perhaps, Croesus thought, they would wander perpetually in its wake, pursuing false rumours and growing old in its shadow, as those in the underworld are eternally locked into some endless task that seems just within reach, but that will never be fulfilled.

After months on the road, they finally came across its trail, the mile-wide wound in the land that the army had left in its wake. They pressed on hard, as though they were homesick travellers returning to their city from exile. Just as the sun was about to set, they finally came upon the army itself, pressed up against the Gyndes river, like a woman curled close against her lover.

The soldiers cried out at the sight of it, thinking of old companions they had thought they would never see again, the new stories that they would tell and hear. Croesus kept silent, and thought of Maia and Isocrates, Gyges and Cyrus.

Slaves and soldiers together made their way down to the camp, to be reunited with their friends.

Croesus had long since become proficient at reading the mood of the army. It took on the character of a single giant creature, and every individual, in his or her own small way, merely manifested the feeling of the whole. Croesus sometimes wondered if kings and generals truly lived apart from this collective as a rider does from his horse, or if they too were parts of this great beast, forced merely to follow its will, not to direct it.

As soon as he entered the encampment, he saw that something was wrong. Most of the men were slumped on the ground. Those who were alone stared out blankly, whilst others clustered together in groups to talk in furious whispers. The captains did nothing to restore order, and no one would talk to the newcomers. When they saw Croesus, they stared at him, uncertain of what to make of his arrival in the context of whatever was troubling them. In all his years of service, the soldiers had yet to decide if he were favoured by the Gods or no. The army had not lost a battle whilst he had been with them, it was true. But bad luck had followed him as a king, and there were many who thought it was only a matter of time before his ill fortune affected the Persian cause.

He thought of plague or famine, but there were no signs of either. Perhaps some great opposing army was too close to run from, and would soon come to butcher them all. Perhaps Croesus had found the army at last only to be destroyed along with it. He wondered if Cyrus had taken ill, and felt a sudden surge of fear.

The soldiers who had travelled with him dispersed, looking for old friends to discover what was happening. Croesus went to find the king.

'Croesus.' Cyrus smiled wearily at his visitor. 'Welcome back. Just in time, as well. We could use your advice.'

Croesus gazed around at the men gathered in Cyrus's tent. Cyraxes was there, looking even older and more distracted than Croesus remembered him. A Gutian general called Gobryas was the only other man he recognized, having been promoted in Harpagus's absence. On every man's face, he saw fear. He looked to Cyrus, expecting to find the king, as always, a centre of calm. He did not see fear there, but there were the beginnings of it – a certain hesitance, an unease that he had not seen before. 'What has happened?' Croesus said.

'One of my horses broke its tether and ran into the river.' When Croesus seemed perplexed, the king continued. 'One of my white horses, the sacred ones. They have been with me all the way from Persia.'

'A horse?' Croesus tried not to give a blasphemous smile of relief. 'That's all?'

'Don't talk lightly of it, Croesus. It is a terrible omen.'

'Of course, master.'

Silence fell in the tent, and Croesus thought of how strange it was, that he alone should be unafraid. He believed in the Gods, for what else was a man to believe in? But perhaps he had lost the faith that they would act on one side or another, that a man could be blessed or cursed by the Gods, rather than by his own choices. He had come to realize that they were neither enemies nor friends to the people of the earth. They were content merely to watch.

'How bad is the mood in the camp, do you think?' Cyraxes said to Croesus.

'It is foul. I thought the king must have died, or that we were on the verge of some other disaster.'

'I do not know what to do,' Cyrus said, and there was another shiver of fear in the tent. 'Did you have to deal with omens like this when you were a king, Croesus?'

'The omens always seemed to be in my favour.'

'Until I conquered your city.'

'Yes. Until then.' Croesus paused. 'Sacrifice is what the Gods value most. Make a great sacrifice, and win their favour back. Or if it is refused, then you will know for certain that you must not cross this river.'

'Yes. You are right, of course.' Cyrus smiled at him – the thinnest of smiles, but Croesus was glad to see it. 'Now, let me show you how a king deals with omens.' He turned, and spoke to Gobryas. 'I have an assignment for your men.'

The general bowed. 'My lord, I don't think they will be fit for anything until a sacrifice is made.'

'That is what I require from them. We are going to sacrifice the river.'

The general blinked. 'My lord?'

'I want that river lowered to such an extent that even a woman can cross it without getting her knees wet. Do you think you can manage that?'

'Yes, my lord.' He thought for a moment, then nodded. 'Yes. Enough channels and the river can be drained.'

'How long will the work take?'

Gobryas hesitated. 'For a river this size . . . at least a year,' he said tentatively.

Cyrus nodded. 'Well. We had better get started then, hadn't we?'

Croesus left the king's tent, and walked through the encampment, searching for Isocrates and Maia.

He asked each spearman and servant that he passed where he could find his friends. Many would not answer, still lost in the ill omen, but he at last found a young boy who knew the tent where Isocrates was sleeping. Croesus hurried then, almost running through the wandering paths of the encampment. Word of his return might spread through the camp, and he wanted to surprise them, if he could.

He slowed as he approached the tent. From within, he could hear an unfamiliar sound, the sound of a woman crying.

He walked close to the entrance, hoping to be mistaken, but the sound persisted, grew stronger. He hesitated, then lifted the flap of the tent a fraction; through the narrow gap, he saw the woman who was weeping. It was Maia.

She had been beaten. One eye was purpled, and blood ran from her nose, half wiped into a reddish smear across her lips and chin. These were only her visible wounds, but she sat hunched and curled up around some other pain.

Isocrates was beside her. He had his arms around his wife and was rocking her gently, whispering words that Croesus could not hear.

He was weeping too. Croesus had never thought that he would see Isocrates cry.

Neither of them had seen him, and before they could, he let the corner of the tent fall, and walked away.

Croesus had heard of men who would beat their wives half to death and then fall about weeping, begging to be forgiven for what they had done. That was not what had happened, he was certain of that. All that he knew was that he had witnessed something he was never meant to see.

9

Croesus sat on the grass at the edge of the river, and listened.

Close to, he heard the rush of the water, ignorant of the hundred thousand men who now worked to silence it; in the distance, the sound of picks biting into wet ground and the cheerful curses of men labouring beneath the sun. Looking across the banks of the river, he counted out the work teams. There were hundreds of groups of hundreds of men, each at work on a separate channel – an army of soldiers, many of them farmers' sons, remembering what it was to work the earth again.

'Cyrus has announced a contest, you know,' he said to Isocrates, who lay on the grass nearby. 'Ten talents of gold shared amongst the men who finish their channel first. A fortune.' He paused. 'I have heard rumours that at night some teams have taken to filling in their rivals' work, hoping to secure the prize for themselves. Imagine if that is true. Imagine if they are all doing that. We might be here for ever, digging trenches by day, filling them in by night.'

Isocrates sighed. 'Must you talk?' he said. 'I was enjoying the quiet. That's why I brought you out here, Croesus. To enjoy yourself, while we have a little time free from our masters. Try it, you might surprise yourself.'

'You're cheerful.'

'Of course. Why aren't you?'

'It doesn't bother you? We're going to sit here for a year, doing nothing but watching them dig away at this river. A year of our lives, wasted here.'

Isocrates shook his head. 'You still have much to learn about being a slave.'

'Tell me then, why don't you?'

Isocrates paused and stretched out, exploring the ground with his hips and shoulders to find a comfortable hollow to fit his back. 'Change is the enemy,' he said. 'For slaves like us. Now we have gained a year where nothing will change. We will eat, do our work and sleep. The army will dig its channels, Cyrus will destroy a river. No wars will be fought, no empires won or lost. Time is frozen, and what a gift that is. To be granted a year of this stillness. There will be no surprises to trap us into making any mistake. If I had my way, I would be happy to wait by this river for the rest of my life.'

Croesus shook his head and said nothing. Looking out at the river, he could see Gyges sitting on the bank some way off. From a respectful distance, Maia watched him closely, for Cyrus had granted Croesus's request to let her see him.

He thought suddenly of what he had seen, and wondered if his son were responsible for what had been done to Maia, if he had always been responsible. Perhaps he could have believed it before, in Sardis, but now, as he sat dangling his ankles in the water and tossing blades of grass to be carried downstream, Gyges looked different. He almost looked happy.

'You are still unsatisfied, I suppose,' Isocrates said.

'I am running out of time. I have wasted so much of my life.'

'And yet here is a year you might not have had otherwise. What is so wrong with that?'

'There must be something more for me to do. Some task greater than survival. I won't find it sitting on this river bank. I thought perhaps I would find it in Babylon. Who knows if we will get there now?' He paused, pulling up grass by the handful and letting the blades fall through his fingers, like grains of sand. 'Do you know what Solon said about happiness? He said he only counted a man happy when he could see all of his life, and especially how he died. What do you think of that?'

'He might have been right. About death, at least.'

'You really think so?'

'Perhaps that is why the Gods created us. They can experience everything we can, and much more besides. They can travel to the heavens and the underworld, transform into a bull, a snake, a shaft of light, a river or a thunderbolt. Shake the earth and reshape the seas. But they don't know death.'

'Very poetic,' Croesus said dryly. 'I've never heard you talk so much, and with so little sense. This river has done strange things to you.'

'Oh, but think about it a little. This event that we shape our lives around, and do everything to avoid. It is so crucial, but the Gods cannot understand it. So they create us. Through us, they get to observe death in countless different ways, and never have to experience it themselves.'

Croesus sighed, closed his eyes, and tried to enjoy the heat of the sun on his face.

'By the way,' Isocrates said, after a moment, 'Solon invented him.'

'Who?'

'Tellus.'

'What?'

'The happiest man who ever lived,' Isocrates said lightly. 'He doesn't exist. In my language, do you know what Tellus means? It can mean perfection. Or death. There was never a man called Tellus, who lived well and died happy. I suppose Solon thought it was a good joke.'

Croesus stared at him. 'How do you know this?'

'He told me, of course. After he had spoken to you. I wish he hadn't . . .' Isocrates smiled. 'You can imagine how I felt when you asked me to find out more about this imaginary man. Years of being terrified that you would remember, and I would have no answer to give you.'

'If I had found out . . .'

'Yes, I know,' Isocrates said. 'You would have had me dragged over a carding comb, or done something even worse. But you cannot be the death of anyone now, Croesus. Count that as some kind of a blessing.'

Croesus looked over at Isocrates. The slave lay utterly at peace on the grass, shifting his face towards the sun. Croesus wished he could let his friend lie there as he was, content and undisturbed. But he also knew that he would never again have the courage to ask what he had to ask if he did not ask it now.

'It isn't you who hurts Maia, is it?' Croesus said, at last.

Isocrates was silent for a long time. 'No,' he said quietly.

'Who is it? Who does it?'

Isocrates turned his face away. 'It is whoever wants her,' he said.

'Why did you lie?' Croesus said. 'Why didn't you tell me?'

'What difference would it have made?'

'If I had known, I would have—'

'What would you have done?' Isocrates said. 'Tell me. I'm curious.'

Croesus hesitated. 'I would have done something.'

'You are a fool.'

'Don't say that.'

'Those slaves and servant girls when you were a young prince. Some when you were a king. Did you think they wanted to be with you? I am sure they acted the part well enough. Not one of them came to you willingly, you have my word about that. They were too terrified to refuse you. Think on that, before you start swearing revenge on these men.'

Croesus remembered his son's wife after the funeral, the memory coming back sharply, like a thrust of pain in his chest. He had almost let himself forget it.

'How can you stand it?' he said instead. 'How can she stand it?'

'It is the way the world is. For a slave like her, anyway. You cannot change that, Croesus. You could not have done even when you were a king. You certainly can't now you are a slave. She has made her peace with it, as best she can.' He hesitated. 'So have I.'

'Well, I can't.'

'You will have to.'

Croesus sat still and stared blankly ahead. 'I don't know what to say.'

At last, Isocrates opened his eyes, sat up, and looked at the man who had once been his master. 'Then, perhaps, don't say anything at all.' He lay back down on the river bank, and closed his eyes once more.

They sat, silently together, and listened to the sound of the dying river.

10

A year before, the Gyndes had looked like a sea that stretched to the horizon. Now, the ruined hulls of boats, previously lost in the depths, squatted in the shallow water like monstrous skeletons. The muddy banks, exposed to the sun for the first time in centuries, teemed with crabs and insects scuttling hesitantly in the open air, distrustful of the new world in which they found themselves. A shallow, uneven trail of water was all that remained of the great river.

The army stood at the water's edge, restless like a pack of children, eager to march on to Babylon. But first, so Cyrus had said, there was a promise to keep.

The king held up a hand for silence, and the deafening sound of the army ceased.

'My people!' the king said. He paused, waiting for his words to pass back through the ranks of his men. Each sentence he spoke took many minutes to reach the rear, as it was whispered from one man to another until it reached the supply train, where the words faded and died. None cared to share the speech with the slaves.

'Our priests are all in agreement,' Cyrus continued. 'The omen of the horse has been overcome. The curse is lifted from our army. We are free of it. Babylon awaits us – the greatest prize this world has to offer. Shall we take it?'

Croesus winced at the sound of the army's roar, and Cyrus raised his hand for silence once again.

'There is one more matter,' he said. He pointed at the river. 'I promised, one year ago, that I would lay this great river so low that even a woman could cross it without getting her knees wet.' He smiled. 'Let us see if that's true.'

He raised a hand and waved, as though ordering his cavalry to advance. At his gesture, the women of the camp came forward through the ranks and assembled at the water's edge.

There were thousands of them. Most were slaves or servants, or village women who had run away after one man or another and had become common property of the soldiers. But there were a few wives and concubines of generals and officials amongst them, mixing unashamedly with the common women.

Croesus was not used to seeing them all together. He tried to pick out Maia from the mass. He couldn't see her, but there was one figure he did recognize. Cyrus's wife Cassandane was poised on the bank, ready to run. She stood quite apart, saying nothing to the other women; Croesus saw a man standing beside her.

It took him a moment to recognize her son, Cambyses, full grown now, who looked around uncertainly at the gathering of women, watching for any who might laugh at his mother or, worse yet, might laugh at him. He stood near her protectively, but also, perhaps, so as to be protected by her, as she hitched up her skirts and prepared to run. Her face was so solemn that it made Croesus smile.

'She is taking this seriously,' Croesus said to the king. 'I would have thought a race like this would be beneath her.'

Cyrus smiled. 'She likes to win,' he said. 'Like me.' The king turned to the mass of women, and raised his voice. 'Gold for any who make it back with dry knees,' he said to them. 'And more for the fastest.'

He let his hand fall, and the women went forward into the river. Some ran as fast as they could, hoping to outpace those behind them. Others worked carefully, moving more slowly on the fringes of the pack, splashing water against the knees of their rivals, defending their own exposed skin with the hems of their robes. Others seemed to ignore the contest entirely, and used the occasion as an opportunity to gather food; moving slowly, squatting over the water, hooking out fish that gasped and floundered in the shallow water.

The army cheered and shouted obscenities at the women as they ran. Their shouting almost drowned out the sound from the river, but occasionally, when the cheering died down for a moment, Croesus could hear the women in the water. He could hear them laughing.

They reached the far bank of the river, and for a moment Croesus found himself thinking that they might not return. That they might keep running, striking out to found some new country of their own, and leave the men to continue their wars without them. Croesus wondered what kind of a world that would be. Just for a moment, they seemed to hesitate on the far bank, on the brink of that new world, before they turned and began to run back towards the army. Out in front, by a short distance, was Cassandane.

In the water, the women had been equal; Cassandane had been forced to work harder than most, as many of the others went out of their way to try and push her into the water, given a rare chance to try and humiliate one of their betters. But she had dodged past them all, weaving through the crowd, running harder than the rest, until she regained the bank of the river, victorious.

Cyrus walked to his wife. He drew close, placing his hands to her sides. She looked up at him and said nothing. He let his hands run down her hips, knelt in front of her, and ran them down her bare legs. He cupped her knees for a moment then looked at his palms. Smiling, finding them dry, he lifted them high and showed them to the soldiers. Then he took his wife by the hand, and led her away to their tent.

Watching them, listening to the army howl their praise for their king, Croesus could not help but wonder about the performance he had just witnessed. How much was for show, and how much was genuine? He doubted if Cyrus himself even knew any more where performance ended and the truth began.

From the banks of the river, he saw Maia coming to him, her husband at her side. Isocrates, perhaps inspired by the king, had for once allowed himself to display affection in public, a single hand curled protectively around her waist.

'I looked out for you, but couldn't see you,' Croesus said. 'Did you succeed?'

'Yes. Look,' she said, and lifted her skirts to show her dry knees.

Croesus turned away, and she laughed. 'Such a shy old man. We slaves can't afford that Lydian modesty of yours.' She turned to Isocrates. 'What do you think? I couldn't finish first. Some of the soldiers' harpies are little more than girls, and they could outrun me. But I finished with my knees dry. What does that make me?'

'Crafty and tricky, is what you are,' he said.

'Like your husband,' Croesus said immediately.

Maia grinned. 'He has you there.'

Isocrates shook his head, but a smile danced briefly across his lips. 'Come on. We need to get ready.' He looked out across what remained of the river. 'We'll be going soon.'

I I

Croesus looked out on the lights of the distant city.

When he was a king, an emissary had once brought him a set of Indian diamonds inlaid in black cloth, arranged to take the shape of Sardis at night. He remembered how the torchlight had lingered on those priceless stones, the way his eyes had connected the separate points of light together to re-create his home.

Even in the darkness, reduced to a scattering of fires and torches, Babylon seemed more beautiful than other cities. He wondered if that were deliberate, if the council of Babylon strictly regulated the torches that were used and where they could be placed, in order to present the city's most handsome face to those who camped outside the city, watching it and wishing they could be inside it.

The Babylonian army had been routed over a week earlier, but the city had still not surrendered. He wondered what its people felt, looking out at the army squatting beneath their city. He remembered gazing down on the same army from his own city. Then, he had felt only despair, the impossible desire to undo what had been done, to relive his life in differently, and make a better choice.

But Babylon was different. Perhaps they were pleased to be separated from a world that was not worthy of them, the way heroes and even entire cities were said to have been spirited away by the Gods, thus freed from the imperfect earth. It would bring an end to contamination by the foreigners who came to gawp at their treasures, the emissaries from lesser nations who came to barter and bargain and plead and threaten, the migrants who tried to find work and make a life for themselves in a city that was already overcrowded. For those who had already established the perfect city, what use was the rest of the world?

'Free of your duties?' a voice said behind him. He started in surprise. He had not heard Maia's approach.

'For a moment,' he said. 'And you?'

'The same.'

She looked up at the city walls, and Croesus turned back to follow her gaze. The thick walls towered high, the battlements fringed with white paint like a snow line, as though they were laying siege to a mountain range. They might as well have been, he thought, for all their army could achieve against those walls.

'How long will it take?' she said.

'Ten years, they say.'

'They are well prepared.'

'They have known Cyrus was coming for a long time.'

'Ten years is a long time for them to live on bread and barley beer.'

'It is a long time to stay out here,' Croesus said. 'Then again, your husband was lecturing me, by the Gyndes, on the virtues of waiting.'

'Ah, yes. That old refrain.'

'You have heard it yourself?'

'Many times.'

'Well, I don't want to wait here. I don't want to die looking up at Babylon. I feel as though I have been dreaming of it my whole life. Don't you want to see Babylon?'

'One place is the same as another for a slave.'

'Now you do sound like Isocrates. I don't believe you,' he said. He gestured towards the city, like some charlatan conjurer directing villagers towards his stall. 'Everything began there. If there is an answer to be found, it must be in there. They have been looking longer than anyone else. What do you say to that?'

'It doesn't matter how grand a city it is. We'll be stuck in the kitchens and the throne rooms, serving our masters. You won't get to see the wonders either way.'

'You may be right,' he said.

She paused for a moment. 'I could be wrong,' she said. 'The Gods have been cruel to you so far.'

'I was king of Lydia. I would not call myself lacking in fortune. Just in wit.'

'I would have rather spent a life as a slave than have lost what you have lost. So the Gods owe you this. They will find a way for you to see the city.'

Croesus considered this for a time. 'Perhaps,' he said. He looked at her.

'They are letting you see Gyges?'

'They are. My thanks for that.'

'And is he well?'

She shook her head. 'No.'

'No? He looked different by the river.'

'He looked happy, you mean.' She sighed. 'I don't know what is wrong. Ever since we came here to the city, he is as he was back in Sardis.'

'I'm sorry. I wish I knew what to do.'

Maia paused. 'Perhaps he wants to see the city as much as you do,' she said. 'And waiting out here in its shadow is what unsettles him.'

'You really think that's possible?'

'I don't know. Perhaps.'

Croesus nodded, half to himself. 'Then we will find a way inside. I promise you that.'

He felt her hand on his shoulder for a moment, then he heard her

261

walk away, back to the tents and to her duties. He was alone with the city once more.

He stayed there for a time, watching one particular light in the city. It flickered in a distant Babylonian window like a dim star seen through passing clouds. It could have been lit for a king, or for a slave attending some nocturnal errand, for all Croesus knew, but for some reason he imagined that it was the light of some ordinary market trader, a butcher or a weaver or a baker. He imagined for a moment that it was his light, his city, that he had never known the burden of kingship, or the shame of slavery.

The light went out. Croesus went to find his tent, to join the owner of the light, his Babylonian counterpart, in sleep.

12

The council met each day in Cyrus's tent. They sat in a circle and drank water and wine, and spoke of the fall of Babylon.

They discussed tunnelling beneath the walls, or raising a mound to go over them. They considered constructing engines to breach them; they thought of ways they might spread disease inside the city, and of deceptions that might enable a band of men to get inside to take the gates. They traded rumours of heroes who were reputed to be wandering in distant lands and who might be drawn into the fight. They summoned bards to sing of the battles and sieges of the ancient world, in the hope that some inspiration might come from them.

One by one, plans were proposed and then rejected. The flaws of some were apparent almost immediately. Other proposals were surrendered reluctantly, giving way only after sustained examination revealed their weaknesses. Sometimes, a plan would take shape late at night when the wineskins were empty, and all in the king's tent would be caught up in the excitement of fresh inspiration. It was only in the sober morning that such plans unravelled. At other times, they would come up with an idea that seemed workable during the day. Only later in the evening, in a haze of sweet wine, would the fatal flaw in the scheme emerge. No conceit was able to withstand their consideration both when drunk and when sober.

Some in the council tentatively began to suggest that Babylon could not be taken. That they should travel north or east or south and find another place to conquer. Cyrus received their opinions respectfully and without reprimand, but he was insistent. Babylon would fall. As months passed, generals and councillors and slaves all grew weary of the endless plotting, but the king never seemed to tire. As time went on, the contrast became too apparent to ignore.

'You looked exhausted, Croesus,' the king said at the end of one such meeting.

'We are all tired, master. Except you.'

Cyrus smiled. 'It would not be satisfying if it were easy. I don't know if it can be done. It may exist in that narrow place between the impossible and the barely possible. But that is where all the greatest things hide.'

'Poetic, master.'

'Thank you, Croesus,' the king said dryly. 'You must be weary if you feel so free to mock me.' He thought for a moment. 'We shan't meet tomorrow. Or the day after that. We will stay apart for as long as it takes. With a little time away, we shall find our solution.'

'Thank you, master.' Croesus tried to smile. 'Perhaps you are right,' he said. But he did not believe it.

On their third day of rest, a familiar figure rejoined the army.

Croesus was out by the banks of the Euphrates, resting his tired feet in the water, when he heard footsteps approach. One pair of feet were treading lightly, making an uneven rhythm against the steady heavy tramp of armed men. He turned, expecting to see Cyrus or one of his advisors. But it was Harpagus and his bodyguards, standing only a few feet away from him.

Croesus started at the sight of him, and Harpagus laughed. 'Did you think I was a spirit, come to haunt you?'

'I thought you were on the other side of the world. You shouldn't creep up on an old man like that,' Croesus said. 'When did you arrive?'

'Just now. I was going to see the king before he slept. I saw you wandering out here, and thought I would surprise you. As I have.'

'You forget that I spent years in fear of you,' Croesus said. He paused, looking on the other man. Harpagus seemed older, he thought, though it had been little more than a year that they had been parted. 'Your wars are over?'

'Yes. The last city fell a year ago. The king's ridiculous work on the Gyndes gave me plenty of time to catch up with you. I would have hoped that you might have talked him out of that one, Croesus.'

'Well, you have come at the right time, if you can find a way into Babylon.'

'What has been decided?'

'Nothing. Cyrus is waiting for someone to give him an impossible answer.'

'You think it can't be done?'

'I am sure it can be done. I just don't know how. We need another trick. As when the king routed my cavalry with his camels.'

Harpagus laughed. 'That was my idea, you know,' the general said.

'Really?' Croesus shook his head. 'I should have known.'

They stared at the city in silence.

'Have you ever been there?' Croesus said eventually.

'No,' Harpagus said. 'It wasn't permitted, when I served Astyages. He found its existence intimidating – the world's most famous city, so close to his borders. He forbade us to even mention its name, and tried to forget it was there.'

'I wanted to hear everything I could about it, when I was a king,' Croesus said. 'Every story.'

'I don't suppose you happened to hear the story of how to conquer it?'

'I am afraid not.' Croesus smiled gently. 'But I did always want to set my eyes on it.'

'Now you will get your chance.'

'If I do, it will be in ruins. I never thought I would play a part in destroying it.'

Silence fell again, filled by the low hum of noise from the army, and the rushing of the Euphrates as it passed by the camp and flowed into the city.

'It was quite something, you know,' Croesus said.

'What?'

'The draining of the river. I have never seen anything like it.'

'Vanity,' Harpagus said. 'That's all. Cyrus cannot do anything simply. He has to find some new way that no one else would think of.'

'I would have thought you would admire that.'

'Originality isn't always brilliance, Croesus. There are good reasons that some things have never been done.'

'Perhaps you are right. Sacrificing a river. Perhaps it is an idea that should have remained in his head.'

There was silence. Croesus looked up, and found Harpagus staring back at him intently.

'What is it?' Croesus said.

'You have given me an idea, Croesus.' He looked out across the city. 'I know a way into Babylon.'

'What?'

Harpagus waved away any questions. 'I shall tell you tomorrow, when I have had time to consider it a little more. Sleep well, mighty king,' he said, and began to walk away. 'Sleep and dream of Babylon. You'll see it soon enough.'

'In ruins?' Croesus shouted after him, as the general disappeared to his tent.

'No!' Harpagus replied. 'I will keep it in one piece, just for you.' He was gone.

*

The next day in the council tent, Harpagus's suggestion was greeted by silence.

Eventually, Cyrus repeated the general's words back to him as a question. 'Drain the river?'

'Yes,' Harpagus replied.

Cyrus cocked his head. 'There are wells inside the walls,' he said. 'Stop the river, and they will still have water.'

'We aren't going to starve them out. We are going to take the city by force.' All in the tent stared at him expectantly, but he said nothing more.

'Continue,' Cyrus said, 'stop toying with us and looking pleased with yourself. Tell me how.'

'The river enters the city at the north wall,' Harpagus said. 'Too high to send men in there, and the current is too strong. But if we can lower the water, we can enter the city.'

'They will notice that the river is sinking,' Cyraxes said. 'They will be ready for us.'

'I have thought of that. We dam it as we dig the channels far out of sight of the city. Maybe even make a show of retreat. Then, open the dams, and drain the river all at once. At night. Then, we go in and take a gate. We need only one open gate, then we have the city.' Harpagus allowed himself a small smile. 'It has never been done before. I should imagine that would appeal to you, Cyrus.'

Cyrus nodded slowly. The others waited as he silently considered the plan, testing it for a weakness, a flaw like the ones that had unravelled all of the others. There was none. 'Thank you, Harpagus,' Cyrus said at last.

'Croesus gave me the inspiration last night. It is him you should thank.'

'He mocks me,' Croesus said. 'I mentioned your sacrifice of the Gyndes to him, that is all.'

'With both of you so eager to avoid praise, let's see whether it will succeed first.' He turned to another general, Gobryas. 'Can you drain another river for me?'

The general looked crestfallen, and Cyrus laughed. 'I am sorry, my friend. I am sure that you are weary of digging channels. Your men too. We are warriors, not farmers. But this will be the last time, I promise you.'

As the others talked, some distant memory, submerged in Croesus's mind, came to the surface. 'In six weeks, they hold a great festival. Belshazzar. The entire city will be celebrating. We won't get another chance as good as that.'

The king nodded. 'Do you think we can do it in six weeks?'

'We won't get much sleep,' Gobryas said. 'But we will manage.'

'Very good. Let us begin.'

'So that was your plan?' Croesus said to Harpagus as they left the tent.

'Our plan, Croesus,' Harpagus replied. 'You also played your part.'

'Don't say that. I have had enough of helping your conquests.'

'Rest easy on this one. You haven't helped to destroy Babylon – you have helped to save it.'

'What do you mean?'

'There are ways to take any city. Even Babylon. But you gave me the only right way.'

'How so?'

'Oh, you will laugh at this. But I want to take it peacefully.'

Croesus stopped and studied Harpagus to see if he was joking, but there was no trace of humour on the other man's face. 'You surprise me, Harpagus.'

The general nodded. 'I saw something terrible out in the west,' he said. 'After you had gone.'

'You saw plenty of terrible things while I was still there.'

'No.' He shook his head. 'This was different.' He lapsed into silence.

'Tell me. If you want to, that is.'

Harpagus thought it over. 'Very well,' he said. 'Let us find a quiet place.'

Finding a peaceful place in the camp was no easy matter. Rumours were already spreading through the army, and orders followed them close behind, like thunder chasing lightning. The paths of the camp were filled with cavalry riding past, carts piled high with picks and shovels, groups of men heading for their assigned places, cursing both the Gods and their leaders for making them labour on yet another river.

After searching for a time, they found a quiet corner. A large store tent had been left unguarded, piled high with arrows wrapped in skin and bound with leather thongs. One hundred arrows in each wrap, ten thousand bundles all told, enough to destroy an army, or murder a city. They went inside, Harpagus stalking about the tent, cursing the captain of the watch for allowing the guards of the tent to slip away, whilst Croesus busied himself with fashioning a couple of seats out of the stacks of ammunition.

The two old men sat side by side on the piles of weapons, listening without speaking to the sounds of the army outside, as Croesus waited for the other man to order his thoughts. Eventually, Harpagus spoke.

'Xanthus,' he said, carefully sounding out both syllables. He fell silent, as though it had cost him much to utter the name again. 'A city in Lycia,' he said, 'one of the last cities in the west to fall. Their army came out to meet us. They would not run, and they would not surrender. Not even when there were a hundred left, wounded and surrounded, up against my fifty thousand. We killed them, to a man. Then we marched on to take their city.' He paused for a moment. 'That's when we saw fire on the horizon.'

269

'They burned their own city?'

'Yes. But not just that. We heard the story from the survivors, fleeing across the plains towards us. Grateful to see us, if you would believe it.' He paused again. 'There were only a dozen or so.'

'A dozen survivors from Xanthus? Many thousands lived there, from what I heard.'

'Not any more,' Harpagus said. 'They told us that when the men heard our army was coming, they filled their temples with every treasure they had. Then they dragged their slaves inside, their women and children. They barricaded the doors, piled wood around them. Then they set fire to the wood. And after that, after they had set light to everything and everyone that had ever meant anything to them, they marched out to meet us. To die.' Harpagus paused, his fingers picking absently at the bundle of arrows beside to him. 'I thought of what must have gone through their minds, as they barricaded their children inside, as they burned their city to the ground, watched their gold run like water and listened to their women scream. What can make a man think like that? Where that seemed like the right thing to do? Then I realized that we had done that to them. I see that city in my dreams now.' He looked sharply at Croesus. 'You can laugh. I know you want to, hearing me talk this way. You must be pleased.'

'It is a little late to have regrets like this, don't you think? That's what you said to me. That there will always be another war.'

'I did. But perhaps we can take Babylon without much of a fight. Who knows what will happen in the next war? But we can fight this one a better way.'

'Perhaps. But it is too late for you as well, you know. No matter what you do now, you will always be considered a monster to the Ionians. They will sing stories to their children. The terrible Mede destroyer who came from the east and put their people to the sword.'

'I thought of you, you know,' he said. 'When I saw Xanthus burning.' He stood. 'Enough. I have matters to attend to.'

'I am sure you do. Good luck, Harpagus.'

'With what?'

Croesus smiled. 'With whatever it is you need to do.'

'The same to you.' Then, shaking his head again, a tired man trying to dispel a troublesome thought, he walked away.

13

It was only on the night before the attack on Babylon that Croesus finally found the courage to visit his son again.

Gyges sat alone in a corner of the tent. All the others stood some distance apart. It seemed that even in the depths of their particular insanities, they had learned to avoid him. When Croesus sat next to him, Gyges made no response. His son was hunched over, running his thumb over the knuckles of his closed fist.

'Gyges.'

His son said nothing. Looking at him, Croesus could feel his fear rise again. No, he thought. I refuse to be afraid of my son.

'I know you are suffering. I wish that I could help.'

'No.' The word came out flat, quiet, and resigned.

'Is it this waiting you hate?'

'No.'

'We are going to take the city tonight. We won't have to wait here any longer.'

At this, Gyges finally looked at him. 'No,' he said again.

Was this the only word he had left? Croesus thought. 'Our lives will be better in Babylon,' he said. 'I promise. There will be a place for you there.'

'No!'

'Please, tell me how to help you!' At this, he thought he saw a sudden weakness, a need in Gyges's eyes, perhaps even a need he could fulfil. Instinctively, he raised his hands and reached out to his son.

Gyges backed away from him. 'No! No! No!' He was standing and screaming at him now, and Croesus stepped back. He saw Gyges cast a hopeless glance over his shoulder, towards the entrance of the tent. He followed his son's gaze, looking on the farmlands out to the west, the horses grazing by the side of the river. In that moment, Croesus thought that he finally understood his son.

'I am sorry, Gyges,' he said. 'I will come again.'

'No!'

His son might have had only one word left to him, but Croesus knew that Gyges spoke the truth. He knew that he would not come back.

When he saw Cyrus sitting on the ground in his tent with many soldiers, Croesus assumed they must have won the honour during the draining of the river. Perhaps they were the fastest diggers, or had hunted down a scout who might have otherwise given away the Persian plan. Cyrus liked to reward such men with the finest wine and drummed music until dawn. But there was something different about this gathering; it was somehow unlike the others that Croesus had witnessed. It was not a celebration.

No wine was passed around, and all the men still wore their armour and had swords belted at their waists. Armed men, aside from the bodyguards, were never admitted into Cyrus's presence. They sat quietly, staring into space. Croesus counted them, and saw that there were fifty.

It was only when he saw the rest of the weapons piled by the entrance, saw the glittering silver and gold at the tips of the spears, that Croesus realized who they were. Fifty of the Immortals, the ten thousand elite spearmen of the Persian army. It was the regiment that never died, for no matter how many fell in a single battle, at roll call the next day ten thousand would answer, the dead replaced by new men. No one knew how many faces the regiment had worn, in its time. They were the finest warriors that the king had.

Cyrus sat beside them, one at a time, talking privately to each man. After he had spoken to all of them, the men gathered in a circle and opened a small, plain wooden chest. It contained a fine black powder – soot, Croesus soon realized, as the men began to coat their skin with it. Cyrus helped them, blackening patches of clothing or skin that the men had missed. His hands were soon black with soot, like theirs.

They worked silently at this strange ritual until they were entirely covered in soot, pale eyes blinking out of black faces, a shocking white, like bone amidst ash. After they had finished, Cyrus stood. The men gathered together at his feet, like children listening to their father speak.

'Some of you will die tonight,' he said. 'Perhaps all of you. All who live will be given land and gold enough to ennoble them. All who die will have the honours passed on to their children.' He paused, and looked at each man in turn. 'But I am not asking you to risk your lives merely for land and wealth. This is your chance to be a part of something greater than yourselves. To build an empire the world will not forget. To take the city that they said could never fall. To become truly immortal.

'No one will forget what you do tonight. Know that your king is proud of you. Know that you shame him with such courage. Thank you.' He clapped his hands once, like a priest completing a ritual, striking soot from his hands in a cloud of black smoke.

They did not cheer. Each man stood in turn, and Cyrus kissed him on the forehead. Then, as one, they bowed to their king, and marched out of the tent and into the night. Almost all of them had gone when the king pulled one aside. 'Hyroeades, wait,' Cyrus said. He beckoned

Croesus closer, a half-smile on his face, and the slave came forward slowly, studying the face of this other man.

He had touches of grey in his hair and a well-lined face, but he did not carry himself like a veteran. He had the awkward uncertainty of a much younger man, and as he stood in front of Croesus he looked at the ground and avoided the other man's eyes.

'Do you know who this is, Croesus?' Cyrus said.

'No.'

'He is the man who found the way into Sardis.'

Croesus stared at him. 'What?'

'He climbed the south wall, and led our people in. I thought you might like to meet him.'

'I see,' Croesus said. He looked at Hyroeades for a time, but could not think of anything to say.

The other man tried to smile at him. 'It is an honour to meet you, Croesus,' he said.

Cyrus laughed. 'An Immortal honoured to meet a slave.' He clapped the soldier on the back. 'Go now. And good luck.'

The man bowed deeply to Cyrus, and then, in an instinctive after-thought, bowed to Croesus as well. Whether it was an honour for his previous station, or some kind of apology, Croesus could not tell. Hyroeades straightened up quickly, as if embarrassed, and hurried out to join his companions.

'It will be tonight, then?' Croesus said.

'Yes. Everything is ready.'

'They are the ones who will enter the city. When the river falls.'

'Yes.'

'Will any of them live?'

'No. Some of them will make it to the gates. They might even reach the palace. But the Babylonians will cut them down long before we can rescue them.'

'I see.' Croesus hesitated. 'You wanted to see me about some matter?'

'I only wanted someone else to see those men before they died. So you can help me to remember them, if I should forget.' The king sighed. 'You can go now. I wish to sleep.'

Croesus stood on the bank of the Euphrates and looked over the city walls, trying to find the same light that he had watched six weeks before. He could not find it. Perhaps his Babylonian counterpart had gone to the festival and had left his home dark. Even from this distance, Croesus could hear the beating of the drums that summoned the people of the city. Though the citizens of Babylon did not know it, the drummers were calling to the invaders as well.

Croesus took off his battered leather shoes, hitched up his tunic, sat on the river bank, and dipped his feet into the water up to the knee. He shivered at the cold.

He remembered walking with his father on a bridge over the Pactolus, looking down and seeing his fortune glittering there beneath the clear water. He remembered the great Maeander, which had run through his old kingdom like a twisting artery, all the way to the coast. And the Halys which he had crossed, dreaming of empire. The Gyndes, where he and Isocrates had traded their secrets. And now the Euphrates. He had heard that the Hellenes believed that they crossed another river when they died. It seemed fitting, that the land of the dead would lie on the far side of a river. His life amounted to nothing more, he thought, than the crossing of one river after another. The shifting flow of water that was always the same, always different, and ever unchanged by his passage.

Croesus sat by the river, listening to the drums of the distant city beat out their alien, syncopated rhythm. He waited for the water to fall.

14

Hyroeades stood on the bank of the river, and the fifty Immortals waited with him, all of them silent, studying the water, waiting for a sign from the Gods.

Some believed that he, Hyroeades, had the blessing of the Gods. The other Immortals, only half in jest, called him the conquerer of Sardis. He remembered that the moon had been thin on that night too, casting just enough light for him to identify the vertical path of hand- and foot-holds that led him to the top. He remembered his hand shaking as it closed over the stone at the very top of the wall; he had been more afraid of finding a Lydian waiting for him than he had been of falling to his death. But there had been no one there.

He had tied the rope and tugged on it six times, and the army had followed him up. Each man, as he crested the top of the wall, touched a hand to Hyroeades's forehead and whispered a blessing before moving on. As the Persians advanced into Sardis and the killing began, none had noticed him quietly slip away, down the north cliff to find a place to sleep and wait out the slaughter.

Hyroeades had felt that he deserved no glory. He had merely followed what he had seen another man do. He had to catch him- self each time he was fêted, restraining himself from praising the Lydian who had first made the climb. After the city fell, he had been summoned by Harpagus to receive his reward. He had hoped they would free him from the army, give him enough land or money to live free of the wars, to take a wife, grow crops, raise children. Instead, they offered him a place in the Immortals, the highest honour a common soldier could hope to receive. He had taken it. There seemed no way to refuse.

Downstream, the captain of the Immortals dipped a long reed into the water. He did so every few minutes, always with the same practised motion, the backhanded, downward thrust of a finishing blow. It had developed the quality of ritual.

When the river fell, it fell slowly, like a man sitting upright who only slowly drifts off to sleep, summoned by his dreams. At first Hyroeades could not be sure that the falling water level was the consequence of their work. He had been fooled several times already by the random ebbing and flowing of the water. But eventually, there could be no doubting it. Now, each man watched the reed as it descended into the river, the water covering less of it each time.

They had asked for fifty volunteers for the attack by the river, and Hyroeades had no intention of volunteering. But when the ten thousand had stepped forward as one, he could not remain behind. What were the odds that he would be chosen, he thought, and so, half a step behind the rest, he too stepped forward. But when they drew the lots from the helmet, his name had come up.

He wondered if his lot had been fixed. If they had ensured that he would be sent inside to help take Babylon, believing his luck would let them take a second unconquerable city. And afterwards, when he saw the relief in the faces of those who had not been chosen, he wondered how many others had thought as he had, how many had come close to not stepping forward. They had been trapped by ideas of honour and duty, unaware that it was dissent that brought the blessing of the Gods, not blind obedience.

For the tenth time, the captain thrust the reed into the Euphrates.

This time, he did not pull it out again. He opened his hand and cast it into the river, and the reed moved slowly with the now sluggish water, leading the way into city. The captain's empty hand rose, and gestured them forward. As one, the Immortals stepped into the water.

Hyroeades kept his eyes fixed on the walls, but saw no sentries there. The few who remained would be high up in the distant watch-towers, cursing that they had drawn sentry duty on the day of the festival. They would be watching for some massed, sudden assault on the gates. None could have suspected that it would be the river, the flowing artery of the city, that would betray them.

They reached the base of the wall where the river met the city, and gazed into the tunnel ahead. The ceiling was low, but there was still enough room for their heads and shoulders to remain above the water. The captain paused for a moment, peering into the tunnel, perhaps thinking that it was a bad place for a warrior to lead his men, his instincts rebelling against the possibility of a trap. He waved his hand again, stepped forward, and disappeared into the blackness. Hyroeades and the others followed close behind.

They kept their arms high to preserve the soot on their skins, their elbows up and hands together like men at prayer. The view ahead was obstructed by the men in front of him, and after only a few steps Hyroeades found himself in perfect darkness. He listened to the steady breathing of the men around him, amplified by the stone and water, as though he were sharing the tunnel with some great creature of the river. He thought of what would happen if the water suddenly rose, if some distant downpour half a continent away flooded down through the Euphrates. He thought of them kicking and clawing to get out, of drowning in the dark.

He reached up and felt the stone above his head, still wet from where the river had touched it not an hour before. Hyroeades remem-bered the feel of the stone at Sardis. Suspended between worlds, he

279

had felt calm and fearless. He had, he thought, never been happier. Perhaps if he had fallen then, he could have died happy.

The quality of the darkness changed, and Hyroeades's trailing hand touched not stone, but air. They were through the tunnel, and into the alien city.

They gathered together, and the captain counted down the line and divided the group in two, taking one man aside as leader of the second group. Hyroeades watched as twenty-five men left silently behind their new leader, circling west below the city wall. They were the men who would take the north-west gate, and Hyroeades watched them with envy. Some of them might still live to see the rest of the army arrive, he thought. But we won't.

They headed deeper into the city. Each man, under his breath, repeating the directions they had been given. They had all sat and memorized them the night before, chanting them together like children reciting a song. Two hundred steps south, and then left along the canal. Proceed until the temple of Nabu, then left again, up the steps and into the royal palace. Keep the ziggurat on your right, and do not go towards the drums.

They were on the canal path, heading east, when the captain waved them to the ground, whispering a curse. Hyroeades was near the front of the group, and he could see a Babylonian walking down the street towards them.

It was a young girl, a slave or a daughter running an errand, occasionally stopping to gaze wistfully in the direction of the drums. She reached a small bridge over the canal and stopped, considering in which direction to go. Right, towards the drums and the festival, or straight ahead, towards the Euphrates. She shrugged and turned to her right, stepping on to the bridge. Hyroeades heard the captain exhale slightly.

The girl gave one last look down the canal path, and stopped, one foot on the bridge and one on the bank. She blinked, and peered more closely.

Hyroeades felt the slinger to his left shift his weight. A slap of leather, the sharp crack of rock against bone, and the girl fell.

They came forward, and stood over the girl. She twitched and jerked on the ground, blood pouring from her head, but she still lived, her eyes looking up at the men who stood over her, her mouth struggling to form words. One of the others knelt over the girl, and drew his knife. Hyroeades turned away. She could not have been older than fourteen.

In front of him was a dark, narrow alley. He could slip down it, perhaps, while the others were not looking. Throw away his sword and armour, wash the soot from his face, and plunge into the crowds. Who would notice a strange face? Babylon was the city of a thousand languages, he had been told. There was no such thing as a foreigner here. He could find a woman at the festival, and if he married her before dawn her family would have to take him in. He might still live beyond this night, if he could find the courage to take a chance.

The moment passed. One of the other Immortals tapped him on the shoulder, and Hyroeades fell into step with the rest of the men. He kept his eyes open for another moment when his companions would be distracted, when he might have an opportunity to escape. But no chance came, and they were past the temple of Nabu and at the palace gates.

The captain divided them again. Ten men concealed themselves as best they could outside the palace gates, and fifteen were chosen to go inside the palace. The ten were sure to die, buying time for the others, but they took up their positions without question. Hyroeades wondered if it were blind chance that he was chosen as one of the fifteen, or if the captain believed that he had the Gods' blessing, and wanted to keep him close to the very end. He felt a strange, useless comfort in the thought that at least he would live a little longer than the men outside.

They headed up the steps, expecting at any moment the shout of alarm, the hail of javelins and sling stones that would end their lives. It did not come. Outside the unguarded entrance, they pulled off their muddied boots and cast them aside. Barefoot, like penitents before a temple, they passed through the gates.

The palace was deserted. Almost all of Babylon was attending the festival, but the king, so their spies reported, would not be there. Only he and a few of his guards would remain in the palace that night for, unpopular as he was, he appeared at as few public occasions as he could for fear of mockery. From time to time they heard someone passing through the corridors. A slave on some late-night errand, a wandering guard, a nobleman creeping from one bedchamber to another. In the empty palace, sound carried and echoed to such an extent that they could not tell if they were on the opposite side of the building or only a single corridor away.

Hyroeades found the emptiness unsettling. Great halls, built to hold hundreds, echoed their soft footsteps back to them. Kitchens with dozens of cooking pots and ceilings black with soot were empty and silent. It was as if the palace, perhaps even the entire city, had been abandoned in the wake of some great disaster, or as if the Babylonians, anticipating the fall of their city, had left it for some other world, melting away into the air in an act of collective magic.

Kings had ruled here for thousands of years, Hyroeades had heard. He could not imagine that the world could be so old. He wondered if, in all the centuries, intruders had ever stepped inside the sacred palace walls, if this was the first time armed foreigners had made it this far. Their presence had the feeling of desecration, of blasphemy. Somewhere, he was certain, a god was stirring to punish them. They had only a short time to complete their mission before he came for them.

They reached the stairwell that led to the royal chambers. After a moment's hesitation, while he listened for some clink of armour above that might indicate that it was guarded, the captain led them up.

They were packed close together in the winding stairwell, designed so that few could hold it against many. A pair of guards above them could have held off fifty men. Hyroeades was reminded of the water tunnel, though now, rather than the smell of the river, the air was rank with the sweat of the men around him. Slowly and silently, they made their way to the highest level of the palace.

They were not alone. Close by, Hyroeades could hear talking in a language he did not understand. Though the tongue was unfamiliar, the tone he understood – bored men passing the time with idle stories. After the long silence it was almost a relief to hear other voices.

The captain looked around the corner and ducked back quickly. He held up both hands and extended all his fingers, repeated the motion. Twenty was the signal. Twenty men guarding the king's chamber. Their luck, it seemed, had finally run out.

The captain pulled the man next to him close and whispered in his ear. The other man listened and nodded, then moved down the line, tapping a number of other men on the shoulder as he went. He hesitated beside Hyroeades, and looked back at the captain, who shook his head. The other man continued down the line, until he had touched nine other men. He beckoned to them to follow him back the way they had come.

The ten made their way silently back down the stairs. The captain, Hyroeades, and three others went into an empty chamber. They waited.

He thought of how easily he and the others would be replaced. The next day, fifty men would be summoned to serve the king. The Immortals, the ten thousand who had worn a hundred thousand different faces, the regiment that could never die. What did his life matter, if his place could be taken so quickly? He thought of how swiftly sons replaced fathers, infants replaced the elderly. Barely had you stopped breathing before you became an irrelevance, as though you had never lived at all. What did anyone's life matter, king or soldier or slave, if they could be replaced in moments and the world go on without them? Our lives mean nothing, he thought to himself. My life means nothing.

Distant sounds, piercing in the silence, reached him from another part of the palace. War cries, the clash of swords. The other Immortals, he realized, had gone to cause a diversion. Somewhere, Hyroeades could hear some great copper gong being struck. The alarm, summoning the guards from around the palace to defend their king, calling the Gods to let them know there were intruders in a sacred place. Either way, he thought, at the Gods' hands or the Babylonians', we will all be dead soon.

They listened as the guards ran past and tried to count how many had gone, how many would remain for them to face. Once the footsteps had faded away, the captain crawled back out to look around the corner again. He looked back, and this time, he held up just two fingers.

The captain looked at each man in turn and nodded, giving an order and asking a question in one gesture. Hyroeades found himself nodding back, giving his consent without thinking. They stood and touched their swords together, then charged out into the corridor.

The two Babylon guards turned to face them, their faces frozen in shock even as they set their spears. The two Immortals in front, the captain and his second in command, died on those iron points. They must have known they would, pitting swords against spears, buying victory with their lives, and before the Babylonians could withdraw their weapons the others were on them, striking them to ground, their swords falling, rising dark with blood.

The others hurried into the king's chamber, but Hyroeades remained at the entrance. He knelt and looked back to the stairwell, listening to the muffled screams from within as the king died.

He had been in Cyrus's army for almost a decade, but he had always tried to find his place away from the fighting. Who knew how many deaths he had caused, leading the Persians into Sardis. But he had never killed a man with his own hands. And he would not kill one now. It was not much of an ambition at the end of a life, he thought. He wished he could have done something else, something better. He wished that he could have lived differently.

He heard the sound of feet pounding up the stairs, echoing louder as they drew closer. A dozen Babylonian guards came into view, their faces marked with the blood of his companions. They looked at him with death in their eyes.

As he saw them, saw their eyes fix on him, a terrible relief struck him. He knew then that he was going to die, that the time for choices was over and only one path lay ahead of him. He understood, at last, what courage was – when there are no choices but one. His dreams had given him other paths to follow, his hopes had made him a coward. Now, at the end of all hope, he knew he could be brave. He knew he could die well. He ran forward, his sword held high, and hoped that they would kill him quickly.

The gates opened, and the Persians entered Babylon.

Marching in close order, row after row of spearmen and archers went into the city. It was one of the largest armies that the world had yet seen, but it had almost met its equal in this vast labyrinth of streets. It was as if the city had been designed to provide a last line of defence if its people failed to protect it, built to swallow up armies like some beast of the ancient times.

The Persians filtered through the city like a medicinal compound absorbed by the blood, past gardens and towers and temples, spreading to every corner of Babylon, as if it were only by traversing every street before the dawn came that the city would be conquered. They wandered, less as warriors now, in the absence of any army to oppose them, and more as curious travellers to a strange and alien place. Gradually, disbelieving that the city could be taken so effortlessly, the Persians were drawn by the sound of the drums to the heart of Babylon, and once there, they gazed on a spectacle that they could never have dreamed they might see.

Perhaps a hundred thousand people filled the main square, equal at least in number to the army that came to conquer them, moving to music that seemed to shake the earth. They gathered in small circles around elderly storytellers, swam like clumsy children in the diminished waters of the Euphrates, made love openly on the ground. They drank and danced, and shouted their welcome to the new arrivals.

If they were aware that their city was being taken, that these were invaders come to impose a foreign rule over them, the Babylonians gave no sign. Even when a regiment of Persian spearmen marched into the square, in a confused and unnecessary show of force, the people of Babylon seemed as delighted by the newcomers as by the arrival of a troupe of acrobats or a great musician from the east. They held up their hands, and asked the Persians to join them, for on the night of the festival they understood the irrelevance of kings and slaves, of cities and empires. They knew that the world would be reordered in the morning, but it did not matter. For one night alone, there was nothing but the dance.

The Persians laid aside their tall spears and wicker shields, their decorated quivers and curved bows. They called for drums and flasks of wine, and came forward unarmed into the square, not as conquerers or liberators, but as revellers.

They drank and danced together under the stars, until the dawn came to banish them all back to their homes the way thought banishes a dream, and time destroys all things.

The sun rose, the people slept, knowing that when they awoke they would be ruled by a new king. They slept contentedly, and dreamed deeply, for they knew that this did not matter. They knew that it changed nothing.

Babylon

I

'What do you make of it?'

'Master?'

'The city, Croesus. What do you think?'

Croesus hesitated. He did not know what to say.

Cyrus had entered the city that morning to find Babylon still sleeping after the evening's revelry. The few who were still awake, blinking at the harshness of the light and heavy-headed with drink, had come out on to the streets to meet their new king.

Cyrus installed himself in the palace even as the slaves still scrubbed blood from the stone floors. It had been the only battlefield in the conquest of the city. There had been no looting and no other bloodshed. It was the most peaceful conquest that Croesus had ever known. The city taken for the price of fifty dead.

Cyrus rested his chin on his hand, and smiled at his slave, reading his silence.

'You are disappointed with Babylon?'

'No, it is undoubtedly beautiful.'

'You do not sound particularly interested.'

'I used to live for wonders, and if one lives for wonders, one must come to Babylon. Now that I am here, I am not so sure.'

'What do you live for now, then?'

'I do not know.' Croesus shrugged. 'I'm hoping I will find out. Before I die.'

'What a morbid thought. Perhaps I should ask myself the same question. The wonders don't move me either. What is my excuse?'

'You too are old, Cyrus.'

The king laughed. 'I should have you beheaded for that. But that's not it. As a symbol, Babylon means everything to me. As a city, it is a troublesome prize. It will make one of my governors over-powerful, and the rest jealous. I desired the essence of Babylon. To be the man who rules the greatest city in the world. The reality is rather tedious.'

Croesus shook his head. 'And they called me a dreamer when I was a king.'

'Perhaps that is my secret. I can dream greater than those I conquer. Including you.' Cyrus toyed with a silk curtain that ran from the ceiling and trailed beside his new throne.

'Babylon,' he said. 'I came to this city not knowing whether I wanted to possess it or destroy it. I almost burned it to the ground.' He turned back to Croesus. 'Would that have been a terrible thing?'

'You would have destroyed a place of beauty.'

'Yes.' Cyrus thought to himself for a moment. 'I had in mind to write something. A proclamation. It is the custom here. First, the king must go north to a temple and perform a ritual of theirs. I have sent Cambyses to take care of that. Then, each new king of Babylon writes of his ambitions on a clay cylinder, declares them to the people, and buries the cylinder in one of the walls.'

'What will you write?'

'Some of it will be straightforward enough. I have to vilify my predecessor.'

'Will you enjoy that?'

'It is hubristic to enjoy it too much. That is the fate of kings like us. Gods whilst we live, objects of mockery the moment we die. I have to win over their Gods as well, proclaim myself as their champion.'

'You aren't afraid of blasphemy?'

'There is only one God, Croesus. He takes many aspects. This Marduk is just another one.'

'What else will you say?'

'I don't know. I have yet to decide how to rule this city.' He turned to face Croesus again. 'I was hoping for a little help from you.'

'I am not much of a man of words.'

'I have scribes for words, Croesus. I am interested in your ideas.' He leaned forward. 'What do you think makes people happy?'

Croesus said nothing at first. He looked at Cyrus's face, that ageless face that had conquered countless nations, but saw no sign of mockery there. 'Master?'

'What makes people happy? Not men like you and me. Ordinary people.'

'How can I answer that?' Croesus thought for a time. 'By the river, Isocrates told me he is happiest when nothing is changing. He just wants to be left alone by his master.'

'I wouldn't have called him an ordinary man.'

'No?'

'Perhaps you don't see it, having known him for so long. But it is an interesting idea. Being left alone. I shall think on it.' Cyrus yawned. 'You may go,' he said. 'I will summon my scribes to begin their work. I will be curious to see what you think, when we are done. And I have a reward for you.'

'What's that?'

'I want you to take a day of freedom,' Cyrus said. 'You and your friends. Isocrates and his woman. Explore the city and see if you change your mind about it.'

Croesus stared at the king for a moment, unsure if he had heard correctly, if Cyrus had really uttered that old, now unfamiliar word. 'Freedom?'

'Yes. No soldiers to escort you. No one will summon you to serve

293

them. You shall have free passage throughout the city.' He paused. 'I will be disappointed if you run from me. I will punish you if I catch you. But do as you will.'

Croesus laughed. 'I am an old man, Cyrus. Where would I run to?'

'Thank you, Croesus. Enjoy your freedom, for a day at least.' He paused. 'I can never free you fully,' he added. 'I am sorry for that.'

'I know.' Croesus tried to smile. 'It doesn't matter. I don't care any more.'

He left the king and passed down through the palace, searching for Isocrates.

Everywhere he went, he saw Cyrus's people at work, once again trying to understand the business of a flawed, alien government. Through doorways that had been carelessly left open or torn from their hinges in the attack, he saw ministers hunched over desks with translators at their sides. Some studied the treaties the city had signed with its neighbours, trying to untangle the knots of alliances and enmities that had built up over centuries of war and diplomacy. Others wrestled with the city's strange, obscure, and barbaric system of justice, noting down laws that should be repealed and those that needed to be enacted to establish Babylon as a civilized part of the empire. The most harassed-looking Persians were those who examined tax receipts and records of expenditure, where, inevitably, the latter was greater than the former by several orders of magnitude. They shook their heads over the profligacy of their predecessors, trying to draw the numbers closer together, to prevent the indebted city from collapsing in on itself.

Elsewhere, guards explored the corridors of the palace and recorded its layout on wax tablets, identifying the paths that an assassin might take, the positions that soldiers could hold secure in the event of invasion or insurrection, the routes by which a monarch could quietly slip out of the palace if it became necessary to make a discreet exit: the palace redrawn as a labyrinth of potential violence.

Croesus observed Persian servants talking animatedly to Babylonian slaves, unable to speak each other's languages yet communicating their needs through tone and gesture. He almost laughed when he saw one give an unmistakable, uncanny impersonation of Harpagus. He imagined the essentials were simple enough to communicate without words. Good masters, cruel masters, stupid masters. The rest was just so much detail.

Several times he stopped and asked the Persian servants to help him find his friend. They stared at him in silence, and the Babylonians mimicked this unspoken aggression. That he was not one of them, that he was neither a master to command nor an equal to be aided, was, it seemed, another concept that could cross the boundaries of language.

He eventually found Isocrates in one of the cellars. After Croesus had told him of Cyrus's reward, he sat down on a sack of barley. He did not speak for a time.

'I don't want to go,' he said quietly.

'What? You must be joking.'

Isocrates offered him a thin smile. 'I don't know what I would do as a free man,' he said. 'I am not scared of much. But that does scare me.' He laughed. 'A day without being at another's command? I think I might go mad.'

'I don't believe that. You are not as weak as that.'

'No. Perhaps you are right. Perhaps I am afraid that I would like it too much. If I can have only one day of freedom, I would rather not have any at all.'

'You are sure?'

'I am quite sure.' He hesitated.

'Something more you want to say?'

'Yes.' But he paused for a long time before he spoke again. 'Take Maia, will you?'

'Maia?'

'Yes. Take her out into the city.'

'You don't think she will feel the same way as you?'

Isocrates smiled. 'No. She is stronger than I am. Smarter, too. She will take it for what it is. A day of freedom. Nothing more.'

'Very well.' Croesus gestured to the heavy bags that filled the cellar. 'You have plenty of work ahead of you, anyway.'

'Yes. A grain counter in the most fertile land in the world.' He laughed. 'How could I take a day off? There is more wealth in bread here than you ever had in gold, Croesus. I could count it for the rest of my life and still not finish before I died.'

Croesus hesitated, struck by a thought. 'How old are you, Isocrates?'

'I don't know.'

'How can you not know?'

'You forget what I am.'

'And what is that?'

'Irrelevant,' he said. 'No royal celebrations marked my birth, Croesus. No priests inscribed the date in their annals. I honestly don't know how many years I have lived. I am a little younger than you, perhaps, but not by much. We are both getting old now.'

'That is strange,' Croesus said. 'Perhaps I envy you. All I see is my age increasing. The time that remains to me ebbing away. Knowing the date of your birth is almost like knowing the day you will die.'

'Well, you have one day back. A day of freedom. Go and enjoy yourself, Croesus. There won't be any more after this one.'

'How do you know? Perhaps Cyrus will reward us again.'

Isocrates paused. 'I had a dream last night.'

'I thought slaves didn't dream.'

'I don't, usually. Perhaps I knew this reward was coming, this little piece of freedom, and took it in my sleep instead.' He picked a handful of barley from the sack at his side, and let it run through his fingers like sand. 'Do you believe in the truth of dreams?'

'I don't know. What was your dream?'

'I dreamed that I was back on Thera. I wish I could show my island to you, Croesus. The red cliffs, the way they plunge straight down, like a diver into the sea. When the sun sets, it is like watching a great golden coin melting into the water, and the sky seems to catch fire. I've never been anywhere more beautiful than that.'

'When were you taken from there?'

'When I was a child. In my dream, I was in my village in the west of the island. The cliff below my village is near vertical, but there are steps, cut or worn by gods or men, that go down to the water. And down there is the port. My father was a fisherman, I think. He used to take me there and teach me knots.'

'Were you a boy in this dream?'

'No. I was as I am now. I went down the steps, but there were no ships in the bay, no fishermen sorting nets or dogs begging for rotten fish. There was only a woman, bathing naked. She was beautiful. A goddess, I suppose. I apologized for interrupting her—'

Croesus laughed.

'It's true, I promise you,' Isocrates said. 'What else can you do if you come across a goddess bathing? But she just looked at me in silence. She seemed to be waiting for me to ask her something.'

'What did you ask her?'

'I had the feeling that whatever question I asked her, she would answer it truthfully. And I knew that there was some question, the right question, that I should put to her. But I couldn't think of it. All I could think to ask, standing beneath those cliffs, was whether or not I would ever find my way back to my village in the waking world.'

'What did she say to that?'

'She looked a little disappointed. She smiled nonetheless. She told me that I would live long, and travel far, but that I would never see my home again.'

'And that was the end of your dream?'

'Not quite.' Isocrates turned to look at his companion, a smile playing on his lips. 'I told her I had a friend,' he said. 'I asked her if she had anything to say to him.'

Croesus laughed, a soft and rueful sound. 'Now I don't know whether you are lying to me or not. I can never tell. If it is true, I wish you hadn't, I haven't had much luck with oracles in the past.'

'Don't you want to hear what she said?'

'Very well. What did this naked goddess have to say about my future?'

'She said that you would live long as well. But that you would never be happier than this day that is to come. That is when I woke up.' Isocrates waited for Croesus to reply, but the other man said nothing. 'What if that were true? What would you do then?'

'I don't know,' Croesus said. Then he remembered Solon, remembered the words they had traded almost twenty years before. He knew then what he must do on his last day of freedom.

2

In the communal room he had been assigned to, he placed his bedroll so that he would be woken first by the sunrise. It was not a hard position to secure, for most of the slaves were keen to sleep far from the light of the sun, to remain in their dreams for as long as possible.

As soon as the dawn woke him, he rolled out of his blankets before he could be tempted to doze. Stepping over the slumbering forms that were packed into the room, he made his way out into the silent palace. Somewhere on the other side of the palace, he knew that Maia was doing the same.

They met like conspirators by one of the great fountains. Laughing together, not quite believing, they made their way to the gates of the palace. The guards, yawning from their long night spent on watch and cursing those who were late to relieve them, laughed at Croesus and Maia as they approached. 'Eloping?' one of the guards asked with a wry smile. But when Croesus handed over a parchment marked with the unforgeable seal of the king, the guards opened the gates without question or hesitation. They left the palace behind, and stepped out into a city that was just beginning to wake.

Most cities grow unplanned. A village that stumbles on some sudden wealth and expands to become a town, a town that is occupied by a wandering warlord and grows larger still. Then there is an influx of migrants, drawn to the promise of work, and the city is finally born. Buildings appear more by accident than any kind of design. Later attempts to provide architectural unity, by kings eager to shape and control their possessions, only serve to highlight the disorder that lies at the heart of every city.

Babylon was different. From the very first brick, it seemed to have been precisely planned, each building carefully placed like a tile in some great mosaic. Or like a miracle of geometry, as though designed by a mathematician to solve a great equation if it were viewed, impossibly, from above.

That early in the morning, the city was almost empty. The dung carts still moved through the streets, and a few revellers from the night before stumbled past, the stale stench of beer following them home. Soon though, the streets began to fill, and with no idea of where they were going, Croesus and Maia followed the trails of citizens like swimmers following a current. Before long they found themselves in Shuanna, the market district.

The merchants gathered as they had done for centuries, each square dedicated to a different kind of produce. In between the ordinary stalls, where cloth was cut by the yard, fresh flatbread sold to hungry workers, piles of worked leather and crafted bronze picked over by merchants, were more unusual tradesmen.

In one, stonemasons carved out the foot-long boundary stones that marked property and court rulings in Babylon, each one etched with a strange mixture of legal formalities and ancient curses. One square seemed to be populated by wives buying perfumes for their lovers, another by worried husbands haggling with shamans over love charms for their wives. The Massagetae, the nomad horse traders from the northern steppes, stood with silent disdain at the edge of the market, making no effort to draw customers to them. They knew their horses, the finest in the world, would bring crowds soon enough. Amongst the traders' stalls moved the translators of Babylon, essential for business conducted in a city of a hundred different tongues, taking a percentage of each transaction as their fee.

Everything was as it had always been in the world of Babylonian commerce; only the guards had changed. Persians now watched over the stalls, breaking up fights when the haggling became too heated, quietly accepting bribes from merchants who wanted to trade in illicit goods. To his surprise, Croesus saw that most of the coins that changed hands were his, the golden ovals marked with the bull and the lion. His coins had clearly conquered Babylon long before the Persian army. That was his legacy.

'Come on,' Maia said. 'I don't want to spend my day gawping at the markets.'

'What do you want to see?'

'Wonders, of course,' she said. 'Wonders and miracles. Let's go and find them.'

After asking for directions, they found the Ishtar Gate, the grand entrance into the heart of Babylon. Its pillars were covered in tiles glazed a deep turquoise, the impossible blue of a sea in a dream, a sea teeming with golden lions, aurochs, and dragons. Remarkable as it was, Croesus had no desire to take his eyes out after seeing it, like the men in the stories. After all, it was just a gate into a city, a gate through which dung carts passed and where beggars loitered.

They continued to the Etemenanki temple, the great ziggurat at the heart of Babylon. The temple was dedicated to Marduk, the God of fifty names, and rose high above any other building in the city. It was said to be the foundation of heaven, seven tiers high, a place where the priests spoke with the Gods themselves.

Maia looked up at it and grinned. 'It is wonderful. Don't you think?'

'I have heard that the Jews have a story about this tower. They say that as it was built, their God grew angry at how tall it was growing, seeing it as a threat to his kingdom. So he cursed its builders by making them speak hundreds of different languages; before then all people had spoken in the same tongue. All misunderstandings begin here, if the story is true.' Croesus looked up at the temple doubtfully. 'I don't think you could talk to the Gods from the top of it, do you?'

'They never finished it, did they?'

'But the people of Babylon say that their priests speak to Marduk here. Their priestesses lie with him up there.'

'Perhaps Marduk lives lower down than Yahweh,' Maia said lightly. 'Come on. There is so much more to see.'

They made their way at last to the storied gardens. As soon as they were through the gates, Maia went on ahead, running along the stone-paved pathways and terraces like a child. She shouted her discoveries from every corner; leather conveyor belts, hung with buckets and turned by slaves, that carried water from the Euphrates up into the gardens; a bed of flowers, purple, gold and red, designed to mimic a sunset; a copse of slender trees that creaked in symphony when the wind blew over them; lush grasses that reached as high as a man's thigh. All of them miracles in this desert city. But Croesus was weary of miracles. He found a stone bench beneath a Persian silk tree, as alien to that land as he was himself. Sitting beneath it, he thought, in an idle kind of way, about escape.

He had told Cyrus that he had no intention of escaping. But why not? They could walk through the gates, the king's seal in hand, and disappear into Mesopotamia. He looked across at Maia, bustling about the gardens, and wondered if she would run with him. They could find a place to take them in, a temple perhaps, and live out the rest of their lives in peace. He turned the thought over in his mind, waiting for a spark of inspiration, for the moment that the idea would catch fire in his mind and drive him to action, but it did not come.

He settled back on the bench, and closed his eyes. He meant to rest for only a moment, but the air was thick with flower scent, like a courtesan's quarters, and in the afternoon heat he soon dozed off to sleep.

He woke with a start to find Maia shaking his shoulder.

'Your one day of freedom, Croesus, and you spend it sleeping?' she said. 'For shame.'

'How long did I sleep for?'

'An eternity. Babylon was burned and built again a dozen times, and you slept through it all.'

He shook his head. 'Sleep is a luxury for a slave. Your husband taught me that.'

'A maxim he observes rather too well,' she said, and sat down beside him. 'He would have spent this whole day asleep in bed, if he had had the wit to take Cyrus up on his offer.'

'Did you enjoy the gardens?'

'They are wonderful. Built for a woman, or so they say.'

'I can't believe that's true.'

'Oh, I am sure they don't like to say so. But I heard it from one of the old Babylonian slaves. I believed her.'

'Is that so?'

'No need to sound so sceptical. I suppose it offends you, to think of something so remarkable being built for a woman.'

'Tell me the story.'

'Well, they say the king's wife was a Persian princess, and she pined for her home when he brought her here to be his queen. He doted on her, and built this – a little piece of Persia in the heart of the city.' Maia nodded approvingly. 'He must have been quite a husband.'

'Don't you think Isocrates would do the same for you, if he had the chance?'

She snorted. 'He would see it as a terrible waste, building me an impossible garden because I was unhappy. Would you have built this place for Danae, if she had asked?'

'Yes. I would have done anything for her. It's an easy thing to say, isn't it? But it wasn't true then. I did little enough for her when she was alive. And I could have made her so happy. She did not ask for much.'

'I am sorry, Croesus. I shouldn't have spoken of her.'

'I don't think of her often enough. Especially now. I can barely remember what she looked like. Isn't that terrible?' He let his head fall and closed his eyes, and for a moment she thought he was going to weep. But when he opened his eyes again, they were clear and dry.

'We were wrong about Gyges,' he said.

'What do you mean?'

'I thought it was the waiting outside the city that was driving him mad. It wasn't.'

'Then what is it?'

'The city itself.'

She said nothing for a time, turning the idea over in her mind. 'Of course,' she said softly.

'I didn't understand before. He hated Sardis, and smiled when it burned. He was happy out on the plains, by the river.'

'It is cities he hates. What they do to people.'

'Yes. Now he will be here for years. He is already forgetting how to speak. He will go mad here.'

She shook her head. 'I won't allow it.'

'There is nothing you can do.'

'Maybe not. But I'll try.' She paused. 'When did he first speak?'

'It was at the fall of Sardis.'

'What did he say?'

'"Do not kill Croesus." He saved my life. I don't know why.'

'He loves you, Croesus. That is all.'

He breathed deeply, tried to breathe away the pain, the shame of an error that could never be corrected. 'I never gave him a reason to,' he said, his voice unsteady.

304

'It does not matter. He still loves you.'

'I don't think so. Not any more. Take care of him, will you? I don't think he will see me again.'

They sat silently for a time, listening to the passing of the Euphrates, looking out over the impossible gardens, built long ago to heal a broken heart. Croesus stared up at the sky, and saw that there was still some time to go before the end of the day. He had a few hours left.

'Can I ask you something, Maia?' he said.

'Of course.'

He hesitated. 'I know the truth.' He gestured to the dim, half-healed bruises on her face. 'About those.'

A shiver of tension ran through her. Then she sighed, and shook her head. 'I wish you had not said that.'

'Why didn't you tell me?'

'I liked it better that way,' she said. 'Isocrates always knew that he would have to share me. I liked it that you didn't know.' A ghost of a smile moved across her lips. 'You are an innocent, Croesus. In spite of all that has happened to you. There are terrible things that happen every day, and you do not notice because you can't imagine people can be so cruel. That is what I like about you. When I am with you, I can pretend these things don't happen either.' She paused. 'Now that is ruined, too.'

'Why do they do it? You are not . . .'

'Not beautiful?'

Croesus looked away and said nothing. She shook her head.

'Why do you men ever do anything?' she said. 'You are just the same, Croesus. That is what you want too, isn't it? To possess things. To control them.'

He stared at the ground. 'You should not fight them,' he said slowly. 'If you did not fight them, they would not hurt you so much.'

'That is the best advice you can give?'

'I suppose so.'

'Well, I don't fight them. I gave that up long ago. Sometimes they beat me anyway. Because they can, and they like it.'

'I . . .'

'Croesus, you are a good friend to me. To me and my husband. But there is nothing you can do about this. And you know it. You are not trying to help me. You are trying to make yourself feel better.' Her voice shook, then steadied. 'And that is wrong.'

He hesitated. 'Does it get easier?'

'No. It gets worse. I try not to think about it.'

'I won't talk about it again.'

'Yes, you will, Croesus. I know you too well.' She reached over and touched him on the shoulder. 'Come on. Let's go back.'

They walked out of the gates of the garden. Out on the streets, the first fires were being lit, and from here and there came the echoing sounds of wine casks being broached, the sweet scent of cooking meat, as Babylon began to prepare for its evening meal.

Maia started out back towards the palace, but Croesus hesitated.

'Is something wrong?' she said.

'I am going to stay a little longer.'

She paused for a moment, then nodded. 'As you wish.' She smiled. 'Goodbye, Croesus. Thank you. It was a good day.'

He watched her go, waiting until she had disappeared into the maze of streets. He began to walk in the opposite direction.

He made his choices at random in the winding paths of Babylon, losing himself deliberately, yet also looking for something. Before long his wanderings brought him to the entrance of a tall building. A temple. And inside the temple, something else – if the stories he had heard were true. Suddenly nervous, he toyed with the idea of going back to the palace. Of forgetting this desire.

He walked into the temple, to find a woman he could buy.

He remembered Sardis. There, one had only to walk through the working quarters to find a woman prostituting herself, like all impoverished, pragmatic Lydian women, to secure a dowry. In Babylon, where all things were made beautiful or sacred, the women gathered in the temple, and the selling of their bodies took on the quality of a religious rite.

At least once in her life every Babylonian woman had to visit a temple, sit down there, and go to bed with the first man who threw a coin in her lap. The tall and beautiful women would sit only for moments before being claimed. The young men of Babylon clustered outside the temple gates, watching the women who entered the temple to fulfil their duty to the Gods, drawing lots as to which of them would choose first. The ugly and the deformed, when their time came, had much longer to wait.

There were stories of women who spent years in the temples, waiting for some man to cast a coin in their laps and free them. Some, it was rumoured, spent the rest of their lives there, growing uglier with age and bitterness, bowed over lower with time like a dying tree on a river bank, until their hearts gave out.

He did not know how or when or why this ritual had begun. If it were a divine decree handed down from gods to men at the beginning of time, or if the cruel joke of an old king of Babylon had somehow found its way into law and now remained, protected for centuries by force of habit, by a stubborn refusal to think differently.

He walked across the temple to where the women sat still and silent, as though they were at prayer, not waiting to be bought. He let chance decide for him. He simply walked along the row of women without looking at them, and counted down from ten. Then he stopped, turned to the woman beside him, and threw a coin into her lap.

She looked up at him, and he saw that she was neither ugly nor beautiful. A merchant's daughter, perhaps, who had spent her life weaving and cooking, until her duty had taken her to this temple. A plain, ordinary-looking face, with calm grey eyes that looked at up him without fear. She had a body like Maia's, he thought, then wished that he hadn't.

He smiled at her. He offered a hand to help her up. She took it, and he led her away without a word.

3

'I am Cyrus, king of the universe, the great king, the powerful king, king of Babylon, king of Sumer and Akkad, king of the four quarters of the world, son of Cambyses, the great king, grandson of Cyrus, the great king, descendant of Teispes, the great king, king of the city of Anshan, the perpetual seed of kingship, whose reign Bel and Nabu love . . .' Croesus stopped reading, and tried to keep the smile from his face.

'Is something wrong?'

He turned to face his king. 'It is a little overdone, don't you think?'

'People expect this kind of thing from me now.' Cyrus paused. 'You didn't have to come here, you know. It is supposed to be your day of freedom.'

'I know,' Croesus said. 'But I wanted to read it today. It's my choice to make, isn't it?'

'Well, come on then. Don't waste your time speaking to me. Keep reading.'

Croesus looked again at the cylinder. It was the length of three fists placed side by side, and every part of the pale clay surface was marked with the strange cuneiform script. Next to it was a wax tablet, marked with the translation that he was reading from. He had never learned the cuniform of Babylon, and even as he read it he wondered what had been lost in translation, what nuances in the original language he would never understand.

He read on. It said that Cyrus came as a liberator to the city, to free it from a tyrant king, with the blessing of the Babylonian God, Marduk. It spoke of how he would not seek to impose his own gods, but would help the Babylonians to rebuild their damaged temples, how he would reconstruct what had been destroyed in the war, to help Babylon prosper, and to worship freely.

'There you are,' Cyrus said, when he saw that Croesus had finished. 'My proclamation. To leave the people alone, as your Isocrates would wish. What do you think?'

'It is a fine piece of writing. I especially like that part about your army. "His vast army, whose number, like the waters of the river, cannot be known".'

Cyrus rolled his eyes. 'One of my scribes. Something of a failed poet. I like to let him add the odd bit of grand language, here and there. It keeps him from pining.'

The king signalled for a servant to take the cylinder away, but before it disappeared, Croesus took one last look at it. It was not in any way unusual, he thought. It was in the form of dozens of kingly proclamations that had come before, and thousands that would follow. Yet it was nevertheless the beginning of something, something that he could not describe because the words for it had yet to be invented. He wondered what strange event he had unwittingly been a part of, what echo down history the cylinder would sound. That was his fate, he thought. Always to be at the beginning, always to be ignorant, never to see or understand the end of things.

Once the cylinder had been taken from the room, to be entombed in the wall of the city, as Croesus had heard the Babylonians used to bury their kings of old, he dismissed his thought as foolish. It was a conqueror's proclamation like any other, to be buried and forgotten. It meant nothing.

'All that talk of free worship,' Croesus said. 'Is there something more to it than just rebuilding a few temples?'

'Yes,' Cyrus said. 'I am going to do something about the Jews. There are thousands of them here.'

'I didn't realize there were so many in the city.'

'Babylon captured Jerusalem some time ago. Apparently they had some trouble with the natives. Insurrections, assassinations, that sort of thing. The Babylonians grew weary of them, and exiled them all to the city where they could keep a close eye on them.'

'You are an expert on their history?'

'I wasn't until recently. One of their elders requested an audience with me. He asked me – no, begged me – to allow them to worship their own god, and not to have to follow mine.' He paused. 'It had never occurred to me to bar them from their worship. What an impious thing that would be. And then I spoke to him a little more. He told me about their exile. We will do something about that as well.'

'Most rulers aren't so permissively plural in how they let their subjects worship.'

Cyrus laughed. 'Permissively plural, is it? I like that. But who am I to keep a man from his gods? If his is a true face of God, surely I would be punished for it. If not, well, the fault lies with him, not with me, for worshipping his empty idols. Don't you think? I am a king, not a god myself.'

'How humble of you to admit that.'

'Mock all you like, Croesus, mock all you like. I am in a good mood today. I shan't punish you for it.'

'You will send the Jews home, then?'

'Yes. We control Jerusalem now. Let them go back there, if they wish to. They have a miserable enough time of it here; the Babylonians loathe them with an impressive passion. Maybe they will find a better home there. There is a temple they want to rebuild. Their elder made it sound very important. We will help them with that as well.'

'Is that wise? They might rise up against you, given their own city.'

'Perhaps, perhaps. But that is a problem for another time. I'll trust they will remember what it was to be exiled, and act with a little humility. I have never understood why the Jews inspire such hatred. Do you?'

'No. It is a customary hatred. Handed down from one generation to the next.'

Cyrus shook his head. 'Hatred should never become custom. It is a poor gift to pass on to your children.'

'You don't believe in hatred?'

'Oh, there are plenty of things I hate. A few people too. But I learned to hate them myself – I would not have anyone teach me. You wouldn't expect to inherit love, would you? It's too important to be passed down. It is the same with hate. A man who hates because he is told he should hate is a fool.'

Silence fell. Croesus stood, waiting for a command, but Cyrus said nothing, apparently without an order to give, yet disinclined to dismiss him. The king's gaze wandered over to a map on the wall.

'I worry about Cambyses,' the king said.

Croesus said nothing.

'He cries too often,' Cyrus said after a time. 'I worry he is too weak to be a king. I sent him to the north, to take part in a Babylonian ritual. The heir to the throne must be beaten by their priest. I thought it would do him some good. But the way he looked at me . . . Was I wrong to do this, do you think?'

'I don't know, master.'

Cyrus shook his head. 'There are many things that I have mastered in this life. But this is not one of them.' He looked at his slave. 'Will you help me to raise him? I want so much for him to be a good king. A good son.'

'I will do my best,' Croesus said. 'But I am an old man. Who knows how long I will be able to help you?'

Cyrus smiled, and toyed with a piece of silk that hung next to the throne.

'Do you know why I like having you as an advisor, Croesus?'

'I thought it was for my unrivalled wisdom. That is what I have heard the storytellers say.'

Cyrus stopped playing with the silks and looked straight at Croesus. 'It is because you do not love me. So I can trust what you say.'

Croesus paused for a long time. Cyrus's face was unreadable. 'You are a king of many talents, Cyrus,' Croesus said eventually, 'but humour is not one of them. It is quite hard to tell when you are joking. This is one of those times, I take it?'

'I am quite serious. Most people do. I don't say it to brag. Just as a matter of fact. Take a man like Harpagus. The last person you would imagine could feel affection for anyone, after the life he has led. But he loves me. I see it in him. And I don't understand why you don't.'

'You don't remember the destruction of my city?'

'I have seen plenty of people love their conquerors. We kneel to power when it has been exercised upon us. Those who do not are men of stronger character than you. So, why don't you love me?'

Croesus shook his head and looked away. 'Cyrus, this is absurd.'

'Is it jealousy? Come on, tell me.'

'I admire you, Cyrus. You know that. I respect you, and obey you. Is that not enough?'

'Give me the truth, Croesus.'

Croesus sighed, and sat down on a cushioned seat. He hadn't asked permission, but Cyrus ignored the breach of etiquette. 'I don't know,' he said. 'I used to want the same things as you. To be remembered. To be a great king. You will be remembered when I am forgotten. Should I not be jealous of that? Or if not, should I not love you for it?'

He paused. Cyrus said nothing, waiting for him to continue.

313

'There is something wrong with us both, I think,' Croesus said after a moment. 'Why do we care how we are remembered? You have spent your life conquering one city after another. What is it to you, once you are buried in the ground, how others think of you? If there is an afterlife, I should think you will have enough problems to occupy you there. You will be leading an army against Death, most likely, trying to install yourself on the throne of Hades.' Cyrus laughed at this. 'And if there is not another life,' Croesus continued, 'well, it matters even less, doesn't it?'

'It isn't just for me. The cities I conquer are the better for being conquered. I bring order, and peace, an end to war, and the only price is submission.'

'At the point of a sword.'

'True.' Cyrus paused. 'Do you wish that you had been born a farmer? Or even a slave? Perhaps you think your life would be simpler. Happier too, not knowing the things you know now. A charming thought, but you are wrong. I was raised as a herdsman for twelve years, Croesus. They live miserable lives.'

'You are right. I think that is what I'm afraid of, more than anything else.'

'What is that?'

'An ordinary life. Aren't you? Can you think of anything more terrible, to live and die as countless others have before you, with nothing exceptional to mark you out? You might as well have not lived at all, living a life like that.'

Cyrus nodded. 'Yes. You are right.'

'I feared for my life for a long time. First from you, then—' He stopped, catching himself. 'Well,' he continued, 'I was afraid.'

'Not any more?'

'No. Why should I be? But . . .'

Cyrus's mouth twitched into a smile. 'But you feel ordinary. A slave and advisor. Not exceptional enough for you?' He spread his arms wide in self-mockery. 'Not even serving a glorious king like me?'

'Forgive me. I meant no insult.'

'Oh, I take no offence,' Cyrus said, lowering his arms. I under- stand perfectly. I don't know if it will ever please you to be in my service, Croesus. I suspect that may be impossible. But I am glad to have you with me. I hope that there is some comfort, at least, in that.' He looked over his shoulder, out through the doorway, over the balcony and across the city. 'You had better go. You have a few hours of freedom left.'

'What will you do tomorrow?' Croesus said.

'I honestly don't know.' He paused. 'There is no one left to conquer. Perhaps we will stay here. It is a remarkable city. Perhaps our wars are done.'

The king spoke these words, and perhaps he even believed them to be true. But Croesus looked into his eyes, and saw that it was not.

The sun was low when Croesus stepped out onto the balcony, and the sky was beginning to redden in anticipation of the sunset. He stood at the highest point of the palace and looked out over the city, his eyes moving from one place to another, from one marvel to the next. The temples and gateways, the houses and canals and hanging gardens, the miracle that was Babylon. He stood, and tried to find the courage to take a few more steps, out into the air, and, perhaps, into another world.

It had come to him the night before, a resolution so strong and sudden that it might have come from the Gods. This had been the happiest day of his life, if he were to believe Isocrates's dream.

He remembered the happy men that Solon had spoken of, and the one thing that united them: their contented deaths. He had thought, ever since he was taken as a slave, that it was his fate to die unhappy, but this was his way out, his final victory. The logic seemed flawless. He would not stay on, to watch his son go mad once again, to remain a slave for his remaining decades on earth. He would end his life as a free man.

He stepped forward, rested his hands on the edge of the balcony, feeling the stone beneath his fingers, and looked down on the ground below. It was high enough, or so he hoped. The king's surgeons would not make any great efforts to save his life. Not for an old slave like him.

He should have died in Sardis, as his wife had. They should have leaped into their city together. He hoped that she would forgive him for taking so long. She had always seen the right thing to do long before he had.

He lifted himself up, and balanced on the edge of the balcony. He looked out, for the last time, on the city. He raised a foot, and prepared to take a last step.

A thought caught him. He remained there for a time, one foot in the air, like a balancing acrobat. If he were to move only slightly forwards he would tip his weight down to the ground far below. Then he lowered his foot to the edge and stepped down carefully. He turned his back on the city, and began to run.

He ran down through the palace, afraid he would lose the thought like a man who forgets a dream on waking. He ran out into Babylon, afraid that he had left it too late, that this last inspiration would come to nothing.

At first, Gyges would not come with him. In the house that the mad had been moved to, Croesus pleaded with him, implored him in every way he could think of, but his son would not come. Eventually, he simply seized Gyges's arm and dragged him out into the city.

If Gyges had fought back, Croesus could not have taken him, but his son submitted. Babylon seemed to have broken his will to struggle, but even so, once they were out on the streets, it was impossible to keep him moving. Such was his horror at being out in the city that he could not move for more than a few feet before stopping and falling to the ground, throwing his arms around his head and howling in distress. He did not speak, and it seemed the trauma of the city had taken the last pieces of language from him.

Croesus, knowing that time was running out, had no time for subtlety. He begged his son and shouted at him, dragged him and slapped him through the streets, as a small crowd of idle Babylonians gathered and followed them, cheering and jeering, entertained by the sport of an old man wrestling with an imbecile like a farmer with a stubborn mule. At last, as Croesus was on the verge of utter exhaustion, they reached the market square.

The market was closing down for the day, and at first Croesus thought that he was too late. But then, past the merchants packing their wares into carts, he saw the people he was looking for.

'They are here, Gyges,' he said. 'Will you come with me? Please?' Gyges, dull eyed and even more exhausted than his father, nodded in defeat. They crossed the square, and came to the stall of the horse-taming Massagetae.

They were a family of six nomads, a man and woman, three sons and a daughter. As Croesus approached the father looked him over with an expert eye and saw that he was a man with no money. The horse trader crossed his arms, preparing to have his time wasted.

Croesus turned to look for a translator to help him, and found a boy of twelve or thirteen already standing at his side. The boy had the dirt-rimmed face of a beggar child, but looked up at him with bright, intelligent eyes and stood with a merchant's confidence. Did he have a family, Croesus wondered? Surely not. He was an orphan who should have starved years before, but had learned to live on words alone.

'You are here to trade?' the boy said.

'Yes. You speak their language?' Croesus said doubtfully.

'Of course.'

'Will you speak for me? I have no money to give you.'

'I need to practise it anyway,' the boy said, giving a small shrug. 'What do you want to say?'

Croesus hesitated. 'Tell him I want him to take this man with him,' he said at last. 'Out of the city.'

As this was translated to him, the horse trader frowned. He spoke a few brief words in response.

'They have no interest in buying your slave.'

'He is no slave. He is my son.'

Hearing this, the nomad bristled. He barked out two short sentences.

'He is insulted that you would sell your son. He asks you to leave.'

'Tell him again that he is mistaken. I am not here to sell him.' Croesus paused. 'I cannot help my son. I want this man to take him in. Take him from the city, and north to the plains.'

The trader threw back his head and laughed. He spoke again.

'He asks you to tell him why he should take this madman into his family.'

'Tell him I can give him no good reason. If he takes this man in, he will save his life. He was meant to be free. This city is a prison for him. Please.'

The nomad listened to the translator. He shook his head and raised a finger in admonishment, but paused before he spoke, his eyes focused behind Croesus. Croesus turned to follow the other man's gaze, and saw his son approaching one of the horses.

It was a white stallion, tall and obviously skittish, but it stood quite still as Gyges approached, then reached out with a shy hand and stroked the horse's cheek. The animal leaned into his touch, snorting its approval, and Gyges took another step forward, placing his arm flat against its head, his elbow on the horse's nose as his fingers curled into the top of its mane.

He took a last step forward and let his arm fall back to his side, and rested his head against the stallion's, like an exhausted traveller placing his head beneath running water, his eyes closed, his breathing slow. The horse whickered in affection, and Gyges gave a small sob in response. Here at last, Croesus thought, in a city of madmen, was something that his son could understand. Something unspoiled by words.

Croesus turned back to the horse trader, ready to argue again, but found him wearing an almost rueful expression, like the face of a man who has made a bad wager. The Massagetae held up a hand to silence Croesus, then called the rest of his family together into a semicircle. They began to debate.

'What are they saying?' Croesus asked the boy at his side.

'They are speaking too fast. I can't understand them.'

It was true that they spoke rapidly, over and under each other, the argument growing increasingly heated. After a few minutes, the divisions became clear. From what he could tell, two of the sons seemed to be of one mind, the mother, the daughter and the other son of another, with the father still undecided. Which of the sides was for him and which was against, Croesus did not know.

At last, the father held up his hands for silence. He looked at each of his family in turn, and they all said a single word in response. He shook his head in disbelief, then turned back to Croesus and spoke.

'They will take him,' the boy said, and Croesus bowed his head and closed his eyes. The world around him seemed to recede, to disappear entirely, as if the entirety of existence, for a single moment, had been reduced to one point of grief. His aching lungs, his weary heart.

When he could speak again, Croesus said, 'Thank him for me.'

He heard a laugh. 'He is telling you to get out of here before he changes his mind,' the boy said.

'I will. My thanks to you as well.'

The boy gave his small shrug once again. 'It is as I said. I am grateful for the practice.'

Croesus watched the boy walk off into the crowd, looking for one last commission before the market broke up entirely. He turned back, and found Gyges watching him. Croesus tried to smile.

'You had better go with them now, Gyges,' he said. 'I hope . . .' His voice trailed away.

Gyges opened his mouth, trying to find the words that he knew his father would want to hear. He seemed on the verge of speech when Croesus waved his son into silence. He knew that there was nothing that needed to be said, that they both knew it all already, had always known, perhaps, but had forgotten until the moment of parting. Gyges nodded, to show that he understood.

Then he stepped forward and took his father's hand in his own. He held it loosely, just for a moment, before he let go and went to join his new family.

The mother threw a sheepskin over his back to keep out the cold and handed him the reins of a horse to lead out of the city, and together, now seven instead of six, they made their way from the market square, to begin their long journey to the steppes and plains of the north, a world of wild herds and wandering rivers, of thousands of people but not a single city.

Croesus stood motionless, and watched them for as long as he could before they were gone from his sight, lost in the crowds of Babylon. He then looked up, back to the royal palace and the balcony at its highest point. If he hurried back, he thought to himself, he might still get back before the sunset. He did not want to die in darkness.

4

Croesus watched the merchant caravans leave the city. He watched the low sun bathe the city in a soft red light. He tried to remember all of the sunsets he had lived to see, to remember how they each compared with this one, whether the last one he saw would be the tenth or the hundredth most beautiful he had ever seen. He stood quite still, and tried to find his strength again. The strength to step up and step forward.

It had been hard enough the first time, and now, even when it felt more right than ever before, it was harder still. His coward's spirit held him by some intangible, compelling force. Each breath came more ragged and painful than the last, and he began to count them. On the tenth breath, he decided, he would jump.

He thought of Isocrates and Maia, and hoped they would be well. He thought of Harpagus and Cyrus, and was surprised by his sadness that he would not see them again. He thought of Gyges one last time, disappearing north to a new life in the wild lands. This was what Isocrates's dream had meant, he thought. That at the end of his foolish, selfish life, he would find the way to save his son. Now, at last, he could die happy. He counted the tenth breath.

'Croesus.'

At first, he did not respond to his name. He wondered if it were some trick of his mind, desperate to save itself, conjuring some aural phantom. But the voice came again, real and insistent.

'I should have known I would find you here,' Isocrates said as he came forward, and leaned against the balcony. 'Well. Did you enjoy your day with my wife?'

Croesus looked across at the other man, and tried to smile. 'Yes,' he said carefully.

'Good, good. And did you find what you were looking for?'

'In a manner of speaking.' Croesus thought for a moment. 'The city disappointed me, but still, I am glad to have seen it. Your dream was not wrong. I think I have been happy here today.'

Isocrates laughed.

'Something amusing?' Croesus said.

'You, you pompous fool. Always talking about happiness as if it is some kind of holy thing.'

'What is happiness to you then?'

Isocrates thought for a moment, then shrugged. 'Eating a good pear with a sharp knife,' he said. 'Making love to Maia, when she'll have me. Falling asleep with the sun on my face. Shall I go on?'

Croesus shook his head. 'Sensation. Relief from pain. That's not enough.'

'It is enough for me.'

'It is not enough,' Croesus said.

'I suppose not, for you. That's why you're out here, isn't it?'

Croesus said nothing. They stood together in silence for a long time, Isocrates running his fingers along the edge of the balcony, Croesus standing quite still, counting his breaths. They were some way past a hundred now.

After a time, Isocrates spoke again. 'Would you like me to go?' he said. 'That's not what I want to do. But I will, if you ask me to.'

'What do you want to do?'

'I'd like to go back inside to my slave's life. I would like you to come with me.'

'For how long?'

'For years. Decades perhaps. There won't be much joy along the way, but I'd like you to be there with me. That is selfish of me, isn't it? But it's the only reason I have.' He paused. 'Croesus. Would you like me to go?'

Croesus said nothing for a long time.

Then he said, 'No.'

'What would you like me to do instead?'

'Stay here, and watch the sunset with me,' Croesus said. He paused. 'It might be a good one.'

'It might.' Isocrates leaned on the balcony, and looked down at the city.

'This is Cyrus's greatest conquest, isn't it?' he said, after a silence.

'Yes.'

'A fine city to rule an empire from. A fine home for a king, and for slaves like us. Is this the end of his wars, do you think?'

Croesus shook his head.

'No?' Isocrates said.

'We shall stay here for a time. But he will grow bored. And one day he will look at his maps, and find another place to conquer. And we will go with him.'

Isocrates gazed down on the streets of Babylon. Then he shrugged. 'Well,' he said, 'let us try to enjoy ourselves until then.'

Far below, the city stretched on as far as an old man's eyes could see.

Babylon. As close to a perfect city as men had yet managed to build. The Persians had come to make it greater, to make it the heart of an empire. They had, instead, initiated its slow decay. It might take centuries or merely decades for it to be destroyed entirely. Some

323

unknown time after that the city would become myth, then die alto-gether, lost to memories and stories alike.

The people of Babylon, had they known this, would not perhaps have cared. They had been taught, ever since birth, that the Gods loved decay as much as they loved creation, that death and rebirth, entropy and regeneration, were the way of things, that nothing lasted for long, least of all a man or a city, a king or a slave, a memory or a story.

If any of the people down below had looked up at the balcony of the palace, they might have assumed that it was their new ruler looking down on them, a trusted slave at his side, though which was the king and which was the slave, they could not have said. Those with keener eyes might have seen the glint of silver in their hair, and wondered whether their wandering lives were over, and they would grow old together and die in the city, or whether their travels had hardly yet begun.

The two men remained outside until the sun had set. If they were still visible through the darkening air, an observer from the streets below might have seen the two men draw together for an instant. It was possible that the blurring of the two forms was a mere trick of failing light and tired eyes. It was also possible that they embraced once, sudden and joyful, the way that children do. Then they returned to the palace, to serve their king, and wait for the next war to come.

Acknowledgements

Very many thanks to Ravi Mirchandani, James Roxburgh, Sara Holloway, and the rest of the Atlantic Books phalanx who have worked so hard on this book, and to Caroline Wood at Felicity Bryan, whose undaunted enthusiasm and keen eye for storytelling have been truly invaluable.

This book has had many readers, and I owe a huge debt to Maureen, Tim, Nick, Gaby, Helen, Vestal, Thom and to all the others who have offered their support and advice along the way. Special thanks to John and Jayme, who set me on the right path in the first place.

Last, but by no means least, I must thank Herodotus, who first told this story so long ago.